Three Grumpy Groomsmen

EMMA FOXX

CHAPTER 1

Ford

"NO. GODDAMMIT, *NO*. THIS MOTHERFUCKER." I'm staring at my phone and reading the message from one of my best friends for the third time. But I still don't believe it.

> Hey, I'm not going to be there today. It's all wrong. I'm sorry you made the trip. Tell Harrison for me.

> That's not funny. Get your ass over here. We're all dressed and ready.

> I'm not kidding. I'm at the airport. I'm not doing it.

> What the FUCK are you talking about? You are getting married today. Stop being a dick.

> I'm not. I can't.

> You're in love, you asshole. It's Ivy. Get your ass over here. You have ten minutes.

> I'm getting on the plane. I have to turn my phone off soon. Sorry.

> You're a cowardly cocksucking chickenshit! Get off the plane.

> I'm serious. Get. Off. The. Plane.

> I am going to kick your ass when I see you. And you can't avoid me forever.

> What did you say to Ivy?

"Hey. What's going on? We're supposed to be out in the garden in a couple of minutes."

I look up as Harrison—yes, I know how our names sound together, ridiculous coincidence—pokes his head around the door to the room where we changed into our tuxes. He's now my *only* best friend. Because the son of a bitch who is texting me right now is dead to me.

"Yeah, well, I don't think they're going to need us out there at all," I say.

He frowns. "What are you talking about?"

I hold up my phone. "Brad just texted me."

Harrison's frown deepens and he steps into the room. "He texted you? Where is he? I haven't seen him all morning. When I texted to ask if he wanted breakfast he never got back to me."

I scowl at my phone. Then hand it over. I can't read it out loud.

Harrison takes it, and his eyes scan the screen.

His gaze bounces back to mine. "He's not here? He's not coming? What the hell does he mean he can't do this?"

I sigh heavily. This is an absolute clusterfuck and I'm so pissed at Brad I almost can't see straight.

My phone pings, and Harrison looks down.

"What does it say?" I ask, somehow knowing it's Brad again.

Harrison looks a little sick when he meets my gaze again. "You have to tell Ivy."

I frown, then start shaking my head. "No. No fucking way."

"I'm just reading the message to you," Harrison says, handing my phone back. "Maybe you shouldn't have called him a cowardly cocksucking chickenshit."

"He *is* a cowardly cocksucking chickenshit. And he wouldn't have told her himself even if I hadn't called him that," I say.

Harrison nods. "Cowardly and chickenshit are kind of the same thing, aren't they?"

"Shut up." I grip my phone and look at the screen.

> You have to tell her. I can't.

That last message from Brad was four minutes after I'd texted him.

I type quickly.

> I am NOT telling her. YOU have to tell her. At least call her. Please be that much of a man.

I suck in a deep breath as I wait.

And wait.

And wait.

"Son of a bitch!" I shout.

Harrison looks grim. "He's really not coming."

"He's really not coming," I repeat. "*Fuck.*"

"And now *we* have to tell Ivy? Seriously?"

"I…guess." I feel my stomach knot. I can't do that.

God, anything but that.

Harrison Reed and I grew up with Brad Richardson. I've known these guys all my life. And yes, I'm stunned that Brad is leaving his fiancee at the altar.

But it's sinking in. Quickly. Ever since Brad moved from Honeysuckle Harbor, South Carolina, to Los Angeles and became a famous chef on his very own television show, he's turned into a prick. We've tried to ignore it—thought once the luster of fame wore off, he would remember who he really is, but this…damn, this is bad.

So fucking bad.

Have I had questions about his relationship with Ivy in the past? Yes. I've always been surprised she agreed to go out with him, not to mention *marry* him. But I wasn't sure if that was reality or just me being jealous because I'd had eyes on her too.

If Brad had broken up with Ivy six months ago, or even a month ago, or even last week, I would have agreed it was a great idea.

In fact, full disclosure, I would have been thrilled.

Not only is Ivy Scott way too good for the new-undisputed-champion-prick Brad, but Ivy is gorgeous, sweet, funny, intelligent, talented, and…the star of several of my dirtiest fantasies.

I'm not proud of that. But it's still true.

And if my fucking friend had done the right thing, realized he wasn't in love with her, and pulled out of their engagement *any time before today*, I would have made a move without a single hesitation.

Yes, I've known Brad since kindergarten, but that doesn't matter. If he let Ivy go, I wouldn't have hesitated to let her know that I was interested. Before the dozen or so other guys who would absolutely be waiting in the wings did.

But do I want to be the one to tell her that her wedding isn't going to happen?

When she's literally five minutes from walking down the aisle?

When the chairs outside in the gorgeous flower garden they've chosen for the ceremony are full to the brim with her family and friends?

When she's spent the morning getting her hair and makeup done and is now wearing what I assume is her dream dress?

Fuck. No.

"I'm not telling Ivy," Harrison says, taking a big step back toward the door. "That's Brad's job."

I scowl at him. "No shit. But Brad isn't here because he's clearly a cowardly cocksucking chickenshit. So if I'm doing it, you're doing it." Then I add, "Please."

I met Harrison playing at the park the summer *before* kindergarten, so he's been my friend longer than Brad has. He was also my college roommate and is now my business partner. We're Harrison Ford together, for fuck's sake. We've been dealing with those jokes—and a reluctant but undeniable love for Indiana Jones (but *not* Star Wars)—for twenty-six years together. We're basically inseparable.

If *he* dumped a woman minutes before walking down the aisle, I would…

No. Harrison would never do that. If he had doubts, he would have pulled the plug before the save the date cards went out. Hell, he never would have proposed unless he was absolutely one hundred percent sure, because he doesn't fall in love easily. He's still very much playing the field, not settling down and committing to one person.

He'd never bail on someone last minute like this. He's a good guy. Though some might characterize him as a playboy, he'd never hurt a woman or a man if he committed to walking down the aisle with them.

"I'm not good at this sort of thing," Harrison says, his face stricken. He looks like he wants to dive under the rolling rack our tuxes had been hung on. "You know that."

He's actually great with people, charming and sociable. But, I have to admit, he's not the best with bad news. He likes happy occasions, parties, celebrations, and wining and dining—be it clients, employees, or dates. He absolutely doesn't want to do *this.*

Fuck, neither do I. The thought of seeing Ivy's face crumple when she realizes she's been stood up ten minutes before her wedding makes my gut clench miserably.

My shoulders slump. "Don't make me do this alone. Not with Ivy."

Harrison knows I have a thing for our friend's fiancee. I've kept it under wraps with Brad and Ivy, for obvious reasons. But Harrison knows me too well to keep it from him.

He tips his head back and groans. "Fine. I'll go with you. But God, I'm going to kill Brad for this."

"Why would you want to kill Brad?"

We both straighten quickly and spin toward the door that Harrison didn't shut fully behind him.

Ivy.

Ivy is standing in the doorway.

In her wedding dress.

Dammit.

"Have you guys seen him? I haven't talked to him all day and I can't find him."

And Jesus fucking Christ I have never seen a more beautiful woman in my life.

The dress leaves her shoulders bare and nips in slightly at the waist, but falls straight to the floor with a short train fanning out behind her. Her light blonde hair is styled in loose curls that frame her gorgeous, sweet face and fall just past her shoulders. All of that skin is gorgeous and golden, but worry has flushed her cheeks and made her big blue eyes bright.

Ivy looks worried. Gorgeous. But worried.

Harrison clears his throat and then elbows me.

I cough and then nod. "Uh, yeah. I've…heard from him."

Her eyes widen, and she visibly relaxes. "Oh, thank God. Where is he?" She frowns. "And why do you want to kill him?"

Fuck.

Harrison looks at me. I look at him.

I don't *technically* know where he is. He didn't tell me what plane he was getting on or where he was going.

But he's not here and I can't believe I'm the one who has to break Ivy's heart.

"What's going on?" Liam Tate, Ivy's best friend, steps into the room behind Ivy. He eyes Harrison, then me.

Liam is both shorter than me and has a slighter build, and yet when he arches an eyebrow like that—with such utter disdain—I feel about two feet tall.

He dislikes me. Because I'm Harrison's best friend. And Liam *hates* Harrison.

It's fair. About a year ago, when Liam and Harrison first met, Harrison was…well, being Harrison with Liam. Charming and flirtatious and…noncommittal.

And now the two of them can't be in the same room without snarking at each other.

"Guys? Where's Brad?" Liam asks, saying it slowly, as if we're not very bright.

"Well. He isn't here with us," Harrison says, clearly stalling.

Liam rolls his eyes. "Thank you for that brilliant observation." He gestures to the small room that couldn't hide a Leprechaun. "So where is he?"

"Where are any of us, really?" Harrison murmurs. "In the grand scheme of things, that is."

Oh, God. Harrison is known as the 'people person' in our company. He's charming, smooth, fantastic on his feet. He can talk even the surliest chef into trying new dishes and even the prickliest food critic into giving second, even third, chances.

But he's *terrible* with Liam.

How he ever got the broody younger man into bed in the first place is beyond me. They couldn't be more different, and Liam clearly thinks Harrison is an idiot.

Which he certainly seems to be whenever Liam is around.

But Harrison still wants Liam. Oh, he denies it but it's obvious to me. I have no idea how Liam feels about Harrison beyond chronically perturbed. I just know that they bicker and bitch whenever they're together, and right now I don't have time for *any* of their usual shit.

My concern is Ivy.

Ivy's relief has turned to agitation again. She's swiping frantically through her phone and biting her lower lip.

"Just answer the damned question," Liam snaps at Harrison. "The officiant wants to talk to Brad before the ceremony."

Harrison stares him down. "Hey, where's your tie?"

"What?" Liam's hand goes to his throat, and he frowns, even as he clears his throat. "With my jacket."

Harrison and I are in tuxes. Liam is supposed to be too, but he hasn't even tucked his shirt in yet. Liam is one of those guys who always looks like he's just rolled out of bed and simply run his hand through his hair—a fact that Harrison has pointed out to me more than once.

Liam is standing up as Ivy's best man, while Harrison and I share the title on Brad's side.

Or that's how it *was* going to be.

Liam suddenly looks a little flustered, and I think it has more to do with Harrison than the missing groom. But he glances over at Ivy and clears his throat again. "Seriously, where is Brad? This isn't cool."

"It's all fine, William," Harrison says, calling Liam the stupid-assed nickname he'd come up with for the grumpy writer.

He'd had to explain to me that William is the English version of Liam. It doesn't matter. It annoys Liam, which is really Harrison's whole purpose for it.

"Don't worry. We're handling it," Harrison says.

His voice is a touch condescending and his expression is... stupid.

I give my friend a look. A look that says *stop being an evasive asshole for no reason, I know you want to bang him but we absolutely do not have this* all at once.

Liam is now glowering at Harrison. "You've got it? No problem? Everything is fine?"

Harrison gives him a nod. "Of course."

"Then where's the groom? And why isn't he answering Ivy?"

Before Harrison can make some other dumbass comment, I decide to just spill it.

I take a deep breath, blow it out, then look at Ivy. "He's...not here. At the venue."

Her brows arch. "Where is he? Stuck in traffic?"

"No. And I'm not sure *exactly* where he is. Well, I know where he is but not where he's going."

Her eyes narrow now, and she props a hand on her hips. "What the hell is going on, Ford?"

I wince. Her words are angry, and there's no getting out of this. It's time to just be honest. And deal with the fall-out.

"He texted me. From the airport. He's not coming. He..." *Fuck, fuck, fuck.* "...doesn't want to get married. I'm so sorry. I'm really, really sorry."

Please don't cry. Jesus, please don't cry.

But then you could hold her. Comfort her. Stroke her hair.

No! You do not want her to cry! This woman is sweet and doesn't deserve this.

Just... please don't cry.

Ivy is staring at me. "What?"

Then she looks at Harrison. "Is this a joke?"

He just grimaces and shakes his head.

Then she looks at Liam.

"Jesus," he breathes, running a hand over his face. "That fucking asshole."

Then Ivy takes a deep breath, swallows, nods, and says. "Okay. So...someone needs to find me some tequila. Right now."

Fuck. This is going to be so bad.

Thanks a lot, Brad.

CHAPTER 2

Ivy

I'M SUPPRESSING the urge to laugh.

I press my lips together and work on swallowing against the snort that's trying to escape. It causes my eyes to water a little and I figure that will make me look sad, which *is* appropriate.

Laughing is not.

I have three men staring at me with varying stricken expressions because my fiancé has skipped town—on our wedding day —and I really do have an overwhelming urge to giggle.

Not because it's funny.

Oh, it's *not* funny.

But ever since I was a little girl, whenever something shocks me or makes me uncomfortable, I laugh. It's a nervous thing, but so, so inappropriate. It either freaks people out or makes them blind with rage, which was the case when I giggled at my grandfather's funeral when I was seven. My aunt Becky spanked me for that because I couldn't explain how the sheer horror of seeing his coffin overwhelmed me, and laughter leaked out.

It's the same feeling I have right now.

Horror.

Liam, who knows me better than anyone on the planet, including my disappearing groom, takes me at face value that I need a drink and stalks over to a side table that has a whiskey bottle and glasses on it. It's not tequila but I'll drink anything short of rubbing alcohol right now.

I'm struggling not to laugh, my face flushed with both rage and embarrassment, and because I'm wearing a skintight fitted wedding gown, my chest is rising up and falling painfully.

This can't be happening.

But it most definitely is.

I watch as Harrison scrubs a hand over his face and mutters, "I'm going to fucking kill him."

Okay, so this is why they were talking about killing Brad.

At least I'm not the only one who wants bodily harm to come to Brad right now.

I look at Ford. He's looking at me with clear concern. He takes a step toward me. He even murmurs, "It's okay. You're going to be okay."

Liam hands me a glass and I toss back the liquor in one big gulp, shuddering as it burns down my throat. Whiskey dribbles on my chin and I don't even care because it has the desired effect —it grounds me and negates the urge to dissolve into hysterics.

"One more, please." I hand Liam the glass back.

He turns on his heel and heads back to the table.

Two hundred.

That's how many guests are sitting in the garden right now. Two hundred people who are here to witness a wedding that isn't going to happen.

There are thousands of dollars in floral arrangements, crates of wine and champagne, a hand-painted sign by a renowned local artist that declares, "Welcome to Ivy and Brad's Happily Ever After!" and an entire *barn* festooned with ivy in my honor, along with a seven-course meal to be served by some of the city's most celebrated chefs as a nod to Brad.

Do you know how hard it is to find a suitable barn in Los Angeles?

Not easy, let me tell you.

And this incredibly gorgeous and insanely expensive wedding is not happening because Brad decided *today* he didn't want to get *married*?

He asked *me*! I wasn't even thinking about getting married until he planned a trip to Santa Barbara for us and got down on one knee and proposed with a hired mariachi band behind us in his favorite seaside Mexican restaurant. He said the theme of the evening was "quaint" and that with me, he felt rooted, grounded. Himself.

So apparently "himself" is a dick and his roots are rotten.

I throw my hand out for the glass Liam is shoving at me for the second time. He has the entire bottle in his free hand.

"This is *bullshit*," I manage to spit out, before taking another fortifying sip. "He could have had the decency to tell me himself!"

Ford nods rapidly. "I agree. I totally agree. This is just cowardly."

"The minute I see him, I'm going to punch him for you," Harrison says. "There's no excuse for this."

There really isn't.

I know we've been fighting lately, but I chalked that up to wedding stress. Even with a wedding planner, it's consumed tons and tons of my time. Plus, we're moving across the country right after the wedding. Brad seemed almost jealous of the time both took away from him, or so I'd thought. Even though both the big wedding and the move were his idea.

Now it seems like all that meant a hell of a lot more than I realized.

That Brad doesn't want to marry me.

Which is ironic as hell.

Because more than once over the last six months I've had the tiny, what-I-thought-was-a-traitorous fear that I don't want to marry *him*. But I stuffed it down. Deep. Because he loves me and I ground him.

"What am I supposed to do?" I groan. "There's all those

people out there. All that food. Oh, my God, we're *moving* tomorrow. To Honeysuckle Harbor, South Carolina."

I don't know why I announce the location. It's not like they don't know. Both Harrison and Ford are from South Carolina, still live there the majority of their time, and Liam knows everything about me.

But I'm starting to feel weird. Hot and slightly dizzy. I sway on my feet and Harrison reaches out and grabs my arms to steady me.

"Whoa there," he says softly.

His hands are warm, and I lean into his touch.

"I quit my job!" I exclaim.

I *love* my job as a food stylist on the hit cooking show *Southern Charm*. Or I did until I quit my job to *move across the country* for Brad.

"Shh," Harrison says, rubbing my arms comfortingly. "There are other jobs."

It's such a dumb thing to say a crack of laughter escapes my mouth. It sounds like a wild cackle. "Sure, there are other jobs but not the job I *love*. And yes, there are other fish in the sea and maybe this was meant to be and God only gives us what we can handle and it's only money, right? Did I miss any other major platitude?"

Harrison winces. "I think you have the big ones covered."

I feel instantly guilty. He was only trying to help. It's not his fault Brad's an asshole. What is Harrison supposed to say to me? I sigh. "Harrison, I'm sorry, I appreciate it—

"Don't you apologize, Ivy," he says firmly with a frown. "This is on Brad. I just wish I could do something. Anything."

"Hey," Ford says, nudging Harrison aside. "Look at me, Ivy."

Harrison's hands do fall off of me, but he doesn't really move out of my personal space. Liam is pacing back and forth behind us, his phone to his ear.

"Answer your fucking phone, you piece of shit!" Liam says, confirming for me that he's trying to reach Brad.

I shift my gaze to Ford.

His hazel eyes are drilling into me with care and concern. I've never really noticed his eyes before, but they're actually very lovely, with flecks of gold in them. Most of all, they're kind.

"Ivy, take a deep breath with me." Ford squeezes my hands gently. "In and out. Come on."

I obey. We breathe in together, my chest and shoulders rising. We breathe out together, Ford's exhalation a controlled stream, mine a hot, anxious burst of air.

But I do feel better.

"I need to go tell everyone," he says, his voice calm, controlled. "I'll be right back."

"I should tell everyone," Harrison says, adjusting the knot on his tie. "As one of the best men. And Brad's former best friend. You stay with Ivy."

Harrison starts to move toward the door, but I reach out and grab his arm. "Wait."

His eyebrows raise. "You don't want to do this yourself. Trust me."

I shake my head rapidly. "Oh, God, no, I don't want to announce that Brad is dipping out on our wedding. But I don't think we should cancel the reception, just the ceremony. People have traveled from all over to be here. The money is already paid, everything is set up, there's so much food that would go to waste…just tell them the ceremony is canceled and we're going straight to the party."

Maybe it's the whiskey winding its way through my veins. Maybe it's being raised by practical parents. Maybe it's my stubborn pride that is refusing to allow anyone to think I'm lying on the floor sobbing about being a jilted bride.

It's probably a little of all of the above.

"You're sure?" Harrison studies me.

"Yes."

Ford's arm has slipped around my waist and I realize I'm

leaning into him. The support is nice, especially considering these guys are Brad's oldest friends.

Harrison looks to Liam. "What do you think?"

Liam's face is red with anger. He's shoving his phone into his pocket. "If that's what Ivy wants, that's what we'll do. Why the hell are you asking me?"

Harrison stiffens. There's no mistaking the venom in Liam's voice and I suspect not all of it is directed toward the missing Brad.

Liam definitely had his feelings hurt by Harrison after they hooked up, though the details are a little unclear to me. Liam isn't big on sharing his feelings, not even with me.

Their obvious tension is actually giving me something to focus on other than my own shock and grief—though is it grief or just a bruised ego? At the moment, I'm not even sure, which is very confusing.

"Liam, go with Harrison, please," I say, determined to focus on the practical matters at hand. "I need you to tell my parents first before Harrison addresses the whole crowd. And my bridesmaids."

I only have two. My little sister, Cece, who is only fourteen, and is going to be devastated, and Brad's sister, Julianna, who has never warmed up to me and vice versa. I suspect Julianna will be shedding no tears today.

Liam grimaces, but he nods. "Of course. Harrison, you're telling Brad's parents that their son is a selfish, cowardly asshole."

"Sure. I'll say it just like that. Word for word." Harrison rolls his eyes. He reaches out toward Liam, who immediately jerks away.

"What are you doing?" Liam demands.

"I want a sip of whiskey. Relax, William."

Oh, boy. That's not going to go over well. I know for a fact Liam hates the nickname Harrison has given him.

Liam stomps past Harrison, taking the whiskey with him, and yanks open the door to exit. "Get your own fucking whiskey."

"That is my whiskey! I brought it with me this morning!" He catches the door that Liam is letting slam in his face and stomps out of the room.

"Good to see they're getting along so well now," I joke to Ford, because if you can't laugh, you'll cry. Another useless platitude. That's not even true in my case.

"Like long-lost brothers." Then Ford looks at me when he realizes what he's said and makes a goofy face. "Maybe not *brothers*," he adds hastily.

I start laughing.

He joins in.

It feels good to laugh. It's releasing some of the tension I've felt since I walked in and knew something was terribly, horribly wrong.

"So I take it you know?" I ask. "About them?"

Ford's expression is making it pretty clear Harrison told him about his night with Liam.

"All I know is that they had a moment and then Harrison fucked it up somehow." Ford rubs his jaw. "He doesn't mean to, but he does that regularly."

"Liam doesn't have the best track record either. He keeps things too close to the cuff then is shocked when people can't read his mind."

"Well, hopefully they can put whatever the hell their feelings are aside and handle all this." Ford clears his throat. "Brad's an idiot. In case you didn't know that."

"I'm getting that impression, yes."

I study him, curious. I don't know Harrison and Ford particularly well. Sure, they've come into town several times over the year that I've been dating Brad and we've all hung out, but I've never *really* talked to either of them. Not one on one, or at anything more than a superficial level.

I'm impressed they're sticking around to clean up Brad's mess.

"Thank you for staying," I say softly. "I appreciate it."

Ford scoffs. "Are you kidding me? Of course. I'm so fucking

pissed right now at Brad. You shouldn't have to handle this alone. Which, I have to say, you're doing remarkably well."

"Should I be crying?" I probably should be, but one, I don't cry. Two, I feel weirdly relieved. I'm not sure I want to admit that to Ford, though. Because then he might ask why the hell I was marrying Brad in the first place, and I'm not sure I have the answer to that right now.

"Definitely. Or at the very least cursing Brad's name or throwing a glass across the room."

"The night is still young. And I'm cursing Brad's name silently in my head. I'm also debating calling him and leaving an angry voicemail, or at the very least, logging out of our joint Netflix account and changing the password so he can't watch a movie on his escape flight."

"I think that's fair."

"So I'm winning at being a jilted bride?"

"You're in like the top one percent of jilted brides."

I laugh softly. Ford is trying to meet me where I need to be met. "You're a very nice man, Ford Anderson. With terrible taste in best friends. Harrison notwithstanding."

"I can't argue with that." He offers me his arm. "Should we do this? Or do you want to change first?"

"The only thing I have on site is a satin robe that says "Mrs." so I think I'm stuck in this dress. Besides, this dress cost two months' rent and I look fabulous in it."

"You certainly do. You look incredible, Ivy."

"Thank you." I actually glance at the mirror positioned for the groomsmen to do tie checks, which is a mistake.

It's a beautiful dress, elegant and form-fitting. My hair has never looked this shiny or effortlessly wavy. The diamond pendant earrings Brad gave me for Christmas sparkle in the sunlight from the window and my makeup, done by my makeup artist friend, Patrice, is slay-all-damn-day amazing.

I do look a little stunned, and a little flushed.

Like a bride who was left on her wedding day by her shitheel of a groom.

Who has not called or even texted me. Which means I'm not calling or texting him because he can't have any explanation for me that could justify this behavior. I refuse to beg for answers as to how he could hurt and humiliate me this way.

Instead, I take a deep, fortifying breath and slip my engagement ring off of my finger. "Here. Do something with this before I flush it down the nearest toilet."

My finger feels empty after the weight of the hefty diamond resting on it for the last four months.

But I'm determined not to make an ass of myself in front of anyone.

Ford takes the ring from me and I shiver at the unexpected brush of his warm flesh over mine. The little jolt of electricity startles me, makes me warm in places only the whiskey should be touching.

He just smiles reassuringly at me. "You've got this."

"I do."

I do.

Oh, the irony of that.

CHAPTER 3

Liam

TODAY WAS SUPPOSED to be a day I was going to just get through. Suck it up, tough it out, don't be a selfish dick and be there for Ivy on her big day.

Not happy for her.

That was never going to happen.

But supportive.

Not for one single second did I ever want her to marry Brad, who is definitely all wrong for her. He's a narcissist, and she's… Ivy.

Brilliant, sophisticated, loyal, confident and caring. Artistic and polished and talented, not to mention drop dead gorgeous. Even now, having been rejected and left in a very vulnerable position, she's rocking that wedding gown, her body shown off to absolute perfection in the white silk.

I am so fucking proud of her for holding her head up high in the face of Brad's horrible betrayal. I never liked the guy, but to stand her up on their wedding day?

He's lucky he's on a plane right now.

I lean against the doorframe at the edge of the dance floor and watch her dancing with a group of her girlfriends and her little sister, arms raised above her head as she dances off beat.

Okay, so maybe she's not perfect. She really can't dance, which I have on occasion informed her of, because I'm nothing if not brutally honest. That is, I am about most things.

I've never been totally honest with her about my feelings for her.

I've never shared with Ivy that I don't just love her as a friend, that I'm *in* love with her. Even if once upon a time, for a brief moment, I'd thought maybe she and I…

But no. It never happened.

When Ivy and I first met three years ago at a launch party for a new celebrity-owned gin, I was dating Anthony, an Italian model. Once I realized that he was all beauty, no brains, and ended it, Ivy was casually dating some guy she met playing beach volleyball. That didn't last long, but by then I was casually seeing someone else.

I'm attracted to women but I haven't dated them as often as men because they usually try to change me. They want more emotion from me, more romance. That isn't me. Never going to be. That's one of the things I love about her. She accepts me exactly as I am—brooding, deep, a little prickly, but fiercely loyal.

For the last few years, the only woman I've wanted is Ivy.

But while I was trying to extract myself from the disaster that was Paul, the podiatrist, Ivy met Brad on set at his cooking show and that was that. Love at first demi-glace.

So because she's my best friend, and she was going to marry Brad, I was going to grit my fucking teeth and endure it because I want her to be happy. More than anything else in the entire world.

Besides, you can't talk anyone out of anything.

Even if they're mistakes.

Like fucking Brad.

Who is still too much of a coward to answer his phone or his text messages.

When he gets back to L.A. he has some fucking explaining to do.

"Let's hear it for the bride!" the DJ says enthusiastically as he launches into a remix of early two thousands pop music.

The guy is trying. I'll give him that.

And truthfully, so is Ivy.

She almost might be drunk.

Ivy yells, "Woo!" with her arms up. Her breast almost pops out of her gown, and she grabs at her dress, almost toppling over.

Okay, she's definitely drunk.

No one can possibly blame her.

The one hundred or so guests who stuck around for the party all clap and cheer.

They're here to support Ivy, because they love her, and probably not because they want to dance to Usher's "Yeah."

Though her aunt Becky is really getting down right now. But mostly, they're out there on the dance floor to protect her, to surround her with her people. Ford is out there, dancing as poorly as Ivy, but he's giving it his all.

Brad's family has left, which was for the best.

Since dinner, this has been my post, watching over Ivy on the dance floor, simultaneously studying her to make sure she's okay and tamping down my feelings of complete and utter fucking relief that she is *not* married and hours away from wedding night sex in a hotel suite with a guy who isn't me.

Sex with Ivy…yeah, I've thought about it once or twice or a thousand times.

I sip my whiskey.

Or rather, Harrison's whiskey.

The thought makes me smirk to myself. I've been carting this bottle around all night at great inconvenience to myself just because I refuse to let him have it back. It's stupidly expensive bourbon, but he can afford another bottle.

He loves to dig at me, so this is my petty revenge. Bourbon theft.

That's another reason I was going to just grin and fucking bear it today.

Harrison.

If my feelings for Ivy are straightforward—I love her but the timing was never right between us—my feelings for Harrison are a tangled and twisted mess.

As an introvert, I'm drawn to the opposite, and Harrison is definitely that. When I first laid eyes on him, my impression was that he was hot as fuck and a lot of fun.

He's both.

The things he can do with his talented tongue…

I shift and clear my throat, wishing I could adjust my dick in my tux pants. I never bothered putting on my tie or jacket.

But after a night filled with laughter and then a whole hell of a lot of naked fun, Harrison sneaked out of my apartment at dawn before I woke up and then didn't answer my calls. I felt like a complete idiot for misreading the signals. I'd thought we had a connection. I'd woken up prepared to make breakfast for him and I don't even cook.

Maybe I'm more of a romantic than I like to think.

Not Harrison.

It was rude as hell.

Even if it was a casual hookup to him, I still think someone who got naked with you deserves the courtesy of a goddamn goodbye.

I'm an adult, I can handle a "this was fun, but nothing else" brush off. But say something.

Then again, Harrison is best friends with Brad, the disappearing groom, so there you go.

"Fuck ghosting," I mutter aloud.

Even as I say the words, I'm looking all over the barn to see if I can find Harrison. He's nowhere to be found.

"Damn right," Patrice says, sidling up alongside me in a plunging red dress with earrings shaped like champagne bottles. "Fucking ghosting. But that's L.A. for you."

Ivy has known Patrice longer than me and they're friends, but

Patrice is a little flaky. She is just as likely to do the ghosting as to be ghosted.

"Bourbon?" I hold the bottle out to her. My wrist is getting tired from gripping the neck and picturing breaking it over both Brad's and Harrison's heads.

I glance over at Ivy. She's throwing back a shot of something, which makes me frown. I feel like she's already had enough to drink.

"I thought you'd never ask." Patrice accepts the bottle and takes a sip. "By the way, it's not weird at all that you're standing on the edge of the dance floor pining for your best friend at her wedding with a bottle of liquor in your hand and your hair artfully disheveled." She reaches over and ruffles my hair. "It's actually a rom com, Liam."

I yank my head away from her touch, frowning. "I have no idea what you're talking about."

"Uh-huh. Sure you don't." The look she gives me smacks of pity. "The whole sad writer thing is really working for you."

"I'm not a *sad* writer. I work on a science fiction show." I also happen to be secretly giddy that Ivy isn't married.

Patrice eyes me up and down. "Uh-huh. Sure. Hey, did you know that if you wear a red dress to a wedding as a guest, it means you fucked the groom?"

That yanks me out of my complicated thoughts. I stand up straight, turn, and stare at her. Patrice has chaotic layered black hair, thin lips, and heavy eye makeup.

Patrice is wearing a red dress. "Did Brad cheat on Ivy with you?" I demand.

If he did, I will track him down and rip his balls off with my bare hands.

She bursts out laughing. "Kidding. Oh my God, what? I would never do that to Ivy, stop. Learn to take a joke. You are sooo obvious."

I rub my forehead and sigh. I have a headache. "That's not funny."

"I literally just heard that tonight. I've never heard that before and someone just told me. Like, what? Have you heard that? Obviously, I would *not* have worn this if I'd known that. But I thought, like red goes with a barn, right? Rustic?"

She's making my headache worse. I need to get some water and ply both myself and Ivy with it.

"I've never heard that. Keep the bottle," I tell her.

When I turn, I almost run into Harrison. I rear back.

Being in his presence makes me hot and angry on a good day.

Today is a *complicated* day. Filled with concern for Ivy and yet, relief for her too, because Brad isn't good enough for her. Hope for me that maybe if I open my fucking mouth in a few weeks when she's recovered from this debacle, I can convince her to give me a shot.

There's also irritation that I think Ford might have a crush on her. The way he looks at her…not cool.

And then here is Harrison, grinning at me, and looking muscular and sexy and casually rich.

There's no fucking way I want to deal with any more of his snarky comments right now.

He opens his mouth—that mouth I can't seem to forget about —to, I'm sure, say something he thinks is funny and that I'll hate.

But the DJ's mic screams with reverb and we both wince and turn. Ivy is wrestling the mic from the DJ.

"That can't be good," Harrison says.

I glare at him and just walk away, heading straight to Ivy to conduct an intervention if necessary.

"Welcome to Ivy and Brad's happily ever after!" she announces with a tipsy cackle. "That didn't last long, did it? No, seriously, thank you all so much for being here, sacrificing your Saturday just to witness me being dumped by a man child."

I start walking faster, hoping she'll spot me in the crowd so I can convey to her that she needs to step away from the mic. Slicing motions across my throat should do it.

But her eyes are darting all around the room, a cocktail glass in her hand. Liquid splashes over the side as she waves it in an attempt at a toast. "Whoops," she says, lifting her hand and licking the back of it. "Never let good alcohol go to waste."

I sense Harrison is on my heels. I walk faster.

"We love you, Ivy!" Patrice calls from the back of the room.

"Thank you, babe. At least someone does." Ivy takes a long swallow of her half-empty glass.

I'm jogging now, my heart hammering in my chest.

"Why is this fucking barn so big?" Harrison asks behind me, echoing my own thoughts.

But I refuse to admit that. "Because it's a barn," I snap. "Why is no one else stopping her?"

Her mother is standing to the side, a hand over her mouth, sobbing. Ivy's father is comforting her mother. The girl I recognize as Ivy's cousin is draped all over Ford, who is trying to shake her loose.

It's time to pull the plug on this night.

"You know, I never wanted to get married," Ivy muses into the mic, swaying on her feet. "I honestly never cared about that. I just wanted to be *happy*. There were red flags with Brad, you know. That I ignored. Big ones, giant red flags, and yet I ran right toward them like a bull to a…what are those guys called? With the black velvet pants?"

I'm sweating as I reach her and yank the mic out of her hand. "Matador! That's what they're called!" I boom into the microphone, way louder than I intend. My fake cheerful voice makes me wince. I turn toward the guests, blocking Ivy from their view. "Wow, okay, this has just been amazing to see how loved Ivy is. Thank you all for being here and supporting her. We're going to wind things down now, so uh, good night."

Harrison is now murmuring to Ivy, who is protesting loudly. "I want to stay! I'm *fine!*"

"Party's over," I tell her.

I hand the mic to Harrison. "You're better at this than me. Get everyone out of here."

His eyebrows raise. "A compliment from *you*, William? That was almost worth today."

I ignore him and take Ivy's hand. I try to gently tug her forward. She resists, digging in her heels. "Liam, stop. I'm staying."

"No, you're not."

She's left me with no choice. She may be mad at me now, but she'll thank me tomorrow.

Bending my knees, I scoop Ivy up under her perfect ass and lift her up.

Then I haul her kicking and protesting out of her wedding reception.

CHAPTER 4

Harrison

I HEAR the clink of glassware and the water running in the kitchenette of the suite.

I crack one eye open and spot Liam at the coffee pot. I'm on the couch, where I've slept fitfully for the past six hours. I glance toward the door to the suite. Ford is still awkwardly draped over the two armchairs he dragged across the room and positioned in front of the door to keep Ivy from sneaking out.

Liam had taken the other side of the gigantic king bed with her, presumably in case she needed anything in the night. But at about two a.m., Ford and I had caught her trying to sneak out to meet some friends who had texted her, asking her to meet them at a dance club.

She definitely didn't need any more alcohol and Ford wasn't about to let the newly single, more than slightly tipsy, no-fucks-left-to-give jilted bride go dancing without us to chaperone. And neither of us was in any mood to hit a club at that hour.

My best friend has had a thing for Ivy for over a year. And while he's too good of a guy to make a move on a friend's girl-friend, and certainly not on a friend's fiancée, I know it's been gnawing at him that he didn't make a move before Brad and Ivy started dating.

Oh no, Ford, ever the good guy, met Ivy, flirted his ass off, then found out she was working on Brad's show and decided he shouldn't mess around with our friend's pseudo-employee.

Ivy was a food stylist on the show where Brad was the star chef. But he was also an executive producer. And had been the one who decided to hire Ivy. She's extremely talented and I'm certain he hired her because of her professional credentials, but it did put him in a position of power over her and boy scout Ford decided that was messy.

He was really angry when he found out Brad was dating her. He even told Brad he didn't think it was a good idea.

When they got engaged, Ford got *very* drunk.

All of which makes his anger at Brad and the fucked up wedding even more intense, I'm sure.

What sounds like a spoon clatters against the inside of the sink and I rub a hand over my face. "Jesus Christ, William," I say. "There are far nicer ways to wake me up."

I make sure both of my eyes are open in time to see Liam swing to face me with his adorable glower.

"You're going to start with your bullshit this early?" he asks.

I know he's referring to my perpetual poking at him.

And yes. Yes, I am.

It's his own fault. He always looks like he just tumbled out of bed, though he typically is fully shaved and at least in jeans or khakis. Right now he's got stubble dusting his jaw, and he's wearing gray sweatpants.

How am I not supposed to want to rile him up looking grumpy and sexy and so damned fuckable?

He's just about the only person on the planet who can get me worked up and thrown off my game. And it's one of my favorite things to see him unsettled ever since I realized that the seemingly shy, introverted writer—who is actually pompous as fuck underneath—is normally cool and composed.

It seems I'm one of the few people who can get to him too.

I like that.

I fucked up with Liam. I'll be the first to admit it. Not because I walked away after our night together, but because I let that night happen in the first place.

He was supposed to be nothing more than a hot, younger guy I had a weekend fling with. I wasn't supposed to develop feelings for him, so I admittedly ran away. I wasn't supposed to still be constantly thinking about him a month later when I was trying to date other people. I certainly wasn't supposed to be getting turned on whenever I saw him a year later. But here we are. So if I'm going to be unable to ignore the chemistry between us, I'm going to make sure he can't ignore it as well.

I sit up, stretching my arms overhead, watching him watch me. I'm shirtless, wearing only a loose pair of athletic shorts. I stand up from the couch, rubbing my hand over my lower stomach, then pad toward the kitchen. Toward him.

"Yeah, I think I'm going to start early."

"For the love of *Christ*, could you two please coexist in the same room for ten fucking minutes without giving me a headache?" Ford asks from beside the door.

He's going to be a bear today. There's no way he slept well on those chairs, plus the woman he's crazy about and who he's assumed is totally off limits is newly single. There's no hope he won't be in a lousy mood.

"What are you doing over there?" Liam asks.

"Ivy decided that more tequila shots and dancing sounded like a good idea in the middle of the night," I fill in. "It took both of us and promises of bacon and Oreos this morning to get her to go back to bed."

Liam frowns. "I didn't hear her get up."

I reach up and pat his cheek. "We know."

He jerks back, then stomps across the small space and opens a cupboard. I don't think he needs anything inside that cupboard, he's just trying to get away from me.

I shouldn't be such an asshole. I was the one who left him sleeping the morning after our amazing night and then didn't return his initial phone calls. And then when I did finally pick up, did so while on a date with someone else.

He has every reason to be pissed at me.

But I can't leave him alone. And I can't admit the feelings I have for him. So I'm resorting to my usual habit of doing whatever feels good and trusting it will work out.

Yes, I am a spoiled rich brat. Raised with a silver spoon in my mouth. Think I walk on water. The whole nine yards. I own it. But usually that's not a problem. The world bends for me, but not Liam.

"Put on a fucking shirt," he tells me.

"Please," I toss back.

He turns and meets my gaze directly. "Do it."

This little fucker. He's younger than me, as a writer in Hollywood makes a pittance compared to me, isn't impressed by my wealth, doesn't give a shit about the fancy restaurants I own or the celebrities I've rubbed elbows with. And yet, when we were together, I was the one saying *please*.

A shirt hits me in the back of the head and I turn to find Ford in the kitchen with us. He reaches for a cup, jams it underneath the single cup coffee maker, and jabs the button to start it brewing.

"Where's Ivy?" he asks Liam.

"In the shower."

Ford's eyes jump to the bedroom door. My friend is clearly interested in the idea of his obsession naked and wet behind that door.

I shake my head. This situation with the four of us is messy as hell.

"I came out to get coffee and find the room service menu," Liam says. "Her hangover is in full swing. She needs caffeine and food before we can figure anything else out."

"What is there to figure out?" I ask.

"Oh, gee, I don't know," Liam says, propping himself against the counter furthest from me, and crossing his arms. "Maybe her entire life? Everything is up in the air now, thanks to *your* asshole friend. She needs to make a new plan."

I don't comment on my asshole friend. I'm no fan of Brad's right now. "As far as I can see, she dodged a bullet," I tell him. "I say she sells that gigantic engagement ring, uses the money on something completely frivolous for herself, then goes back to her life as if nothing happened. Screw Brad."

Liam's eyes widen. "You mean the life where she worked for the show where Brad is the big star? Where all of the viewers of that show knew they were getting married? The life where she *quit that job* because Brad convinced her to move to South Fucking Carolina?"

"Hey now," I say as I pull my shirt over my head and jam my arms through the sleeves. "Leave South Carolina out of this. It's not South Carolina's fault." It's home. It's where Ford and Brad and I grew up. It's where Ford and I live the majority of the time. It's where we fell in love with the restaurant business and opened our flagship restaurant, Raw.

Liam rolls his eyes in a pretentious way that makes me want to grab him and kiss him until he admits that he likes at least one thing that came out of South Carolina.

"She doesn't have a job. She doesn't have a place to live. She's been living with Brad. They were going to move into some house in South Carolina. What is she supposed to do now? She needs a new plan. She's basically homeless," Liam says.

"So we'll help her make a new plan," Ford says easily.

My buddy is a problem solver. I'm the people person in our business, charming and schmoozing people. He's the get shit done guy. He deals with numbers, obstacles, and keeps hiccups from turning into disasters. It does not surprise me one bit that he is already in fix-it mode for Ivy.

"Oh, shit." I turn and walk over to the coffee table. "I helped Ivy's parents deal with all the gifts, but there was this one left over." I pick up the flat rectangular box and head back to the kitchen. I hand it to Ford.

"What is it?" he asks.

"I have no idea. But look who it's from."

He flips the tag on top and reads. Then he scowls. "This *fucker*. What is he up to?"

Liam frowns. "What is it?"

"It's from Brad," I say.

Liam leans in and grabs the box from Ford. He rips the paper off.

"Hey, you think you should do that?" Ford asks.

"Preemptively check what other fuckery Brad is up to?" Liam asks, pulling the box top off. "Yes." He pulls out a short stack of papers, letting the box and wrapping paper drop to the floor. He reads the top page, then flips to the second, then the third.

"What is it?" Ford asks.

Liam looks up. "Brad gave her the house."

"What house?" I ask. But a second later, the answer hits me.

"The house in South Carolina," Liam confirms.

"What do you mean, he *gave* me the house?"

We all turn to find Ivy standing just outside the bedroom door.

Damn, this girl keeps sneaking up on us. She's like a ninja.

I hear Liam sigh. He steps past me to stand right in front of her. "This is a gift from Brad." He hands her the papers. "Apparently, the house in South Carolina is fully yours. It's all paid for. But everything connected to it is in your name." He pauses. "Only your name."

Ivy takes the papers, staring at the top page for several seconds before looking up at her friend. "I don't want the house in South Carolina."

Liam nods. "I know."

"So why would he do this?" she asks.

"His letter says it's an apology. For leaving you. He didn't want you to be without anything." Liam says the last word weakly.

Ivy holds her hand out for the letter, and Liam passes it to her. I see her scan it, lips pressing together. It must be short but it's mere seconds later that she's looking back up at us. "That's literally all it says," she says, sounding mystified. "No explanation for anything."

I look at Ford. Brad has turned into a gigantic dickhead over the past couple of years since his cooking show has taken off. But still, I can't believe this is the guy that we grew up with.

Ford looks murderous.

"We will fix this," he says firmly. "You don't have to keep a house you don't want."

She looks at him. "So what am I going to do?"

Ford uses that as a reason to walk past me and go to stand in front of her with Liam.

I've never seen my friend like this about a woman. Ford gets plenty of attention from the female variety. Sometimes male too, but he doesn't care about that. Ford dates. He's very romantic. He's a great guy. He takes care of everyone around him. But I've never seen him actually enamored with any of the women he's dated. It's like none of them have really fit before.

But I remember the night he met Ivy. And how he reacted after he realized he shouldn't pursue her.

I also remember the night he found out that Brad was dating her. I don't think Ford has been that drunk since college.

He has tried to drink her out of his system, work her out of his system, fuck her out of his system with other women. And none of it has worked. He tries to hide it, but every time we are around her, even when it's with Brad, I can tell it kills Ford a little.

And now she's single.

And in need.

This is Ford's fucking kryptonite.

He is in so much trouble.

I study her now as Liam and Ford flip through the pages of the agreement Brad left for her.

She really is beautiful. I've always thought so, of course. And she is funny, and sweet, and has this elegant sophistication about her that I find fascinating. She has amazing taste in everything, but it seems second nature. Even now, hung over, fresh out of the shower, she's wearing an outfit that is clearly supposed to be for lounging, but is made of expensive material and is matched and perfectly fitted to her trim frame. Her hair is pulled into a loose but stylish French braid that hangs over one shoulder, and even without makeup and hungover her skin is glowing.

She carries herself with an easy, confident air, and is always composed. In fact, yesterday at the wedding was the first time I've *ever* seen her anything but totally put together. And yet, even with all of that, she makes everyone around her feel at ease.

I am amazing at working a room full of people. I'm not at all intimidated by power, status, or wealth. But my charm is more exuberant. I've seen Ivy do the same thing I do—mingle, and charm, and convince everyone around her that she's right about whatever she's saying—but with a soft, sophisticated ease.

Studying her now, I think about that and the fact that the two of us together could probably run the United Nations easily and peacefully.

"I don't want this fucking house!" she exclaims.

I have to grin. I'm not sure I've ever heard Ivy say the word fucking. That's not only amusing but it makes it more impactful honestly.

"You'll sell it," Ford says, his tone calm and confident.

Of course I would've never asked Ivy out. When I met her, Ford was already enamored—that took about five minutes—then Brad was dating her and then engaged to her. And then there's Liam.

I study the guy again while he's unaware.

Ivy and Liam are best friends. I never would've met him if it wasn't for Ivy. He had been invited to the same party because of her. Ford and I were there because of Brad. It was some celebration for their show getting picked up for the second season.

Yes, I find Ivy absolutely attractive and I love dating women, too. But once I met Liam, he was my focus that night.

"How am I going to sell a house in South Carolina?" Ivy asks Ford.

"Well, it probably would be best if you went to Honeysuckle Harbor," he says.

Ivy sighs and looks like she might cry for a moment.

Liam reaches out and takes her hand. "You were going to make that trip anyway. Just go. Sell the house. Then you can come back here. You know you can stay with me as long as you need to."

She gives a short little laugh. "I love you, but your apartment is not exactly…"

"Sleep on the street then," Liam says with a shrug.

But Ivy is giving him a very affectionate smile. "Thank you." She lifts a hand and rubs it over her forehead. "I guess I'm driving to South Carolina."

I frown, but Ford says what I'm thinking before I can.

"You're *driving* to South Carolina?"

She lifts a shoulder. "We were moving there. I need my car to get around once I'm there. And all of my worldly belongings have already been taken there by the moving company."

That all sinks in. Brad was going to be driving with her. Now she's alone.

"You are not making that trip by yourself," Ford says. "I'll drive with you."

Her eyes widen, and for a second I think she's going to protest. I should tell her there is no point. Ford will absolutely not let her drive by herself.

But Ivy's smart. She nods. "Okay. Thank you."

"I'll come with you," Liam says. He shoots a quick frown at Ford.

I want to laugh. He's incredibly brilliant. I'm not surprised that he has picked up on the fact that Ford has feelings for his bestie. Plus, Ivy doesn't know Ford that well. And it's a long ass trip from California to South Carolina.

"You're going to come?" Ivy asks. "Can you take the time?"

"I can write on the road," Liam says, seemingly unconcerned.

She looks up at Ford. "Well, then you don't have to come. Liam can keep me company."

I grin, waiting for Ford's very predictable answer.

"I'm still coming."

There's obviously no reason for Ford to make this drive with Ivy. Except that he wants to.

I decide to help my buddy out. Plus, this will really rub a certain broody writer the wrong way.

"Road trip!" I say enthusiastically. "I'm in."

They all turn to look at me.

"You don't need to come," Liam says bluntly. With that cute glower.

"But I'm going to," I tell him with a grin. "It's been a long time since I took a good road trip. But I'm telling you right now, it's Twizzlers all the way. No fucking Red Vines."

Liam just studies me.

And I know my grumpy onetime lover is figuring out there is no way out of this.

He might be bossy as fuck in the bedroom and pissed as hell at me, but I'm stubborn and have nowhere I need to be any time soon. I'm coming on this road trip. Whether he likes it or not.

Ford looks from me to Liam to Ivy and then back to me. "So the four of us are going to road trip from California to South Carolina?"

I nod. "Looks like it."

Ford shakes his head. "What could possibly go wrong?"

CHAPTER 5

Ivy

"CAN I borrow ten million dollars?"

Ford is sitting next to me in the backseat of my Prius. He looks over and grins. "Sure."

I don't know if he's grinning about my question or my appearance.

Liam rolled his eyes when I walked out of the inn to get in the car. Harrison's eyes widened, and he said, "Right this way rock star," as he opened the back door and helped me into the backseat.

Maybe I'm being a little dramatic, but I love the pink, orange, and yellow headscarf and oversized yellow sunglasses I'm wearing. The scarf because I didn't feel like doing my hair. The glasses because the sun is really freaking bright this morning.

But besides the headache, scratchy eyes, and general regret over my life decisions, I feel very Elizabeth Taylor. I'd feel even more glam if I was drinking out of a martini glass instead of my pink Stanley cup, but I didn't want to spill anything when we hit the bumps in the road.

Yes, I'm day drinking.

I was left at the altar yesterday and I am now on my way to

South Carolina to deal with a house I apparently own and don't want.

If anyone deserves an oversized thermal cup full of vodka and soda water at ten a.m., it's me.

Ford hands me the water bottle that he has been routinely passing to me over the past three hours.

I sip to make him happy. Ford has been very sweet. He hasn't said a single judgmental word, and has just been plying me with water, food, and ibuprofen while I tip back my Stanley cup. But because of him I'm only mildly buzzed and my headache has faded and I actually feel okay instead of like, oh, every decision I've made in the past six months was terrible and the consequences have all smacked me in the face at once.

I take a long pull on my straw, then ask him, "Actually, can I just *have* ten million dollars because 'borrow' makes it sound like I'll pay it back and there's no way that's going to happen."

He chuckles and I feel a strange swirly heat in my stomach. I'm aware that is probably inappropriate, everything considered, but it's undeniable and I have enough vodka in my system to just enjoy it instead of trying to squelch the attraction to my ex fiancé's best friend.

Brad has a lot of faults, but his taste in friends is top-notch.

"Yes. You can *have* ten million dollars, Ivy."

Wow, I guess that confirms that he has ten million dollars that he could just part with on a whim, and it's pretty nice to think that he would give it to me without question.

I give him a smile that I think is possibly a little wobbly from the liquor, but is no less genuine.

"You're not even going to ask me what it's for?"

"I'm sure you've got a good reason."

I look toward the front seat, roll my eyes and look back to him. "I'm going to pay them to shut the fuck up. I assume you'll agree that's a good reason."

He glances at the front seat, where Liam is driving and Harrison is lounging in the passenger seat, wearing an irritated look. They've been bickering almost nonstop, completely ignoring Ford and me.

"Getting them to shut up is a great reason," Ford agrees. "But you realize for ten million dollars we could just buy a new car and hire a driver and leave these two on their own."

I salute him with my cup. "Very good point. Why haven't you brought that up before now, Mr. Multi-millionaire?"

He chuckles, then shrugs. "I suppose I'm trying to keep them both alive and I don't think that will happen if they're left alone?"

Just then, Liam slams his hand onto the dash of the car. "I'm not fucking listening to any more Miley Cyrus. If you sing *anything* about buying yourself flowers, I'm kicking your ass out of this car."

Harrison hoots. "So you do know the song."

It's been like this for three hours. They've argued over the music. They've argued over the temperature. They've argued over the route we're taking. They've argued over the stops we've made.

Liam wants to listen to a podcast, though he had agreed to listen to Frank Sinatra or something classical.

I swear he did that just to annoy Harrison. Because Harrison wants to listen to heavy metal or good old-fashioned rock 'n' roll. Liam likes both.

Why my best friend can't just agree to get along for this road trip, I cannot understand.

I study them as I sip on my straw.

Well, that's not entirely true. Liam and Harrison have some history.

History that means that Liam hates Harrison. I have to admit Harrison is not one of my favorite people either, because of that history. Somebody messes with my best friend and they are on my shit list, too. But Harrison is Ford's best friend and for some reason, I really feel good about having Ford along on this trip.

The second Liam agreed to go with me, Ford was off the hook. There's no reason for me to want him here. I don't *need* him here.

Still, I'm glad he is.

I love Liam. He knows everything about me, never judges me, and will absolutely get me through this…whatever this is in my life. A bump? A low point? A glitch?

Yes, I'm aware that my broken engagement and ruined wedding should probably register as more than a glitch.

But I'm already past being sad and angry.

I'm not hurt.

I'm frustrated.

And I'm frustrated because I am on my way to my ex fiancé's hometown to sell a house he gave me that I absolutely do not want. What a pain in the ass.

But my feelings today actually have nothing to do with not marrying Brad yesterday.

Still, as much help as I know Liam will be, Ford makes me feel stable. Grounded. Like everything is going to be okay.

Liam will help me solve any problem. He'll listen to me rant. He'll let me bounce ideas off of him. And he'll do anything I ask him to do.

Ford, on the other hand, will just make things happen.

I won't need to problem solve or come up with ideas.

It's not that I *can't*. I just…don't want to right now.

I would love to have someone take care of this.

I'm an extremely capable and independent woman.

I just planned an entire wedding with zero help from my fiancé.

And then it was for nothing.

So I'm tired. And I don't want to deal with any more contracts or advice or planning or *people*.

Ford will take care of it and I love him for it.

I don't know how I know that about him. I don't know him that well. But it's just a sense I have of him. He's so confident. He never seems to blink. He just steps in, says it'll be okay, and something inside me believes him.

Brad must've talked about him, told me stories or something, right? That has to be why I feel this way about this man.

I tune back into the conversation as Liam tells Harrison,

"Because of you, we are already two hours behind schedule. Can you just *please* sit there and shut up for five minutes?"

I'm honestly not sure that Harrison can do that. He is a talker. And even though he is on my shit list because he hurt my best friend, I find him amusing. I would never admit that to Liam, but Harrison has definitely made this road trip more fun already. When he's not pissing Liam off, he's funny and interesting and his enthusiasm is contagious.

Actually, even when he is pissing Liam off, he's fun. I was all for stopping at the rubber ball museum he saw the hand-painted sign for. And I laughed just as hard as he did when we found out it was just some guy's garage and his collection of, well, rubber balls. Harrison still paid the guy our ten dollar "admission" and accepted a warm can of root beer from the "snack bar." All with a grin.

I giggle even now, thinking about it.

He teases, and picks at Liam though, and I have to say I have never seen my friend like this. Liam is quiet, unassuming, laid-back. He's an introvert for sure, but he's also just very uninterested in most other people. The fact that he is so easily riled up by Harrison is fascinating. I can't wait to talk to him about it later.

"Seriously?" Harrison asks Liam. "We don't have a schedule." He laughs. "We can't be late for something none of us intended to do."

"Not all of us have vats of money we can just dip into when we run a little low," Liam snarks. "Some of us have to work."

Harrison stretches his arm out along the back of the seats and twirls his finger in Liam's hair. "Do you need a little pocket change, William? I've got a few tasks you could do for me."

Liam slaps his hand away. "Not if I was down to my last dollar."

I shoot Ford a look. "Do you think we can find a car dealership at the next stop?"

He chuckles. "Maybe we can just send them in to watch the armadillo circus and we can take the car while they're not paying attention."

"Armadillo circus?" Harrison asks, pivoting in his seat to look back at Ford. "Did you make that up?"

"Saw a sign a few miles back," Ford says.

I study him as I take another pull on my straw. I can't tell if he's kidding. That's hilarious.

"Oh my god," Harrison says, pulling out his phone and swiping over the screen, obviously looking up *armadillo circus.* "Fuck, it's real," he says, almost in awe a moment later. "William…"

"No." Liam scowls at Ford in the rearview mirror. "We're *not* stopping and definitely not for fucking armadillos." He mutters something under his breath but I definitely hear 'or a fucking circus'.

"Come *on,*" Harrison says. "When are you ever going to be back *here* with *this* opportunity?"

"Holy shit, I hope *never,*" Liam says, looking over at him. "I can't believe we're on this damned road in the first place!"

"William," Harrison says again, his tone pleading. "*Liam…*"

I see Liam's hands tighten on the wheel. "Stop it." His voice is a little gruff.

"I'll do that thing you like," Harrison says.

I actually feel my brows arch. I glance at Ford. He gives me a *should we be here for this?* look. I shrug.

Liam clears his throat but then says, "Which thing? The thing I like, or the thing I *really* like?"

Harrison grins. "The thing you *really* like."

"Say it out loud," Liam demands.

Harrison puts his hand over his heart and declares, "I'll do whatever you say, and *shut the hell up* the whole time."

I laugh.

Harrison glances over his shoulder and winks at me. "The circus is a few miles off this road, so that's a lot of quiet time for our little introvert."

Liam sighs. "How far off this road?"

"Just a few miles," Harrison says noncommittally. "Turn here."

Liam does, but he asks again. "How far?"

"A little over ten miles."

"How much is 'a little'?" Liam asks resignedly.

Harrison just says, "I'm not supposed to be talking."

Liam actually growls.

I giggle and sip.

Harrison settles back in his seat, smiling. And not talking.

"Okay, when we get there, I'll distract them and you go for the keys from Liam," Ford says with a grin.

I look over. "Oh. Well…"

Ford sighs, but he's smiling. "You want to see the armadillos?"

"It's a *circus*, Ford," I say.

Harrison laughs. "That's my girl."

Liam growls again, louder. Maybe about me and the armadillos. Maybe about Harrison speaking. Maybe both.

Ford just shakes his head. "You know it's probably just two armadillos in some lady's backyard."

"But we kind of have to find out why she calls it a circus, right?" I ask, actually laughing now.

"Do we?" Liam asks. "Or are we just asking to be tied up in her basement with the other decaying remains of people who thought 'armadillo circus sounds totally normal and interesting'."

I laugh, and sip from my cup, and then, just to make Ford happy, I reach for the water bottle he's holding and take a long gulp.

He gives me a smile and I feel lighter. Actually happy. Less than twenty-four hours after being left at the altar. That's pretty amazing.

"And to think, you could have been on your way to your honeymoon right now," Harrison stage-whispers to me.

Obviously Liam can hear him, but instead of growling, he meets my gaze in the rearview mirror. I know he's checking on my reaction to the mention of the wedding that wasn't. I owe him a huge thank you and a hug for carrying me out of the reception before my drunken speech went any further.

But I just nod and say, "I can honestly say that an armadillo circus with you guys sounds a thousand times better."

And I really mean that. Even without knowing what exactly an armadillo circus entails.

CHAPTER 6

Ford

"NO," Harrison says, forcefully. "Absolutely not."

Ivy and I exchange a look in the backseat. She looks exhausted and I don't blame her. It's been a long hot day in the cramped backseat of this car, with Harrison and Liam going at each other most of the time.

The armadillo circus was a bust.

Well, maybe it was amazing, but we never actually found it. If it did exist, it was more off the beaten path than we were willing to search. After several turns into random driveways and Harrison's GPS glitching, Liam called it and got back on our route headed east.

Harrison can't let it go and he's not going to allow Liam to win this next round.

They're locked in battle over which hotel to stay in and where. Liam wants to push on and drive for another hour or two so we can get to South Carolina as fast as possible, but Harrison is determined to set a leisurely pace with stops at luxury hotels.

"I'm not staying in that 'motel.'" He even uses air quotes for the word motel as if Liam is suggesting we all sleep in a flop house for the night.

"Can you just compromise?" I demand. "We're already stopping earlier than Liam wanted."

"Yes, because we're not going to just drive past an iconic town like Winslow, Arizona without stopping," Harrison says, glaring at me from the passenger seat. "We're going to stand on the corner like any true American."

"What are you even talking about?" Ivy asks, leaning against the glass window as we're idling in front of a budget motel Liam has picked for us to spend the night.

I feel really bad for Ivy. After the first few hours of driving, she stopped talking, mostly just fiddling with her phone and gazing out the window. I can't tell if she's just tired or if she's devastated over her canceled wedding or something else entirely. Her mouth is pinched, and she's kept her enormous sunglasses resolutely on her face.

At least she's stopped drinking alcohol, and she did nap for a while but I'm still worried about her.

"It's from a song," Liam tells her. "It's old, so you wouldn't know it."

It's a reminder to me that Liam knows Ivy really well. I feel a pang of jealousy that is totally unjustified. He was her best man, or meant to be her best man. Of course they're close.

"From the early two thousands?" she asks.

"No. The seventies."

"Oh. Yeah, no, I wouldn't know it."

"If you heard it, you would know it," Harrison assures her. "Let me play it for you."

Liam turns the car off. "I'm going to check into the hotel."

"Motel."

Liam shoots an irritated look at Harrison. "There is absolutely nothing wrong with this hotel. It's a well-known chain with a highly regarded free continental breakfast. We don't all have piles of disposable income to blow on fancy hotels for the next week."

"I'll stay here with you, Liam," Ivy says, sitting up a little straighter and reaching down to grab her purse off of the floorboard.

"No," Harrison says. "Absolutely not. If the starving writer wants to stay here for a free bagel and bedbugs, he can, but I'm getting you a room at a decent hotel. My treat. It's the least I can do after my former best friend left you with a mess."

Ivy doesn't look like she cares one way or the other. "Fine. Thank you. I just need a shower and a bed."

I shouldn't envision Ivy in the shower, but I do. All five foot eight inches of her, rivulets of water trailing down her golden skin, over tight breasts right down to her…

I clear my throat and force myself to focus.

God, what the hell is wrong with me?

She's exhausted and heartbroken, and I'm picturing her naked.

I can't help it. Being this close to her for hours and hours is fucking with my head. And my dick. I'm aware of every move she makes, from shifting to get more comfortable, to sighing, to flips of her blonde hair back off of her shoulder under that headscarf.

At one point, Liam asked her to take it off because it was blocking his view in the rearview mirror.

She'd said, "Absolutely not. I'm channeling Elizabeth Taylor, who suffered many heartbreaks in her life."

"Wasn't she married a dozen times?" Harrison asked. "That's not really your problem."

Her answer had been a lifted chin and a withering glare that had actually brought Harrison to a shamed silence, which was no easy feat. He had muttered a hasty, "Sorry," then went back to tormenting Liam with his musical selections.

Sometimes Harrison speaks before he thinks.

Liam gets out of the car and retrieves his bag from the trunk. Then he opens Ivy's door and ducks his head in to talk to her. "I'll see you in the morning. Text me if you need anything. I'll be five minutes away and I can walk over."

She nods. "I will. I love you."

His eyes soften, which sets off alarm bells for me.

"I love you too," he murmurs and kisses her forehead. When he pulls back, his expression is fierce and intense.

Our eyes lock behind Ivy's head, and he stares me down defiantly.

Holy shit.

He's in love with Ivy.

Now I know why Liam has been suspicious of me and Harrison. He has feelings for her himself.

I thought Liam exclusively dated men, but I have no idea why I think that. It's not like we're friends and we've only met socially a few times. Ivy has never said much to me about him, but I also haven't spent much time with Ivy off-set or beyond work functions to promote the restaurants and the show.

I'm lost in all my swirling thoughts as Harrison gets out and jogs around to the driver's side and hops in. He presses the button to restart the car. "Now we can all relax and enjoy ourselves. The grinch is gone."

"You shouldn't give him such a hard time," Ivy snaps. "Liam is hardworking, talented, and always there for me. He's a great guy."

Yesterday I would have assumed she was just defending her friend, but after seeing Liam's expression, I have to wonder if there's more to it.

Not that it's any of my business.

But you've made it your business.

Because you have fucking feelings for Ivy, you idiot.

My inner voice is annoying, so I say, "I thought you were going to play the Eagles song, Harrison."

"Thank you for reminding me." Harrison swipes on his phone and music starts playing through the speakers as he pulls out of the parking lot and drives two minutes down the road to a historic hotel we saw on our way into town.

To call it luxury is a bit of a stretch, but there's a steakhouse on site and I need to eat. Road snacks are not filling me up. Ivy has spent the day eating like a five-year-old let loose in a gas station with forty bucks. She's had chips, candy, beef jerky, and some kind of chocolate cake sandwich that looked like it was made from plastic.

As a guy who's spent my adult life around farm to table restaurants, it's a little horrifying, but at least it distracted her from the vodka in her Stanley cup. Though any port in a storm, I suppose.

Harrison is singing at the top of his lungs.

Ivy rubs her temples. "I've never heard this song in my life."

"You hungry?" I ask. "Their website said there's a nice restaurant off the lobby."

She shakes her head. "I'm going to go to bed."

"It's six o'clock," Harrison protests. "You'll wake up in the middle of the night if you go to bed now."

"Not if I finish the vodka."

I don't think so. Not on my watch. She may think I'm heavy-handed but I'm not going to let her drink alone in her room.

Harrison seems to notice her shift in tone, because he meets my gaze in the rearview mirror and frowns, but then we're pulling up to the front entrance of the hotel.

"No valet?" he asks, glancing left and right.

For some reason that makes Ivy giggle, which makes me feel better.

Thirty minutes later, I'm juggling two dinners in to-go boxes and knocking gently on the door to Ivy's hotel room.

Harrison is eating downstairs in the steakhouse, but I'm worried Ivy hasn't had enough protein today. I'm also worried that she's just sitting in a dark room swigging vodka like its water.

When she opens the door, she's dressed in a tank top and tiny cotton shorts. She isn't wearing a bra. My mouth waters and it's not because of the loaded baked potato in the bag in my hand.

Holy Jesus, she's just so fucking gorgeous.

"Hi," I manage to say. "I brought you some dinner, in case you're hungry after all."

She gives me a smile. "Thanks, Ford. You're a good guy."

"Food fixes almost everything," I tell her. "Or at least it makes it a little bit more tolerable."

"Come on in," she says, pulling the door open wider.

"Are you sure? I don't want to interrupt anything."

She scoffs. "What? Me spiraling? If you can tolerate my sad girl summer mood, you're welcome to join me."

"I can handle sad girl summer. I have three younger sisters."

That makes her laugh. "Oh God. I can't even imagine. I was an only child until I was thirteen. Then my mom popped up pregnant with my sister and I cannot even tell you how devastating that was for me."

I follow her into the room and set the bag on the dinette table. "Wow, that would be a life change after being an only child for so long."

"Not just that, it was also really embarrassing to be in middle school and have a pregnant mom. No one at that age wants to think that their parents have S-E-X."

I grin at her. "No. I guess not. How was it after your sister was born?"

Ivy goes over to the dresser and retrieves two bottles of water. "Oh, after she came, it was amazing. She was my little baby doll, and I loved playing with her, feeding her, dressing her. I like to think we're as close as can be, considering I left for college when she was only four. Are you close to your sisters?"

"As close as you can be when they're triplets and you're the older brother." I open the bag and pull out the two boxes and a foil bag filled with silverware and butter packets.

"*Triplets*? Your poor parents." Ivy pops open one of the boxes. "Oh, this looks yummy."

"Yep, triplets. Frannie and Fiona are identical twins and then there's Finley, who is at law school at Clemson. Frannie and Fiona live in Honeysuckle Harbor and work at our restaurant. They're both pastry chefs. They definitely have the twin connection."

"Oh, I met them then at the holiday party! I had no idea they were your sisters."

I nod, placing a napkin down for her. That party had been pure torture for me. I had watched Brad parading her around the room, introducing her to everyone, peppering kisses all over her at random intervals. He'd shown me the engagement ring he was planning to give her on their upcoming trip to Santa Barbara.

The ring that has been tucked in my pocket since she shoved it at me.

It was also the only time that Ivy had been in Honeysuckle Harbor and somehow we'd both wound up on the back deck of the restaurant, staring out at the water and casually chatting. I think it was the only time I'd ever been alone with Ivy until now, and I had wanted things I knew I could never have.

Now we're alone again, and there is no Brad in the picture.

But still, the timing is all wrong.

"So...have you talked to Brad?" I ask, since he's the damn elephant in the room.

I pull out a chair for her and she looks a little startled, but does sit down. "No. I blocked his number, though, so I have no idea if he's tried to text or call me. But I can't even imagine what he could possibly say and I feel like any way he tries to explain it is just going to make me feel worse."

"I'm sorry." It's not enough, but it is sincere.

I sit down across from her.

Ivy shrugs and opens a butter packet. She spreads it liberally on the dinner roll in the takeout box. "Thank you. But it's weird. I feel like I should be more upset than I am. I'm angry. I'm embarrassed. I'm questioning everything about the last year of my life. But I'm not devastated. My heart isn't broken and I think that's very telling. I should be in a puddle on the floor, don't you think?"

"I think everyone handles tough situations differently. But I'm glad you're not crying on the floor. That would break *my* heart." I cut my steak and take a bite. "This isn't bad."

She laughs a little. "You were expecting it would be?"

I shrug, a little embarrassed. "I've become a food snob. I can't deny it."

"Because Brad's an incredible chef." She doesn't pose it as a question. We both know it's a fact.

"He is. But he's also a dick."

"Yes, he is." Ivy lifts a water bottle. "A toast. To the universe stopping me from marrying the wrong man."

I'll definitely toast to that. I raise my own water bottle. "To new beginnings."

"To getting there without Liam and Harrison strangling each other."

"To fast cars and a hot real estate market."

"Yes. To a quick sale of the house I've never even seen because Brad bought it without talking to me about it."

I wince. What a prick. I feel worse and worse about being friends with him. "Yes. Definitely toast to that."

We click our plastic bottles together, then both take a sip. We eat silently for a few minutes, but it's comfortable between us. Ivy is mostly focused on the baked potato, but at least it's not fake food.

"I feel like I don't know anything about you, Ford," she says. "Have you ever been married?"

I swallow the bite in my mouth, surprised at the unexpected question. "No. I believe in marriage, though. I just haven't met the right woman."

Though the night I met Ivy, I'd thought I had. For three beautiful minutes when we'd been introduced, it was love at first sight for me. Then she'd been whisked away by a production assistant to meet Brad and that had been that.

"Are you a romantic?"

"I am. I'm also loyal."

She fiddles with her fork, dragging it through the potato. "With a strong moral compass."

"I like to think so."

"Have you been in love?"

"I don't think so."

"I don't think I have either."

That shocks me a little. "No?"

Ivy looks up from her plate. "I *thought* I was. But I think if I had really been in love, I would be more upset. I think I got caught up in the whole "it looks good on paper." It worked at first and we were happy—at least I was—and we just sort of fast tracked the whole relationship. I may have been drunk last night but I was right about ignoring red flags. Granted, they were subtle, not huge like I claimed, but I'm so mad at myself for that."

"Don't be so hard on yourself. We've all done that. I ignored the huge red flags that Harrison and Liam can't be in a car all day together."

Ivy laughs. "I think that's called sexual tension."

"Oh, is that what it is? I thought it was bitter resentment," I joke with a smile.

Raising her fork, she licks the tines with the tip of her tongue and I fight the urge to groan. I want to kiss her with every fiber of my fucking being.

If she had any idea the thoughts running through my head…

Strong moral compass, strong moral compass.

"What's in the minibar?" I ask.

CHAPTER 7

Ivy

"THIS IS the tiniest and cutest bottle of champagne I've ever seen in my life." I hold up the bottle from the minibar for Ford to see as I crouch on the floor. "I must drink it."

"That is extremely tiny and cute," Ford agrees, dropping down beside me in a squat. "And probably costs forty bucks."

"I put my room on Brad's credit card." I try to twist the top off of the champagne but nothing happens. "I figure paying for me to get to South Carolina with tiny champagne bottles along the way is the least he can do."

"I agree. In fact, we've just found our snacks for the road tomorrow. Why pay two dollars at the gas station when we can pay twelve here?" Ford holds his hand out to me as I continue to struggle to untwist the top.

Without thinking, I pass the champagne bottle over to him. "That is very true."

He opens it and hands it back.

I'm startled to realize we just silently communicated with each other.

Granted, it wasn't like a mind meld—it was just non-verbal cues, but still…it's intriguing to me. Being around Ford is so easy, comfortable.

"Thank you," I tell him.

He's digging around in the minibar as I sip the champagne.

He turns back to me. "For what?"

"Being here. I appreciate it."

"I'm happy to be here."

"Me too," I say softly, and I actually mean it. "Happy you're here, that is."

"Open your mouth," he says. "But first, close your eyes."

Sexy. That's another thing being around Ford is.

When did Ford become so damn hot?

He looks exactly the way he always has. Attractive, fit, with a warm smile.

But now I know more about him.

He's caring, compassionate, fiercely steadfast and loyal, and he's patient. I spent the majority of the day wanting to throttle Liam and Harrison, but Ford remained calm and collected.

He also makes me feel safe. And cared for. He was looking out for me, making me eat and drink, letting me nap, and I felt like I could just *be*. I didn't have to worry. Or *do* anything for anyone.

I never felt that way with Brad. I always worried. About how he was feeling, what he was thinking, if things were going the way he wanted them to, if I was pleasing him.

I frown. When had *that* become my life?

I shake it off. Fuck Brad. I'm here with Ford now. And I'm in very good hands as long as Ford's around.

"Is this a trick?" I ask Ford. My tone isn't suspicious, it's flirty.

I'm flirting with Ford without planning to.

But now that I'm aware of it, I don't really want to stop. It feels freeing to be here with him.

"No. It's a treat. See if you can guess what I put in your mouth."

He has his hand behind his back. I assume it's chocolate or nuts or candy, but the phrasing makes me giggle.

"Absolutely not. I fell for that one in high school," I joke.

"Along with my boyfriend asking me if I wanted a facial for my birthday. Imagine my surprise when the time came."

Ford gives a choked laugh. "Wow. Okay, fine. I'll show it to you first."

I raise my eyebrows. "That still sounds dirty."

"Everything sounds dirty if you think about it too long. Take fruit, for example. Ripe with sexual innuendo."

"Ripe." I giggle. "Juicy. Peach. I get what you're saying."

Ford holds his hand up in front of me and unfurls his fingers to reveal the chocolate in his palm. "It's a chocolate and hazelnut truffle. Tell me if you taste anything else."

He gently eases it between my lips, and I take a small bite. The chocolate melts in my mouth and overpowers the sweetness of the champagne. I flick my tongue over my lip to catch an errant crumb, but I also catch the tip of his finger. He sucks in a sharp breath.

I swallow the chocolate, heat suddenly pooling between my thighs.

His thumb strokes over my bottom lip. His gaze sweeps over my face before studying my mouth.

It feels like the most natural thing in the world to close the distance between us and kiss him.

For a brief second, when my mouth covers his, I hesitate.

Maybe I read him wrong. Maybe he's horrified or offended.

But then Ford kisses me back.

It's not a friendly kiss. Or a sure-why-not kiss.

It's commanding, hot and confident.

It's an unexpectedly fierce and demanding tangling of his tongue with mine, his fingers climbing into my hair to grip the strands tightly as his mouth dominates mine. He draws me onto his lap on the floor and a wave of heat floods my body, settling in my core, and weaving its way out.

When I gasp, he growls.

I never would have taken Ford for a growler. I shift my arms around his neck, grind myself deeper into his lap, the distraction welcome, wanted. "*More.*"

But Ford draws back, breathing heavily.

"*Ivy.*" He runs his thumb over my bottom lip. "This isn't what you want."

"Yes, it is." I reach for him.

But he resolutely eases me off of his lap and stands. I'm face to face with his very hard, very large erection. My nipples harden even as my cheeks flood with heat. I'm angry he's turning me down when he so clearly enjoyed the kiss.

"Let me rephrase that. Maybe you want this—and trust me, I fucking do too—but your relationship with Brad just ended. I don't want you to wake up and have regrets tomorrow."

I sip my tiny champagne. It's almost entirely gone.

What the hell am I doing? My emotions have been all over the last forty-eight hours.

He's probably right, damn it.

It confirms that Ford is a nice guy.

I nod. "That's fair."

Ford holds a hand out to help me to my feet. The touch of his hand is light, and he's put space between us. But he digs in his pocket and comes out with my engagement ring.

The giant diamond startles me, makes me feel off-kilter.

"I've been walking around with this in my pocket since you gave it to me. It's been a lodestone, reminding me not to act on the attraction I have for you. I think you're incredible and gorgeous and funny as hell and I've thought that since the first time I met you."

I suck in a breath. I don't know what to say.

"When you ask me for the ring back, I'll know you're ready to do whatever this is." He points between the two of us. "Do you want the ring back?"

For a second, I almost say yes, because I want to feel Ford's lips on mine, have his taut muscular body moving over me, making me forget the sting of Brad's rejection.

But the thought of taking that ring makes me hesitate, and I know Ford is right.

I shake my head. "Not yet."

He nods and slips it back in his pocket.

"You're a wise man, Ford. And like I said before, you have a strong moral compass."

Ford drags his hand over his beard scruff. "I hate myself for that right now, but I try to do the right thing."

I give him a smile, to let him know I appreciate his stance. "It's orange," I tell him.

"What?"

"The hint of flavor behind the hazelnut. It's orange."

The corner of his mouth turns up. "Bingo. Beautiful and a foodie. I'm officially an idiot for hitting the pause button."

The magic of the moment is broken, but it doesn't feel awkward with Ford. I just give a soft laugh. "Thank you for dinner. Goodnight."

When he leaves, I wait for the door to close with a soft snick and I lock the deadbolt behind him. I sigh as I take in the takeout boxes and the minibar mess.

Being a jilted bride sucks.

"I'm driving today," I announce, as Harrison and Ford meet up with me in the hotel lobby at eight the next morning. "You two can take the backseat."

Maybe if we split up Harrison and Liam, they won't bicker nonstop.

I actually slept well and I feel refreshed today. Maybe all the stress of the last couple of days has caught up with me and I slept hard. Or maybe Ford's kindness reminded me that there are decent men in the world still.

God, Ford is a great kisser.

Which is confusing.

Or is it? Why wouldn't he be a great kisser?

But it *is* confusing that I did it in the first place.

I just was staring at him and it felt like the most natural thing in the world.

But he broke it off and left my room and he was wise to put a halt to it. I don't need to hook up with my ex-fiance's best friend and complicate my life any further.

At first, when he pulled back, I was angry at what felt like yet another rejection, but that's not what Ford intended. He was worried I was behaving impulsively, which I was.

If we'd had sex, it definitely would have been a rebound situation.

And yet I sneak a peek at Ford, who is glancing down at his phone. Given that kiss, I can only imagine what else he could do with that tongue…

"Works for me," Ford says with a smile.

I've forgotten what we were even talking about.

Right. Me driving. "I'm ready to take on the rest of this road trip and sell the hell out of the house I never wanted," I tell them.

Harrison just gives me a grunt of acknowledgement, his hands buried deep in the pockets of his shorts. He's wearing sunglasses.

Ford gives me a smile. "Wise move," he murmurs, leaning in closer to me. "Harrison is hungover. Apparently, he decided to stay in the hotel bar last night and try to drink Liam out of his system with some bikers from Wisconsin. It didn't go well."

"Oh boy," I say, smiling back at Ford.

I'm grateful he's not being awkward around me in the aftermath of that amazing kiss.

"Where the fuck is the coffee?" Harrison mutters, glancing around the lobby.

"They don't do breakfast here. We can grab some on the road."

My answer draws a grimace from Harrison. I hand him my Stanley cup. "Have some water. You should hydrate."

He doesn't take the cup from me but he does lean over and puts his lips around the straw and takes a sip. His sunglasses slip down his nose so that I can see his eyes, which are locked on me.

He has deep brown eyes that are usually filled with mischief. Right now, there is something else there…

Holy shit.

I'm startled to feel a bit of heat sizzle between us.

Maybe it's just how close I am to his mouth, or maybe it's because he's an attractive guy.

Maybe it's because I'm suddenly single.

But for whatever reason, I am suddenly very aware of men.

These men.

This man.

That other man two feet away.

How can I want to kiss *both* Ford and Harrison?

I fight the urge to swallow audibly.

Once Harrison stands up straight, I take my cup back and head toward the front door resolutely. I text Liam to let him know we're on our way. I have yet another text from my mother that is a picture of a kitten, inexplicably with a herd of elephants. "This is tough, but you're tougher!" the meme declares.

I know she has no idea what to say to me right now, but I have no clue how to respond to this either. I just send her back a kiss emoji and start driving.

As we pull up to the motel, Liam is standing outside with a cup of coffee in his hand.

"Are you fucking kidding me?" Harrison mutters from the back seat. "He has coffee."

"He told you they have free continental breakfast here," Ford says.

"No coffee for us?" Harrison complains as Liam gets in the passenger seat and closes the door.

"Why would I bring you coffee when you're staying in the Winslow, Arizona, version of the Ritz? You should have had a fancy coffee maker in your room."

There were no coffee makers in the rooms, a fact Liam knows because I texted him to complain about it this morning. But then I remembered there was an iced coffee in the minibar and that had satisfied my caffeine craving.

Clearly, the bickering is going to continue.

"How was your bagel?" Harrison asks.

"I had a fresh waffle, bacon, eggs, and fresh fruit. It was quite delicious, thank you."

Harrison grunts. "We're still standing on the corner," he says. "I want to take a picture."

"No." Liam sips his coffee and sighs in exaggerated delight. "Damn, this is good coffee."

"Pull over here," Harrison says, pointing to the town center, where several people are gathered around the Route 66 sign.

I obey, because I slept great and Harrison's enthusiasm is always contagious. I also realized again this morning I do feel genuinely grateful that the wedding didn't happen. Brad clearly didn't want to marry me and if I'm attracted to both of his friends, I shouldn't be marrying him either.

"I'll take the picture," Ford says, getting out of the car.

Harrison's ability to enjoy himself even when he's hungover and craving coffee makes me appreciate his zest for life.

Even now, the first thing he does is offer to take a picture for an elderly couple who are standing under the street sign attempting to take a selfie.

"Okay, say rock 'n roll," he tells them when he holds up the man's phone.

"Rock 'n roll!"

"Thanks. Let us take your picture now." The older man gestures to me. "Hop on in here with your friends, sweetheart."

"Yes, perfect, thanks, man!" Harrison shoves his sunglasses up onto his head and throws his arm around me.

On my other side, Ford slips into place and his hand immediately rests on the small of my back. They're both leaning in and I feel very crowded by muscular men. It's a...pleasant experience.

"One, two, three...okay, one more." The man finally lowers the camera.

Harrison removes his arm to take his phone back. He gives the man a handshake and waves to his wife as we head back to the car. Liam is silent in the passenger seat.

Harrison passes his phone to me from the backseat. "Want me to post this and ruin Brad's day? You look like you don't have a care in the fucking world."

It's the picture of us.

I'm wearing loose linen pants and a sleeveless tank in ivory. I look tanned and relaxed. My hair is cascading over my shoulders and both Harrison and Ford are leaning into me, protectively. When I zoom in, I see my nipples are hard.

"Sure," I say, striving for casual as I hand Harrison his phone back. "If you want."

Liam shakes his head, frowning a little.

"What?" I ask.

"Nothing." He looks down at his phone. "Let's go. We need to get to Texas by tonight."

"Are you our navigation princess?" Harrison asks.

Liam ignores him.

Which doesn't do anything but make Harrison more determined to get some kind of response. "I'll give you fifty bucks for the rest of your coffee, William."

"Seventy-five."

"Done."

Liam hands his coffee back to Harrison.

"There's only like two sips in here!"

"You didn't ask how much I had left."

"I'll pay both of you two hundred dollars to drive in silence for the next two hours," Ford says. "And Ivy picks the playlist."

I glance at him in the rearview mirror and mouth, "Thank you," with a smile.

He smiles back and I feel my stomach swoop.

Eight hours, three memes from Mom, and two more bribes by Ford later and we're Somewhere In Texas.

I spot a honky-tonk on the side of the road with a giant sign that declares, "BBQ, live bands, and bail bonds."

This obviously needs to happen. I pull into the parking lot, which is filled with trucks.

"I just found our dinner plans, boys." I grin happily at them one by one.

Liam looks horrified.

Ford looks uncertain.

And Harrison looks thrilled.

Which, let's face it, makes this place perfect for this road trip.

CHAPTER 8
Liam

WHAT FRESH HELL IS THIS?

Not only have I spent the entire day driving through the middle of nowhere with the woman I love and the man I'm stupidly attracted to, but now Ivy wants to enter my idea of the seventh circle of hell—a country dive bar.

"We do need to eat," Ford says from the back seat. "I love barbeque."

Ivy beams at him. "Thank you, Ford."

Not only is Harrison driving me insane and I'm worried about Ivy, but when the hell did Ford become Ivy's yes man? I don't like the way he's been looking at her all day. Like he wants to cuddle her and then fuck her. Or fuck her, then cuddle her.

Even worse, she keeps giving him soft smiles whenever they make eye contact.

I regret staying in the separate motel last night.

But my bank account is already screaming at me and I couldn't resist poking at Harrison. He brings out my competitive side. Or some might argue my petty side. Yet now I'm fixating on the fact that maybe something went down between Ford and Ivy—like him between her thighs.

She would tell me, though.

I think.

She usually tells me everything.

Now I'm in my head and there's no choice but to open the car door. "I'm in." A bargain dinner will be easy on the wallet too.

Harrison steps out of the car. "My God, it's a thousand degrees here. I need a cold beer the size of my head."

That might be the most he's said since this morning. He slept half of the drive, which makes me curious what he was doing last night. He doesn't have the look of a man who went to bed alone at ten p.m.

Not that I care who he went to bed with.

Harrison stretches, his T-shirt pulling up and tight across his chest, revealing the hard pecs that I thoroughly enjoyed running my hands over when he was naked…

Fuck. I do care who he goes to bed with.

I want it to be me again, because while we might bicker nonstop when our clothes are on, when we were together that night, not only did we get along, it was electric between us.

Which makes his behavior the next day and every day since even more annoying.

I'm determined to despise him, no matter how fucking hot he is.

As we cross the parking lot, I move in step beside Ivy. I put my hand on her shoulder and give a light squeeze. "You doing okay?"

"I'm fine. I slept really well."

Because Ford gave her an orgasm?

The thought pops in and I can't get rid of it.

"That's good to hear."

I slept horribly.

I tossed and turned and alternated between visualizing Ivy's expression when Ford told her Brad was a no-show and Harrison naked. Neither was relaxing. So I waffled between worried and turned on all night long until I finally dozed off and had a dream where I was having sex with *both* Ivy and Harrison. At the same time.

Which has sparked a fantasy I didn't even know I had and now can't get out of my head.

"What's our cover story?" Harrison asks. "Should Ivy be a famous actress and we're her bodyguards?"

"What do you mean?" she asks.

"You need a story in a place like this. We can't just be ourselves."

"Who are we going to be talking to?" I ask.

An hour later, I have my answer—everyone in the whole damn bar.

That's who Harrison is talking to.

After ordering four plates of food that could easily feed eight people, Harrison has the older female server laughing and calling him "handsome." He's turned and made small talk with the table behind us when he borrowed their hot sauce sampler caddy and then before I could blink he was in a pepper eating contest with a man introduced to us as "the cayenne king."

Everyone loves Harrison, including the band, who has invited him up to play drums, which, amazingly, he can.

Meanwhile, Ivy smashed on a whole pulled pork platter, gifted her sunglasses to a toddler who admired them, and is laughing and dancing on the sticky floor with a very elderly man when the band dedicates "California Girls," to her. I don't even know how they know she's from California.

Ford is keeping one eye on Ivy and the other on the bullseye as he has suddenly become the stiffest competition in wherever-we-are-Texas's charitable dart tournament. He paid the entry fee and added an extra five hundred bucks when he heard it was to help a local family whose young daughter has cancer. He's gotten more kisses on the cheek from middle-aged women than I would have thought possible.

Then there's me.

Sitting in a corner.

Legs sprawled out in front of me, a beer I'm ignoring resting on the table next to me.

I'm an introvert. The observer. I enjoy watching people interact and have a great time. People are fascinating and I apply all of that to my writing. My friends understand me well enough to know that just because I'm sitting doesn't mean I'm not having fun.

My role when I usually go out with friends is to make sure no one ends up in jail or leaves their credit card behind the bar, and I'm good with that.

Harrison doesn't get that.

He alternates between trying to coax me into having fun and snarking at me about not being capable of anything enjoyable.

"Seriously, does anything at *all* give you pleasure?" he demands, after putting the drum sticks down and returning to the table for his beer.

For once, I don't think he meant it as an innuendo.

But as I eye him, allowing my gaze to wander from his head and on down the length of his sexy as fuck body, the corner of my mouth turns up. "There are a few things that give me pleasure," I murmur.

His eyes darken, and he drops into the seat beside me. "Like what? Me being quiet?"

I run my fingers over the sweat on the side of my beer bottle. "You being quiet because my cock is in your mouth, yes." I shift my legs apart on the chair, needing more room. "While I yank your hair."

Harrison leans forward, resting his chin on his palm. "Tell me more."

But I'm not making it that easy for him. I sit back, creating more distance between us again. "I like to dance."

His jaw drops, then he breaks out in laughter. "You do not."

"How do you know?" I ask calmly, casually. "It's not like you know me. You didn't stick around long enough for that."

He makes a face. "Look, we didn't talk about what came next, if anything, that night. I thought we were just having good, clean, naked fun."

"Sure," I agree, because I'm not going to insist it was more than that, even though he knows full fucking well it was.

There was chemistry, yes, but there was a connection that went beyond sex.

But if Harrison wants to keep me at arm's length, that's his right.

"I'll give you a thousand dollars if you line dance in front of all these people. Like all in. Hips and hands moving, William. Don't let me down."

I sip my beer. "Easiest thousand bucks I've ever made."

Harrison snorts and stands back up. He goes over to the band, who are on break, and has a chat with the lead singer.

"Okay, folks, we're going to do a little classic Texas two-step for our Cali friends. Everyone get on out here and show these folks how everything is bigger and better in the Lone Star state!"

There are whoops and hollers and a dash to the dance floor.

"South Carolina!" Harrison calls out.

"What?" the singer asks.

"Two of us are from South Carolina. Two from California."

"Then we have a real dance off! Three states represented."

Harrison makes a face like that backfired on him. "Can't dance?" I ask.

But Harrison, being Harrison, says, "I can do anything."

That makes me snort and shake my head. He probably doesn't even know the two-step is a partner dance. I stroll over to Ivy. "Dance with me?"

She nods, grinning. "I thought you'd never ask."

As Harrison makes his way to the floor, he realizes about a heartbeat too late he needs a partner. A woman grabs him by the arm with a big smile. She's about half his height and twice his age, but as I start the dance and take Ivy's arm, I see the woman is literally dancing circles around Harrison. He's just standing there bouncing on his heels, looking bewildered. She gestures for him to lift his arm to twirl her, but he doesn't get the message. He just lifts his arm.

Meanwhile, me and Ivy have a nice rhythm and flow. We've danced swing together before and this shares some common roots with it. So even though I've never technically done the two-step, it's easy to follow, especially since the singer is calling out directives to be helpful.

She smiles up at me. "You haven't lost your touch. You been dancing without me lately?"

Since Brad. That's what she means.

I shake my head. "No. You're my only dance partner." I turn her and tug her in tight up against me, closer than the dance calls for.

She collides with my chest. "Well, hello."

"Hi." I turn her out. When she comes back, I murmur, "You're amazing, you know. I'm proud of you for how you're handling this."

"Thanks." She strokes my cheek. "You're the best."

There's a moment hanging between us and I feel my heart swell. I want to kiss her.

The music suddenly cuts out with a loud scratch. Ivy jumps. I wince.

"Whoops, sorry, folks!" The DJ laughs over the mic. "Our Cali couple is doing an amazing two-step! Well, our young lady is anyway."

It's a poke at me that I can't let stand. Not with Harrison watching.

The two-step focuses on the woman.

I need to show off a little more.

I make eye contact with the singer. "Something faster?"

He gives me a grin. Then he says into the mic, "Cali Boy requests we crank up the speed. We've got you covered."

The man isn't fucking around. He plays "Footloose," which allows me to really move next to Ivy, who is suddenly shrieking and laughing as she tries to catch up. It's silly and fun and yes, I am enjoying myself. I'm also sweating.

Harrison has given up on dancing and is leaning on the bar watching us.

The "Git Up" follows, and it gives me some wiggle room to add a little hip hop edge to it.

People are yelling and clapping and pointing fingers at me. "Go, Cali!" a woman calls out.

Ivy yells to me, waving her arms, "I can't keep up! I'm out."

She squeezes her way through the throng over to Harrison. Ford has joined him.

It doesn't bother me that there are a lot of eyes on me. I even give a few hip thrusts that have people screaming. But two more songs and I'm officially out of breath.

"A big round of applause for our Cali Boy!"

I grin and wave as I pretend to wipe my brow and slide off of the dance floor.

"That was…something," Harrison says.

I shrug. "I can dance."

He's trying to be cool about it, but at that, he cracks a grin. "Yes. Yes, you can. Nice thrusting, William. Here's your payout."

He pulls cash out of his wallet, which momentarily stuns me. He has a grand in his pocket? But then I take it with a feigned nonchalant "thanks," and head right over to where they're collecting donations for the family of the little girl. Her picture is emblazoned across a plastic jug with her name on it. I give the money to the woman who is in charge of it.

Her eyes widen. "Bless you!"

"My pleasure. I hope Alyssa has a speedy recovery."

When I return to the table, Harrison looks at the others. "Are we ready to leave now that William has made me look like a complete dick?"

"I'm ready." Ivy pinches off one last piece of cornbread from her platter and pops it in her mouth.

Ford nods.

"Works for me. I can drive."

Except when we open the front door and step outside, it's pouring down rain. An absolute torrential downpour.

We all pull up and pause under the overhang. "Now what?"

"We could find a hotel," Ivy says.

"Or wait it out," Ford adds.

"Oh, this is an all-nighter," a man says as he steps outside and lights a cigarette. "If you're looking for a place to stay, there's a hotel a mile up the road. The Armadillo Inn."

"That sounds appropriate," Harrison says with a smirk, sticking his hand out into the rain like he can gauge how long it will last by touch.

"That's probably our best bet. I'll drive. Wait here, I'll get the car," I tell them.

I dash through the rain and jump in. Once I pull around, Ford has taken his shirt off and is holding it over Ivy's head in some overblown chivalrous gesture. I frown, but then they're in the car. Driving in the direction the man pointed, I can barely see the road. I'm going twenty miles an hour and the only way I know we're still on pavement is the tires aren't spinning.

Relieved, I spot the motel and turn in.

There is a debate in the backseat between Ford and Harrison over who will go into the lobby. Ford has put his wet shirt back on at least. I don't need Ivy ogling him. I don't offer to go in because I'm not putting four rooms on my credit card.

For whatever reason, they do rock-paper-scissors and Harrison wins—or loses?—and he opens the door and jogs through the rain.

"This is crazy," Ivy says. "It never pours like this in California."

"It does in South Carolina."

"Oh, goody," she says, dryly, before shooting Ford a grin over her shoulder.

What *is* going on with those two?

Harrison comes back and jumps into the car. His shirt is soaked through, outlining his chest in a way that makes my mouth dry. Water is running down his face, and he swipes a large hand over it and through his hair, torturing me further.

"Bad news. There's only one room available." He holds up a classic motel key. "Be prepared to get cozy tonight, kids."

I sigh in defeat. A whole night crowded in a room with a wet Harrison and Ivy and Ford sneaking glances at each other?

Fucking fabulous.

CHAPTER 9

Harrison

OKAY, so I'm going to be riding out a monsoon in Texas in a roadside dump with my best friend, my ex-lover, and my other friend's ex-fiancée. Oh, and that ex-fiancée is the woman who both of the aforementioned men are in love with. Yes, I'm aware of Liam's not-just-a-friend feelings for Ivy. I'm not an idiot. I just play one…most of the time.

I watch them all run from the car to the door to the motel room.

It's one of those places that has the doors on the outside. It opens right up to the parking lot. It's just one thin piece of wood between us and the rain storm. Or the serial killer with the chainsaw.

I sigh.

This is the craziest road trip ever.

So why am I having such a great time?

I watch as Liam unlocks the door and lets Ivy precede him into the room. Ford lugs his bag and Ivy's suitcase inside. The door shuts behind them.

I take a breath.

Okay, so this is it. The four of us in one room for the night. The guy told me there are two beds. Two queens. Not even king-sized beds. That means it's going to be two and two. It's gonna be a tight fit.

And something *is* going to happen.

There's no way the four of us will emerge from that room in the morning unscathed.

This sexual tension amongst us is ridiculous.

And yet, I don't think I like three other people on the planet as much as I like the three people in that room.

I've liked Ford for most of my life. I love him like a brother. I'd do anything for him.

I've liked Liam since I met him. Fucking him was just the hot caramel, crushed cashews, and whipped cream on top of the grumpy-sexy-bossy-intriguing sundae. I could just listen to him talk or watch him do, well, anything for hours. And that was before I knew he could dance.

Fuck, that was hot. And surprising. And watching him smile and actually *laugh*…God, I wanted to push him up against the wall and kiss the hell out of him just for that.

And yes, I definitely like Ivy. She's spunky and funny and has been up for absolutely everything I've tossed at our entourage. She's supposed to be heartbroken and down on her luck and was even hungover for a good portion of the first day. But the girl rallied. She was fun, adventurous, and curious about everything from the new sour candy I found at the gas station to the rubber ball "museum" to the armadillo circus. I love her smile and making her laugh gives me a warm feeling that I want to keep producing. Yeah, I absolutely like her.

Something *needs* to happen in that room. We all have a lot of emotion to work off and we need to really connect somehow. We've been getting closer. Between the wedding debacle, getting Ivy through that first night, the silly stops that first day, the honky-tonk…now we need something more absolute. Something real. I can't explain it better than that.

So Ivy was just left at the altar. Big deal. It wasn't her fault. Brad is an asshole. We all know that now. It's time to move on.

What good does it do for her to hold herself back from Ford because of Brad? That's stupid. She probably should have been with Ford all this time. No time like the present to correct that mistake.

As for me and Liam, I know I hurt him, but he wants me as much as I want him. I just need to make the first move since I was the one who bailed last time. Fine. I can do that.

We're grown-assed adults. The three people I'm with just need a little nudge.

Or a Let's Fucking Go shove.

I get out of the car and jog up to the door. I step into the room and immediately strip my shirt off, and head for the bathroom.

"Whoo! I'm soaked." I grab a towel from the rack and run it over my hair. "How about you, Ivy? Bet you're pretty wet, aren't ya'?"

Both Ivy and Liam are standing in the middle of the dinky room, between the beds, watching me as I rub my hair with the towel. I'm not *totally* full of myself, but I don't spend an hour and a half in the gym every day because I like the smell of sweat. It keeps me healthy and strong, and the people I like to fuck seem to appreciate the muscles it produces.

I drag the towel over my chest and down my abs. "Ivy?"

She's following the path of the white cloth. "Yeah?"

"Are you wet?"

It's a stupid question. She is, of course. We all are. It's pouring outside and even running the thirty feet from the car to the motel drenched us all.

Her blonde hair is hanging straight, and water is dripping from the ends. A drop of water runs from her hairline down her temple, over her pretty cheek, to her jaw.

Her tongue pokes out and slides over her lower lip. "Um," is all she says as she watches me drag the towel over my arm.

Liam steps in front of her, blocking my view. Except that I'm tall enough I can see her over his head.

"Knock it off," he tells me with a frown.

I chuckle. "Oh, don't worry, William," I say. "I'm paying attention to you, too." I step forward and lift the towel to his face, dragging it over his cheek and down his neck.

His lips fall open. "Just..." He clears his throat. "Leave Ivy alone."

"If she wants me to," I agree. I loop the towel around his neck and look past him at Ivy. Then I drop my hands to my button and zipper, undoing them and pushing the wet shorts over my hips. "You feeling bothered by me, Ivy girl?"

She's watching me strip, her eyes wide. Her gaze goes to the mirror on the wall behind me, where she's got a good view of my ass.

"No." Her voice is soft.

I grin at Liam as I toe off my shoes and step out of my shorts. "See? No problem."

"Harrison."

I look over at Ford. He's standing by the window with the bed between him and Ivy. *He* looks bothered. He's watching Ivy watch me.

"Everything is good, buddy," I tell him. "Just go with it."

I'm in only my black briefs. They're a little wet too, but I don't intend to keep them on for long. I step into Liam, grabbing both ends of the towel around his neck. I pull him close and kiss him. It's a hard, short kiss. Just a warm-up. Just to let him know what's coming. "Save my spot," I say against his lips before letting him go, pushing him down to sit on the bed to my right, and stepping past his knees to Ivy.

I take her by both upper arms. She's staring at my mouth, maybe replaying my kiss with Liam.

"I'm going to share a bed with Liam, so you're going to be over here with Ford, okay?" I say, turning her and walking her one step to the other bed.

This room is so fucking small it's going to feel like we're all in bed together, anyway.

"Oh," she looks over her shoulder at Ford. "Okay."

"That's not—" Liam starts.

"Ford and I are too big to share a bed," I cut him off without even looking at him.

As if I don't know Liam has feelings for Ivy, too.

An image of Liam and Ivy together, kissing, naked, in bed…with me…flashes through my mind.

I freeze, staring down at the woman before me.

Wow. What was that?

I do like Ivy. I find her incredibly beautiful. But I've written her off as off-limits. First, because of Brad. Then Ford. Then Liam.

But fuck, the idea of having her *and* Liam shoots a bolt of heat straight through me.

Yeah, I'd be into that.

"You have to ask Ivy if it's okay and if she's comfortable," Liam says behind me, interrupting those unexpected thoughts.

"It's okay, Liam. They are bigger than you and me," Ivy says. Then she casts an almost shy glance at Ford. "If it's okay with Ford."

Right. Ford. I can't have Ivy and Liam together because Ford wants Ivy.

I was intending to give my best friend a chance to heat things up with his dream girl. And this is my perfect chance to wear Liam down further. I need another chance with him. I need to kiss him again. I *need* tonight in his arms.

Should I just say that? Maybe.

But I'm a little chicken. I'll admit it. I'm rolling the dice here and hoping that being naked in bed together will make it harder for Liam to continue to reject me.

Ford gives a short laugh. "Yeah. It's fine with me."

Her cheeks are pink when she says, "Okay." She looks up at me. "It's fine."

I squeeze her arms. "You should undress, though. Don't want to get the sheets wet."

Her cheeks get even redder.

"Everyone needs to undress," I announce to the room. "Quit

dripping on the carpet." I step back from Ivy, strip out of my briefs, and toss them toward the bathroom door.

They're all still dressed. I'm bare-assed naked. And it doesn't bother me at all.

Ford's seen me naked. Liam's seen me naked. Ivy has not, and she is actually not my focus here tonight. But when her gaze drops to my cock, it hardens, and suddenly, I find myself studying her mouth.

I can easily picture her sinking to her knees, my hand tangling in her long, wet hair, guiding her forward, those pretty pink lips parting, and my cock sliding past them as she makes a gorgeous, needy, moaning sound.

I bet her mouth is so fucking soft and hot.

She wouldn't suck me the way Liam does. It would be softer, sweeter—I'd have to talk her through it. I'd be in control with her.

Liam is in control when we're together. He's the boss.

But I could boss this pretty little thing.

And her pussy...God, I bet she's tight. She'd be so gorgeous riding me.

Would she like to watch Liam and me together? Would that turn her on? How would her pussy feel around my cock while Liam fucked me?

"Harrison?" she says softly. "Are you okay?"

I shake my head, realizing that I'm staring at her, not saying a word or moving.

I'm naked, hard as steel, intending to push her into bed with Ford, itching to get my hands on Liam, but suddenly having very vivid, very dirty thoughts about Ivy.

I clear my throat. "Yeah, Ivy. I'm okay. Really, really okay."

I think our road trip just got a lot more interesting.

And yeah, I'm okay with that.

"You should get undressed and go to bed," I tell her.

Suddenly Liam is there, pushing between us again.

He literally shoves me back onto the bed he was just sitting on. "Here." He hands Ivy what looks like her pajamas.

What a mood killer.

Then he steers her toward the bathroom. He pushes her inside, shuts the door, and then turns toward me and Ford.

"Jesus Christ, Harrison."

I just grin because he says it to my cock.

He pulls his shirt off, and my grin dies.

He is not my usual type, but I remember every inch of his body. The way he moved against me, the things he made me feel, the way he seemed to just know me.

I have had dominant lovers before, but not like Liam. Liam owns his sexuality in a way I've never experienced. He knew exactly what he wanted, but he gave me what I needed first. Over and over. In fact, that was what he wanted, I realized later. My pleasure was what drove him.

It was the hottest night of my life, and the way he read me, the way he made me surrender over and over, was what freaked me out. It was like he knew a part of me I didn't even know. And I wanted more and more.

I had to get the hell out of there the next morning and I couldn't face even a text conversation for about forty-eight hours after.

I'm suddenly wondering if this road trip and the sleeping arrangements tonight were really terrible ideas.

"You know what?" I say, pulling the duvet and top sheet back and sliding under them. "Ford, get over here. Obviously, Liam is upset."

Liam strips his pants and underwear off. He gives me a look. "Seriously?"

"Yeah. We still have a long trip ahead. I don't want you to be all pissy tomorrow. I'll stop teasing you and Ivy."

"No, you won't." He comes to the side of the bed naked, his fully erect cock bobbing.

"I will." My eyes will not leave his cock, no matter how many times I say look away! "I don't want to upset anyone."

Ford snorts.

But Liam is fully focused on me. "All you've done is upset me since I saw you that first night a year ago. Certainly, since you arrived in California for the wedding. Definitely since you planted your fine ass in the car for the road trip. And now you're naked in my bed. It's way too late to be apologetic now, Harrison."

His tone is ominous. His expression is full of dark promise.

My cock pulses, and lust courses through my body.

God, he's so fucking gorgeous.

"So…"

"So scoot the fuck over," Liam says, pulling the covers back and kneeling on the mattress.

I do, and he climbs in next to me.

He plants a hand on either side of my head, bracing himself over me.

"I knew you were going to be trouble the second I laid eyes on you," he says.

"But no regrets, right?" I ask as he leans closer, his lips nearly on mine.

"Oh, so many fucking regrets," he says.

And then he's kissing me.

CHAPTER 10

Ford

THIS IS SUCH A BAD IDEA.

I'm going to be in bed with Ivy while Liam and Harrison fuck in the bed next to ours.

I quickly strip down to my underwear and pull on a pair of athletic shorts and a T-shirt, then climb into bed. Then I hit the lights. Liam is kissing Harrison like he's a starving man and my best friend is a five-course meal.

But the dark just intensifies the sounds.

I pull a pillow over my head.

Fuck.

This is bad.

And pretty much what I thought was going to happen.

I knew Harrison had plans for Liam. I hadn't been sure if they'd work out. Liam is stubborn as fuck. But Harrison is charming and the fire between them is hot enough to burn those of us standing too close.

But hell, then Harrison had that moment with Ivy and I'd been seconds away from vaulting out of bed and stepping between them, marking my territory, I guess. I hadn't expected that.

Now Ivy is in the bathroom, clearly taking her time to gather

her thoughts—or her courage?—and I'm not sure what to expect, or what to do, when she gets in bed with me.

I can hear Liam and Harrison's groans and the mattress creaking even through the pillow.

Jesus.

Do I just lie here and listen?

Do I leave?

Sleep in the car?

But I can't leave Ivy in here with them.

Can I?

Hell, Liam wants her. I'm certain of it. Not just *wants* her but is in love with her. And just a few minutes ago, I swear Harrison was about to kiss her. Out of the blue. I haven't sensed or seen anything from my buddy to indicate that he's attracted to Ivy or that he has feelings for her beyond friendship, but for a second there, they were standing there, staring at one another with definite sparks jumping back and forth. Sure, he was naked, his dick at full mast, but I thought that was about Liam.

Of course, Harrison dates and fucks women, too, so…it's possible. Of course. Ivy is gorgeous, and she and Harrison get along great.

So if I leave her here with them, they might invite her into bed with them…

Harrison totally would.

Liam would likely punch him in the face for it, though.

But would it be because he was protective of and jealous of Ivy? Or Harrison?

Or…would having both Harrison and Ivy together be Liam's ultimate dream?

I can't help the images of the three of them, naked, kissing, the men's hands all over her body, her writhing, moaning, pleasure etched on her gorgeous face from flashing through my mind.

And what would she say to that invitation?

Not only do I wonder if she's attracted to either of them, or both individually, but would she be open to a threesome?

That has my blood pumping faster for some reason.

What about a foursome?

Jesus, where did that thought come from?

I have never thought about sharing a woman before. Not with Harrison, not with anyone. That's not really my thing. Especially a woman like Ivy, who I have real feelings for.

But now I can't *stop* the thoughts.

The moaning and rustling sounds from the bed next to me, knowing Ivy is changing clothes in the bathroom and will be coming out here to get in bed with me, don't help.

Just then, the bathroom door opens.

"Okay, I—oh!"

I hear her surprised gasp.

"Ivy, get in bed," I hear Liam say, his voice tight. "With Ford."

"I...can't see anything," she says.

She's lying. The light from the bathroom illuminates the room enough that she can see Liam and Harrison together on the bed closest to the bathroom. And she's definitely looking.

"Come closer, Ivy girl. We'll give you an eyeful," Harrison says, his voice teasing.

"Go to Ford," Liam says, his voice commanding.

"Come here, Ivy," I tell her softly.

Her eyes find mine. A spark arcs between us.

"Okay." She hits the bathroom light switch, plunging the room into darkness.

The sounds in the bed next to me have quieted, and I know the two other men are watching her dark form move through the room, the ambient light from outside filtering in through the curtains and making her look like she's floating over to me.

She stops and arranges some of her wet clothes over one of the chairs. Then she turns toward the bed.

I hold the blanket up so she can slip underneath. She moves up to the side of the bed and I feel the mattress dip.

"Okay, so...uh, I guess goodnight every—" Harrison starts.

"Where do you think you're going?" Liam growls.

Harrison gives a low groan.

"Don't fucking move," Liam tells him. "I want you right…"

Harrison groans again.

"*There*," Liam says thickly.

"Oh my god," Ivy whispers.

And…fuck it.

I reach over, wrap an arm over her, and drag her across the mattress and up against me.

She burrows close, putting her face into my neck.

I thread my fingers into her hair. "I can distract you from what's going on over there," I say against her ear.

"Okay," she says.

"Are you sure?"

She puts her hand on my chest. "Yes."

I feel something hard pressing into my left pec. Realization dawns quickly and adrenaline shoots through me.

I cover her hand with mine. "Ivy."

"I'm sure."

I move her hand and feel for what she was pressing against my chest.

Her engagement ring.

"I dug it out of your pocket," she says. "I'm ready to take it back, sell it, move on."

I let out a long, shaky breath. "Fuck. That's…"

"Just say yes, Ford," she tells me softly.

"How about fuck yes?"

"That will work."

I'm done. She's over Brad. If she was ever in love with him in the first place. She's sober, in this bed of her own free will, and I'm a mere mortal. I can *not* resist her any longer.

"Okay, pick your distraction," I tell her as a loud moan from the next bed fills the room. "Bedtime story or…" Screw it, I'm taking a chance here. "Orgasm?"

She pauses for just a moment. Then stops my heart when she

says, "Orgasm. For sure. But you can talk to me the whole time to, you know, cover up the noises."

Just then we hear, "Fuck, Liam, yes."

My fingers curl into her hair momentarily. Then I say, "Anything you want."

She reaches over to the bedside table and sets her ring on it, then snuggles closer. "I'm ready."

Holy shit.

She feels so damned good. God, I want to touch every inch of her. I want to make her feel good. In absolutely any way I can. If she just wants to snuggle, I can do that. But she wants an orgasm.

So that's what she'll get.

She's on her side, one hand tucked under her cheek, one on my stomach.

"Do you have panties on?" I ask.

She nods.

"Take them off."

She shifts against me without hesitation, her hand dipping under the big T-shirt she's wearing. Her wiggling against me and the knowledge that she's going to be bare from the waist down takes my cock from semi-hard to achingly hard in a second.

Ivy puts a tiny scrap of silk on my chest with a soft giggle a moment later. I crush it in my fist.

"Good girl," I tell her thickly. I move my hand to cup her bare ass, pressing her against my hip. "Now lie on top of me so I can reach you."

She immediately slides up and drapes herself over me.

She feels so fucking good. She's light, but I can feel the press of her sweet body from her breasts against my chest to her stomach to where her pelvis nestles against my lower abdomen.

I take advantage of the position, the situation, hell everything Fate has put, literally, in my hands. I slide my hands from her waist to her ass, then down the backs of her thighs, pulling her legs wide so she's straddling me.

She shivers and her breath escapes on a little moan, warm against my cheek. My hands feel huge on her body.

"Before we start, you can stop me at *any* point, okay?" I ask. "I mean that. This only goes as far as you want it to."

She shimmies up a couple of inches and presses her lips to mine in a sweet, brief kiss. "I trust you, Ford," she says against my lips. "And I want you."

I squeeze her thighs. "I've been dreaming about this body for so fucking long, Ivy." I run my hands up and down the backs of her thighs, my thumbs sliding over the curve of her ass, my fingertips tantalizingly close to the heat I can already feel between her legs.

Her arms are around my neck, her face against my throat. I can feel her hot breath and her sweet mouth against my skin. "Have you really?"

"You have no idea. You are a part of every dirty dream I've had since we met."

"I like that," she tells me.

"Yeah?"

"Definitely." She pauses. "Did you have dirty thoughts about me sometimes when Brad was around?"

I groan softly and run my hands up and down her thighs again. This time my fingertips brush over her pussy. Her little intake of air kicks me in the chest. "Yes."

She shivers in my arms. "Tell me about one time."

I slide my hands up to her lower back, under the shirt she's wearing. Then I keep going up her back. "Let's take this off. I want to feel you totally naked against me."

There's a low moan from the bed next to ours. I don't know if Harrison and Liam are responding to one another or to the idea of Ivy getting naked over here. The idea of them listening in on what I'm doing to her gives me an unexpected jolt of heat.

"Okay," she tells me, pushing up to sit, straddling my thighs. "But I want your shirt off, too."

I start to pull my shirt up, but pause as she grasps the hem of her shirt and slides it up her body. I can't see much in the dark, but I don't want to miss even the shadow of the movements of her stripping for me.

The shirt slides over her head and she drops it next to the bed. I start to reach for her, but she covers her breasts. "Take your shirt off, Ford."

"Grip me harder," I hear Liam growl. "You know how I like it."

Ivy wiggles her hips. I wonder if that's in response to Liam. She's not sitting high enough for her pussy to be where I really want it. She's still straddling my thighs. So I whip my shirt off, then grip her waist and haul her up my body.

I'm still wearing shorts, but I settle her pussy against my rock hard cock, pressing up into her.

She moans. "*Ford.*"

I press a hand against her ass, grinding her against me. "They're listening to us," I tell her, low and husky. "They're going to hear everything I say to you. Every sound you make."

She moans again and grinds herself against me.

"It's going to be such a fucking turn-on for them to hear me make you come, Ivy." I rock her against my shaft, making sure her clit is getting pressure and friction. "Because you are going to let me make you come, aren't you, princess? You're going to let me make you feel so good."

"Please." It's so soft it's almost a sigh.

"Oh, you're going to have to get louder than that." I slide her higher, bringing her breasts to my mouth. "How about I tell you about how much I've wanted to suck on these sweet tits ever since the dinner we had with you and Brad in Malibu?" I flick my tongue over one nipple and she gasps, pressing her pussy against my lower abs. She's hot and wet. "You were wearing a cream-colored jumpsuit that tied behind your neck." I move to her other breast and lick, then suck lightly. She moans. "It left your entire back bare and meant you couldn't wear a bra." I suck harder. "But you should have worn those little stick-on pads or something, because I could see your nipples through it." I suck harder and longer. She's gripping my shoulders and pressing closer. "They were hard most of the night, too. It was killing me." I move to the other breast again, sucking hard, then giving her a little nip.

"Ford!"

"If you had been mine that night, I would have dragged you into the closest alcove, untied that top and done this until you came." I lick and suck and bite as she grinds her hot, wet pussy against me.

I slide my hand down to cup her pussy, pressing the heel of my hand against her clit, giving her something firmer to press against.

She grinds harder.

"Yep, just like that," I tell her. "I would have let you get off against my hand and gotten that expensive jumpsuit all sticky and wet." I drag my mouth up her throat to her mouth. "Because you weren't wearing panties that night either, were you?"

More groans from the next bed. Liam hadn't been with us in Malibu, but Harrison had been there. There was no way he'd missed Ivy's nipples in that jumpsuit. Though Brad had seemed to. He should have given her his jacket. That's what I would have done if my girlfriend had been making every other guy in the place hard the way she was. But Brad was oblivious. He'd never appreciated Ivy the way she deserved.

But I appreciated her. So fucking much.

She shakes her head. "No."

"I know. I studied every fucking inch of you that night." I press against her clit. "Every night." I circle my hand. "Every fucking time I was around you."

She's breathing hard when I pull her down for a deep kiss. I stroke her tongue with mine as I let her grind against my hand.

I pull back, looking up into her gorgeous face. Her hair is falling forward and her breaths are coming in hot, quick pants against my mouth.

"I went back to the hotel and jacked off in the shower thinking about you that night," I tell her.

She moans.

"Of course, I did that every time I spent even five minutes with you."

"*Ford.*"

"Fuck yes," comes the muttered curse from Liam.

I feel Ivy's rhythm picking up, so I pull my hand away.

"Ford," she protests.

"Don't worry," I tell her. "I just need my fingers inside this sweet pussy when you come. I need to feel that."

"Jesus Christ."

That's Harrison and though their mattress is still squeaking and they're breathing hard, I know they're also listening in over here.

I'm a good friend. I decide to give them even more commentary.

"Your tits are perfect, Ivy," I tell her. "Sweet and perky. Your nipples hard and so sensitive." I give one another nip. "Now let me feel this perfect cunt."

She hesitates for just a second. Then she asks, "How do you want me?"

Three men groan in unison.

I bring her head down and kiss her again. "That was the perfect answer," I say against her lips.

I shift her back. "Like this. This way you're filled up but that greedy clit can get what it needs too."

She's spread wide over my thighs again. Her clit is against my cock and I run my big hand over her ass, then down between her legs, sliding two fingers into her.

She moans. "Oh, God."

"You're so tight. You're so fucking wet. Perfect," I tell her. And the guys.

I move my fingers in and out. She shudders against me.

"Damn, princess, you grip cocks so well, don't you?"

She squeezes around my fingers, and I press up into her.

"Grind against me, Ivy. Get yourself off against me."

"I...want..." She does what I tell her, but she wants more. I'll give her anything.

"What, baby? Tell me."

"I want your cock."

"I don't want to stop and get a condom," I tell her honestly. "Let me get you off this way."

She nods. "Okay. But I want skin on skin."

I realize what she's saying a second later and heat rockets through me. "You want me bare up against that needy little clit?"

She nods quickly.

Fuck, this woman is so...surprising. Sweet and hot and...fuck. Better than I even imagined. She's funny and flirty and has this naughty side that I want so badly to explore fully.

"Take what you want, Ivy," I tell her through gritted teeth.

"Suck me," Liam orders harshly.

I hear their bed creaking as Ivy lifts herself off me enough to lower my athletic shorts. Her hand brushes over my cock and it aches.

"Fuck," I grit out.

She wraps her hand around me and strokes. "You're so hard."

"Rub your pussy against me, Ivy," I tell her firmly. "Want you to come."

She immediately moves, pressing her clit against my bare shaft. The contact makes air hiss out between my teeth. I feel like electricity is filling my veins.

I still have two fingers buried in her pussy and my other hand presses down on her ass as she rocks against me.

She lifts one hand to her breast, playing with her nipple.

I feel her pussy clenching around me and I thrust in and out.

"I love watching and feeling you take what you want," I tell her. "You know just how to move, don't you? You know just what this sweet body needs. That's right," I praise. "Move just like that.

Your pussy wants more than fingers doesn't it, my sweet, dirty girl?"

"*Yes.*" Ivy picks up her pace and I fuck her faster with my fingers.

But we're not fucking. It's *very* heavy petting. But I'm going to come. This is too much. Too fucking hot.

I feel Ivy's pussy clench hard. "Oh, God! Ford! I'm coming!"

"Yes. Fucking yes. Let me feel it, Ivy."

She cries out, the prettiest, "Oh, *yes!*" as she clamps down hard around my fingers and comes.

I'm right behind her, spilling between us, over my stomach.

She slumps forward, despite the mess. My fingers slip from between her legs and I cup her ass.

"Fuck. Fuck, fuck, fuck," Liam is chanting.

There are two low groans.

Then Liam shouts, "Fuck, Harrison!"

The next sound is the bed creaking and Harrison saying, "Goddammit, Liam. Yes, fuck, like that."

There's more creaking, some skin slapping, muttered curses.

Then Harrison roars, "Liam!"

We hear kissing sounds next.

And then the room is quiet except for all of our heavy breathing.

That was...unexpected.

And maybe the hottest thing that's happened to me in...ever.

CHAPTER 11

Liam

I WAKE UP EARLY, because of course I do. There's a hot, hard body up against mine. And my body is reacting to that.

Fucking Harrison.

I never should have given in. I know it seems to everyone, including Harrison, that I am in charge when the two of us are together. But I wish my heart would get the message.

He has me twisted up, has from the very beginning, and my chances of resisting him last night were negative zero.

I think I put on a pretty good show, but he had been slowly chipping away at my self-control and when he started stripping, I knew I was done for.

Then the charged moment between him and Ivy was my definite breaking point.

Watching the two of them just stare at one another ignited lust inside me that I have never felt before.

And they were just *looking* at one another.

If they ever touch, or kiss, if Harrison ever wraps her hair around his fist, says the dirty fucking things that I know he can say to *Ivy*, if I ever see her naked in his arms, I might combust.

I shift away from his body, knowing that he might wake slightly, but then he'll roll over, get comfortable again, and go right back to sleep. Harrison doesn't let things like someone else being awake keep him from his own comforts, like sleeping as late as possible.

I swing my legs over the side of the mattress and stand, quickly grabbing clothes from my bag and ducking into the bathroom. I shower and brush my teeth, getting ready as quietly as possible. I'll head out and find coffee and breakfast for everyone and hope that they're all stirring by the time I get back. The sooner we get on the road, the sooner we get to South Carolina and the sooner I can put real distance between me and Harrison.

I'm almost to the door of the room when I hear Ivy's soft voice. "Liam," she whispers.

I look over at her bed. I had avoided that until this moment, not wanting to see her snuggled up against Ford.

She's sitting on the edge of the bed, pulling her shoes on. She must've gotten dressed while I was in the bathroom. Her hair is up in a bun on the top of her head, and she's wearing a sundress.

Fuck.

Do women know what sundresses do to men? It's what gray sweatpants on men do to women. And other men.

I have double the temptation in this room. Harrison has a pair of gray sweatpants along.

The bastard.

And now my girl is wearing a baby blue sundress that hits her mid-thigh when she stands. The thin straps leave her shoulders and arms bare, and the dress molds to her perky breasts.

The ones Ford sucked on last night.

I groan. Not only because she looks adorable, slightly sleepy, and sweet, but because I just so naturally thought of her as 'my girl'. Hours after she spent the night in another man's arms. A man who sucked on her nipples and made her come.

I don't know the details—I was a little distracted myself, but I heard it. Harrison did too. And I know it turned him on.

The sounds—those fucking sounds—of Ivy coming apart in

pleasure…*fuck*. I wasn't responsible for them and yet I don't know that I will ever get them out of my head.

"Are you going to get coffee?" she asks me, keeping her voice low as she comes to stand beside me.

I nod instead of speaking.

"Can I come?" she asks.

You come prettier than anyone I've ever heard. Of course I don't say that. Or the next thought either. *Harrison doesn't come pretty.* No. He comes loud and with my name on his tongue. Exactly the way I order him to.

Yep, I can distinctly remember how he sounded with my hand wrapped around his cock, pumping him until he spilled, hot and sticky, all over my hand.

Jesus. It's not even eight in the morning and I am hard as a rock.

I open the door and usher her out with a hand on her lower back.

Once the door shuts behind us, I say, "I saw a place a few blocks over. It's just a diner, so I'm not sure what they'll have to offer. But hopefully to-go cups. Unless you want to stay there."

Maybe that's a good idea. We can sit and eat and let the other two sleep for a while.

I wouldn't mind some alone time with Ivy. I don't know where her head is for sure—this road trip has been intense—and I would love to know how she's feeling about everything. Okay, specifically about Ford.

I should be wondering how she's feeling about Brad.

But I know her. She's okay about her ruined wedding. I can read her well enough to know that. I was worried that she wasn't madly in love with Brad to start with. I'm definitely relieved that the wedding got called off, of course, and yes, some of that is selfish because of my feelings for her, but it's also because I know her feelings for Brad were not strong enough. And he's a dick. He was never good enough for her.

But my curiosity isn't about Brad. It's all about Ford. There's clearly something there. Something more than what happened last night.

He wants her. Has for a while, I know. But now she's available and she's interested, I can tell.

And if fucking Harrison wasn't here distracting me, I'd be more tuned in to what's going on between her and the other millionaire playboy.

Hell, that's probably not even fair.

Ford's a good guy. He dates, sure, but he's not the man whore the guy *I'm* stupidly crazy about is.

Ford has been taking care of Ivy this whole time. While I've been dealing with Harrison.

But has he taken advantage of her vulnerable state? Is she looking at him with a little hero worship maybe?

We should talk this out.

She's been quiet on the drive to the diner, so as I pull the glass door open I say, "Let's stay and eat here."

"What about the guys?" she asks.

I step in behind her and frown. "They're big boys." But then I say. "We can take them something to go. But I'd like a chance to talk, just the two of us. We haven't had any time alone since the wedding."

Her blue gaze meets mine. She nods. "That would be nice."

My heart trips. Damn. This woman has me wrapped around her little finger and she has no idea. She could have anything from me. I'd even let Ford have her if that's what she wants.

But fuck. This is the first time we've both been single at the same time since I met her. How can I just step aside without at least telling her how I feel?

The diner is busy, and a harried waitress with medium brown skin, curly black hair, and a big smile hustles over and grabs two plastic coated menus and tells us, "This way." She leads us to a booth in the far corner and we slide in on opposite sides.

We peruse the menu, but the offerings are pretty basic and we decide quickly.

I order eggs, sausage, and toast while Ivy gets an omelet. The waitress pours us both coffee and I say, "We'll need a couple of the breakfast burritos and some coffee to go as well."

She notes that on her pad and heads for the kitchen.

I look across the table at my best friend.

"Okay, how are you?"

She takes a deep breath and blows it out. "Good. Actually, really good."

"Really?"

She nods. "Really. I'm relieved that things with Brad are over." She gives a short laugh. "As sad as that is. I'm feeling stupid that he was the one who had to end it. But also glad he did. I'm actually having fun on this road trip, though I'm dreading dealing with the house. I know you guys, you and F-Ford, will help me." She stumbles slightly over his name. "And things are..." Her gaze drops to the tabletop. "Good otherwise."

"You mean things with you and Ford." I feel a cold ball gathering in my chest. Fuck. She's already taken. Again.

"Oh, I don't know," she says with a shrug.

My heart kicks with what I can only describe as hope. "Really? What about last night?"

She blushes. "Well, that was fun," she says with a little smile. "But before last night, I kissed him and he pulled back. He doesn't want to rush things and I think he's right. I am very, *very* attracted to him. And he's a great guy. I do feel *something* there. There's a ton of chemistry. More than I ever had with Brad, sadly. But...I don't know. Maybe the timing is wrong."

"So last night was only sex?" I shouldn't ask. It's probably none of my business. But I'm in love with this girl. And she's my best friend. Best friends talk about this stuff, right?

Okay, that's not it. I need to know how she feels about Ford. I need to know if they've talked about any future. I need to know what I'm up against.

"Not sex," she says, lowering her voice. "Just messing around."

I lean in. I've always kept things friendly and fun with us. I've never pushed things with Ivy. Again, one of us has always been taken, and that wouldn't have been appropriate. But neither of us is taken right now. Not officially. Not in a committed, in love way. So I say, "I heard you come last night, Ivy. That wasn't just messing around. I heard what he did to you."

She stares at me, as if she can't look away. Her cheeks are pink, but her mouth falls open, and she's breathing a little faster. The air between us heats slightly.

Her tongue darts out and wets her bottom lip. "He made me come. But it wasn't sex. Just...touching." Her gaze darts around as if she's trying to figure out if anyone can overhear us. When her eyes come back to mine, she gives me a little half grin that looks sexy and satisfied.

I can't help but grin in return. I've been there. "Well, it sounded really good."

Her eyes widen slightly. "I could hear you, too."

Heat arrows through me sharply. "Is that right?"

"Yeah. Both of you. It sounded like you were having fun, too."

I nod slowly. "Yeah. It was fun. Also just touching. No sex."

She watches me without speaking, and I wonder if she's picturing it. Me and Harrison together, hands around one another's cocks. The pink in her cheeks is darker now. And dammit, I'm again assaulted by images of her and Harrison. Him kissing her, her mouth around his cock, her riding him.

They would be so fucking hot together. And I would be there too. Definitely. I'd be telling them both what to do to each other. *Fuck*, that would be hot as hell.

Just then, the waitress arrives with our breakfasts, setting plates of eggs and sausage in front of us. The scent of fried potatoes, onions and peppers surrounds us and my stomach growls. Ivy immediately reaches for the butter and strawberry jam.

We both get busy salting, pouring ketchup, and digging into the good old-fashioned breakfast.

We eat without talking. We're very comfortable being quiet

together after our years of friendship, and I am struck by how much I like just being with her.

But it does feel different between us at the moment. We've never talked about sex like this. We've never been in the same room together while having orgasms. At the hands of other people.

And I really want to do it again. And I really want to know what she's thinking.

And I really need to tell her how I feel about her.

We make small talk about getting on the road, how far we're going to drive today, if we think the guys are awake yet.

Our waitress brings our check, along with a paper bag with two burritos, and a drink holder with two paper cups of coffee. She tells us there's also cream, sugar, and plastic stirrers in the bottom of the bag.

I pay, rolling my eyes inwardly about buying breakfast for two fucking millionaires, but I do find some satisfaction in it being greasy diner food.

As we approach the car, Ivy laughs. "Here, you should carry the coffee." She starts to hand me the drink carrier.

I frown. "Why?"

"Your boyfriend will like it if you bring him coffee," she says with a grin.

My boyfriend. She just referred to Harrison as my boyfriend.

I stop walking. She takes two steps before she realizes I've stopped. She turns back. "What's wrong?"

"I need to tell you something," I say, realizing this is the moment.

"Okay." She frowns, clearly realizing from my serious expression and tone that I'm not joking around.

"We have never been single at the same time," I tell her. "Every time I'm single, you've been seeing someone. Every time you've been single, I've been with someone. Ever since we first met."

Her brow furrows as if she's thinking about this. She nods. "I guess that's true."

"Now, we're both single, but we're kind of on the verge of possible relationships again. With Harrison and Ford."

"I don't know what's going to happen with Ford," she says.

"If you want something to happen with him, it will," I tell her. She needs to know that. I need her to know that. "I think he's had feelings for you for a while. And there's very clear chemistry between you. He's being a good guy right now because you just had a breakup. But the ball's in your court. And I know you really like him." I take a breath. "He'd be good for you."

She takes a step back toward me. "And you have big feelings for Harrison. Are you admitting that to me finally?"

I pull in a breath and blow it out. "Fuck. Yes, fine, I do have feelings for Harrison."

She is not surprised by my admission. "But they live in South Carolina," she points out.

"Yes. It's a little complicated with both of them, but that's not what I want to talk to you about. This isn't about them."

"Okay."

I take a step toward her. Now we're directly in front of one another. I study her beautiful face. It's so familiar it makes my chest ache. I've looked at her a million times and wished that I could reach up and cup her cheek, tuck her hair behind her ear, drag my thumb along her jaw, lean in and kiss her.

Fuck it.

Why can't I do those things now?

She's my best friend. I love her. She's single. I'm single. And I might not ever have another chance.

I drop the bag with the two burritos to the ground, reach up and take her face in both hands and pull her close.

"Ivy."

"Yes?" she asks, her voice soft.

Her eyes are wider than I've ever seen them. But she's not pulling back.

"I do have feelings for Harrison. And if you have feelings for Ford and something can come of that, I'm very happy for you. If that's what you want. But there's something you should know."

"Okay," she says, her voice almost a whisper.

"You are my best friend, and I love you, the way we've always said. But it's more than that. I want you. I want to be with you. I am *in love* with you."

Then I do the thing I have been aching to do for three years. I pull her close as I lean in and I *finally* kiss her.

CHAPTER 12

Ivy

LIAM KISSES LIKE A DREAM.

That's the only thought in my head as I give myself over to him, pouring all of the love I've always felt for him into our unhurried, yet passionate, embrace.

The way his hands cup my cheeks is strong, sexy, and oh-so-Liam. Confident, quiet, commanding. Yet worshipful at the same time. We kiss again and again, a yearning, questing, completion of what's been simmering under the surface for years.

He's in love with me.

That's what he said.

I suppose on some level I've always known that. Or at least sensed it. I've felt it too, a secret understanding that what we are —what we could be—is more than friends.

There are actual tears in my eyes when he finally releases me, soulful blue eyes sweeping over me, seeking a confirmation of our connection.

"I'm in love with you too," I whisper.

"You're crying," he murmurs, stroking up the length of my cheeks to gently brush across the moisture that is clinging to my lashes, but not falling. "Why are you crying, my precious?"

That makes me give a watery laugh. Liam has a definite nerdy side and one time he told me that when he finds the love of his life, he'll call her or him 'my precious' in a nod to Gollum. It had been a joke, and he's using it now because he doesn't know if my tears are good or bad. Liam doesn't like it when he can't interpret a person or a situation.

Which is why Harrison makes him crazy. He can't figure out why Harrison does the things he does.

But I won't keep him guessing with me. It's time I tell him the truth.

"I'm crying because I've always loved you, but I love our friendship so much too, and I've never wanted to risk losing it."

He's tracing my eyebrows, down my temples, and across my lips. "Why would you lose our friendship?"

"If I told you how I feel and you didn't feel the same way, that would ruin what we have. So, instead, I just ignored my feelings. I'd rather have your friendship than not have you at all."

He studies me, lowering his hands to my shoulders. "But if you could have all of me, you'd want that?"

I nod. "Yes," I say simply.

Liam understands me completely, on every level. We had a bond from the very first time we met and it's only grown deeper and deeper over the years as our lives have shifted and grown and moved around each other. Through relationships and moves and career changes, he's been my constant.

"Then you have me," Liam says. "All of me. I'm yours."

A shiver rolls through me. I throw my arms around Liam and give him a hug. He kisses the side of my head. I feel giddy and excited. "I love you."

Liam squeezes me tight. "I love you too. Now I guess we should go back. You've seen Harrison without coffee. It's not pretty."

I give a soft laugh as he bends over and picks up the bag he set down with the breakfast burritos. I bite my lip, a little nervous over having to face Ford in the light of day. I don't know what I feel for him. I like what I know of Ford—he's kind and caring and has been a safe haven for me since that disastrous moment when I walked in on him texting Brad.

Last night he made me feel incredible…but I have no idea what he's thinking. I feel a little guilty for pushing him away two nights ago, then pulling him back in last night.

There's an attraction between us, chemistry. We like each other.

But does that mean anything beyond a few days on the road?

I have no idea where his head is at or where mine is surrounding Ford, to be honest.

Now there's Liam.

This is a different level entirely.

Liam predates even Brad. He's my best friend. My go-to. My rational, steadfast, honest, and solid-as-a-rock ride or die.

"How do we do this?" I ask nervously.

Liam opens the car door for me, something he doesn't normally do. He grins. "I have no idea."

"I feel like they're going to know."

"How would they know?" He shuts the door and goes around the car. Once he's in the driver's seat, he says, "We have to tell them, anyway. It's the only fair thing to do. There's a lot for all of us to unpack."

I nod. We all need to figure out what we're doing together, if anything.

I know what I want with Liam.

Now that he's kissed me, I want more. As soon as possible. I'm already envisioning Liam touching every inch of me, sliding his hands down my body in the same worshipful way he cupped my face. "If we're in love with each other, we're going to have sex, right?"

Liam turns to me quickly. "Uh, fuck, *yes*, we're having sex. That's what was in my head, anyway. Tell me you're on the same page."

His very Liam horrified reaction makes me laugh. "Yes, we're on the same page. I was just checking." I reach over and touch his knee. "I want you."

"God, I fucking want you. I've wanted you every day for over three years."

I can't stop smiling. It's ear to ear. "You actually hid it very well. We're going to have to have a chat about that later."

"Can we be naked when that happens?"

I pretend to give him a stern look. "I want to know *everything*, Liam. If you remember what I was wearing the first time we met—

"Black pants and a sleeveless beige shirt with a gold necklace."

Interesting. And delightful. "And what you thought of the guys I dated—

"Idiots. All of them. Not good enough for you."

"Are you saying I have bad taste?"

"Until today, yes, I could argue that. Of course, Ford seems like a decent guy."

That makes me feel weird all over again. "He does. Are you jealous?"

"A little. Are you jealous of Harrison?"

"A little. But at the same time, because we've been friends for so long and dated other people, it doesn't feel as maddening as it should, if that makes sense."

"I totally agree with that."

Though what that means for the future, I have no clue.

Maybe Ford isn't interested in anything beyond last night. Maybe he was comforting me. With an orgasm. My nipples harden at that memory.

We get out of the car at the motel and walk up to the room. I'm carrying the paper bag and Liam has the drink holder in one hand. He takes my hand with his free one right before we reach our room. "Hey."

"Hmm?" I turn toward him.

"I love you. I just wanted to say that one more time."

"I had no idea you were so adorable when you're in love."

He leans in and kisses me, softly, briefly.

But then a fire sparks inside us and we're suddenly on top of each other, pressed up tightly chest to chest, kissing with sizzling heat and tangled tongues. I moan low, wanting more. His hand traces over my lower back and onto my ass, cupping one cheek to rock me against his hard cock.

The door opening behind us barely registers in my sex-soaked brain.

"Ivy."

I break away from Liam and turn to see Ford standing in the doorway in a towel, his hair damp from the shower. He looks stunned.

"Ford, I…" I have no idea what to say.

This is not how I wanted to bring this subject up and I fumble around for words and don't find any.

Harrison is behind him, fully dressed in shorts and a polo shirt, his arms crossed over his chest. He's wearing a grin, but it looks strained. "William. I hope you at least brought coffee."

"We did," Liam says, lifting the drink holder, seemingly fully composed. "Let's go in the room and talk about this."

"I don't really see what there is to say." Ford turns on his heel and heads straight to the bathroom, grabbing his overnight bag on his way.

I hear the lock on the bathroom door click.

My heart sinks. This mixture of emotions is confusing as hell and I hate the idea that I've hurt Ford in any way. It has me frozen in place.

With his hand on the small of my back, Liam gently pushes me into the room, edging me past Harrison, who steps out of the way. Liam pushes the coffee at Harrison, who takes the cardboard tray. I drop the bag with the burritos on the small dining table.

"So you're friends with benefits?" Harrison opens the bag and peers inside. His words are casual, but there is some hurt in his tone. "Did Brad know about that?"

Liam bristles. "Not that it's actually any of your fucking business, but there was nothing for Brad to know. This just happened."

"You went for coffee and decided to make out?"

This feels like a Liam-Harrison private conversation, so I walk over to the bathroom door and knock. I need to explain. "Ford, can we talk?"

The door opens, and he's fully dressed. He's on his phone, swiping. I can see he has a car service app open.

I frown. "What are you doing?"

He finally looks up at me. His gaze drills into me. "I'm going to the airport and flying to South Carolina. I don't really think I'm needed on this road trip after all and this all feels very…messy."

My jaw drops. "I…"

I don't actually know what to say. I feel awkward and guilty and yet, at the same time, I don't feel like I did anything wrong. We're all adults. Hell, we were four feet away from Liam and Harrison in bed last night, and that wasn't a problem. This hasn't exactly been a straight-forward friends-only road trip.

And yet…there was a spark between me and Ford. I don't intend to deny that, but it looks like he does.

"Ford. This was unexpected with Liam. Just like between us was unexpected."

"But you're in love with Liam," he says flatly.

"Yes. But—

Ford throws his hand up. "I don't need to hear the rest. Seriously. It's fine. This was a crazy fucking week. You don't have to explain yourself."

"But—

"Stop. Seriously."

Frustration creeps in that he won't let me speak. So I just decide to let him do what he needs to do. He looks *very* determined to leave. "Okay. Thank you for your help, Ford. I appreciate it."

He scoffs. "You're welcome."

He sounds hurt, which hurts me, I have to admit.

"You got an Uber?" Harrison asks, even as he starts shoving his clothes in his bag. "I guess they're everywhere now. Even the middle of nowhere."

"Are you leaving too?" Liam asks him, sounding as astonished as I feel.

"Uh, yes. I'm Ford's wingman. He goes, I go. That's the best friend code." Harrison takes a bite of his burrito and shoves his feet into his sandals as he zips up his bag. "Good luck selling the house, Ivy."

This is happening so fast, my head is spinning.

"Well, that's just ridiculous," Liam declares. "We can all have an actual conversation, you know. We are adults. Or at least three of us are."

Harrison's eyebrows shoot up. "So me, Ivy, and Ford?" Then he reaches over and kisses me on the cheek. "Don't let William boss you around or pull his grumpy bullshit."

I wait for Liam to try harder to stop them both, but he looks as astonished as I feel.

I just nod. "Thank you, Harrison. For everything." Ford is already at the motel room door. "We can drive you guys to the airport if you want," I tell them. At least that would give us time to talk.

"No, thanks." Ford waves his phone. "Uber is already on its way."

"Oh. Sure." I bit my lip and watch them both step out as a car pulls up almost immediately.

Harrison gives us a wave. Ford climbs in the vehicle without a glance back.

A minute later, Liam and I are just standing there, staring at each other.

"I don't know how I saw that going, but that wasn't it," I admit.

"Me either." Liam frowns at the closed door.

"Are you okay?" I ask, worried that he might be feeling rejected by Harrison for the second time.

Liam smiles, but this time it doesn't quite reach his eyes. He glances at the car pulling out of the motel parking lot. But then he says, "Yes. I'm not surprised by Harrison, though I'm sorry that was so awkward with Ford."

"Me too," I murmur. "But he made it clear he doesn't want to talk about it."

"Well." He glances around the room and heads for his bag. "Should we hit the road?"

"Yes. This room has bad vibes now." I make an effort to just shake off feeling suddenly and summarily abandoned by Ford. That's not fair. He didn't even have to come on this road trip. I'm still a little disappointed though, which also isn't fair. He saw me kissing Liam. "What a week."

Liam actually chuckles. He sets his bag on the bed and comes over to me. He pulls me into his arms. "Best week of my life so far."

That makes my heart full again, in spite of my convoluted feelings about Ford.

I snuggle into Liam's chest, grateful for him, as always. Even more so now that we've admitted our love for each other. "It's going to be even better tonight."

"I guarantee it."

CHAPTER 13

Ford

I CAN TELL Harrison is as rocked by what happened with Ivy and Liam as I am because he hasn't said a word since we left them in front of the hotel.

Harrison is never this quiet for this long.

He might be trying to play this cool, as if he couldn't care less that Liam and Ivy were kissing in front of the motel room door, but I can tell he does care. A lot.

I do too.

A lot.

More than I would have expected.

Sure, I'd entertained dirty thoughts about watching her kiss and touch—and be kissed and touched by—Harrison and Liam, but seeing it happen the way it had was…different.

They were kissing passionately. Privately. Like two people in love.

That was not a caught-up-in-a-dirty-moment. That wasn't a product of being stuck in a motel room together.

That was clearly the culmination of long-held feelings.

Obviously reciprocal feelings.

Fuck.

Now Harrison and I are on our way to South Carolina.

Did we need to charter a private plane? Of course not. Did we do it so we didn't have to drive to Amarillo to the airport, and then sit in a busy terminal waiting, and then sit on a full plane with a bunch of other people when we are both feeling big hurtful feelings? Yes. At least that's why I did it. Harrison did it because it's second nature. He loves to fly private.

He's always told me that he's not built for commercial air travel, and he even proved it to me once when I made him fly a regular airline in *coach* to spring break, telling him it was part of the experience.

He was amazed by everything about it.

Not in a good way.

It really is less annoying to just pay to fly my spoiled baby friend private for as long as I can afford it. Someday I might not be able to. At which time I will simply stop traveling with Harrison.

He's staring out the window and I study him as I lift the glass of whiskey to my lips.

Should I be on my second whiskey without any food in my stomach at ten a.m.? Of course not.

But this is how I am choosing to handle the fact that Ivy is already taken. Again.

And the fact that I had two chances to fuck the woman of my dreams and I passed them both up.

I glance at my phone, then I'm annoyed with myself for doing so.

I left. Do I really expect her to immediately start texting and begging me to come back?

Okay, yes, a small part of me does.

Which is ridiculous. She owes me nothing. She certainly shouldn't have to chase after me. It's beneath her and I respect her for not indulging in my bullshit. I stomped off without talking and I get what I get.

Which is drunk on a plane.

My phone buzzes and hope blooms in my chest.

It's an unknown number, so I ignore it.

"I'm happy for them."

I take a long draw of my whiskey as Harrison looks over at me. He's lying, of course. I simply lift a brow.

"No, seriously," he insists. "Liam's been in love with her for years. Obviously, he finally told her how he feels. Good for him."

I swallow, welcoming the burn of the liquor. I set the glass down and link my fingers over my lower stomach. "You are so full of shit."

"I'm a good fucking guy," Harrison protests. "I am happy that Ivy got rid of Brad, that she's moving on with a great guy, and that Liam finally gets what he wants after all this time."

I am Harrison's rock. I know this. It has always been our dynamic that I am the steady anchor and he is the fun one. If everything was left up to me, our bank account would probably be twice the size that it is, we'd have opened three more restaurants, and it's possible that we would both already be settled down, married, and maybe even have kids.

But I will admit that we don't need more money, or more restaurants, and we probably would've married people just because we should rather than because we wanted to.

Harrison, on the other hand, makes sure that we enjoy the things we accomplish. Because of him, we've traveled far more broadly than we would have otherwise. We've spent our money on fun and frivolity, but we've had amazing experiences and met amazing people. We're not settled down and married, but neither of us feels like anything is missing from our lives.

At least we didn't.

Before now.

Before Ivy and Liam.

How is it possible that these two people could be with us for two days and three nights on a crazy road trip, stuck in a dumpy motel room, and turn our fucking lives upside down?

"You don't care that the only man you cannot get out of your system no matter how hard you try, woke up this morning after spending the night in your bed and declared his love to the woman who spent the night in my bed?" I ask. He doesn't need to answer. I know him well enough to know the answer. But he is not going to gaslight me. "You don't care that you finally got to kiss him again, got your hands on him again, actually spent several hours not fighting with him, and then found him kissing Ivy and announcing that they are now in a relationship? That doesn't bother you at all?"

Harrison's entire body is tense, but he leans back in the expensive leather seat across from me, links his hands behind his head, and takes a deep breath. "Nope," he lies straight to my face. "Everything's good. Obviously, he got me out of his system and is able to move on. Good for him."

Is that what happened? I let myself wonder about that for a moment. Is that what happened with Ivy? She got me out of her system? Because there was definitely something between us. Yes, chemistry, for sure. But I think it was more than that.

I don't think it's my ego talking when I say that I was good for her. She relaxed around me. She was able to let go of the prim and proper, sophisticated side that she seemed to always be putting on. She is effortlessly elegant, independent, creative and sure of herself. But it's clear to me, even in the small amount of time I've been around her, that no one takes care of her or carries any burdens for her. She actually took care of Brad—that was always clear. And Liam lifts up her independent, strong side. He encourages her to make her own decisions and be his equal in every way. Which is amazing. She deserves that.

But she also deserves to be worshiped. To have someone fully focused on her and her needs. To be someone's princess.

That's me.

I'll be her cheerleader too. I absolutely admire her and want to see her succeed in whatever she wants to do. But I have a burning desire to take care of her. To be the one to hold her when she's sad, to be sure she's eating well and drinking enough water, and to be there when she's hungover or has the flu.

I shove a hand through my hair.

She and Liam are friends. They have history. She's in love with him.

Fine.

But I can't shake this feeling that she still needs *me*, too.

My phone buzzes with a voicemail notification. I read the text version of it. The FBI wants to talk to me about Brad? What the hell?

I relay this to Harrison, who frowns. "That's fucked up. Do you think that's why he ran?"

"I have no idea." If he did something illegal, surely there would be more signs of it. "Maybe they want to ask him about someone else and are just trying to find him."

Harrison grunts in acknowledgment.

"Should we try to get in touch with him? What if it's serious?"

Harrison gives a very Harrison response. "Call him if you want. I figure the hell with him. He's the reason we're both in this mess. He's on his own, as far as I'm concerned."

"True." Yet I still text him, because it's the FBI. That seems serious.

No surprise, I don't get a response.

We fall back into silence, and I let out a hefty sigh as my thoughts drift back to Ivy.

Fuck.

"Man, you need to get over it."

I look up to find Harrison studying me. And obviously reading me clearly.

"That would be nice." I say. "But I don't think it's gonna happen."

"You need to go out with someone," he tells me.

I roll my eyes. I date. I'm no monk. "That's not the solution."

"Well, it's going to have to be," he snaps.

I frown. Harrison never snaps. Except at Liam. And even then, it's not until the other man has *really* gotten to him.

"Are *you* going to go out with someone?" I ask.

He nods. "You and me. Amelia and Cara."

Amelia and Cara are two women we know in Charleston. They are friends who own a marketing firm together and who did some work for our restaurant about four years ago. They have often been our plus-ones when we need casual, no-strings dates who can handle the sophisticated, wealthy, gossipy social circle we sometimes have to interact with.

"I'm not going out with Amelia in an attempt to get over Ivy." The two women have some things in common, but there is nothing *real* between Amelia and me. There's no way she'll successfully distract me from my feelings for Ivy.

"Well, I'm going to see Cara."

Yes, it's interesting to me that my friend is going to try to get over a man by getting into bed with a woman. I notice he is not calling his guy-friend-with-benefits Wes, instead.

"Yeah, I'm sure being with Cara will be the same as being with Liam." I reach for my whiskey again.

"That's the point," Harrison insists. "I need something totally different."

And that's probably as close as I'm going to get to a confession from Harrison that he is, in fact, upset about Liam.

"That's the thing," I say. "I don't want different. I want *Ivy*. Exactly as she is. Different will only remind me constantly of her and all the things I want instead."

Harrison frowns, but he looks thoughtful. "Okay, how about Kendall? She's a lot like Ivy. Sweet, creative, stylish, smart."

But I take a gulp of whiskey, then shake my head. "I want Ivy. Just Ivy."

"So you're just going to die alone, then? Is that right?"

I'm *finally* starting to feel the happy buzz of the alcohol in my brain. I salute him with my now empty glass. "Well, I've always got you."

Harrison just shakes his head. "God help you."

CHAPTER 14

Ivy

I DRIVE for the first hour after we leave the motel. I'm lost in thought, mixed up over what happened with Ford and Harrison, wondering if I should call or text and if I do what I would possibly say.

Liam is just as quiet, though. He has to be thinking about Harrison.

And strangely, even though we just confessed our feelings to one another and are now officially in a relationship, it doesn't bother me that he's upset over Harrison.

I know that's a little weird. But everything has been different, unexpected, since I walked in and found out Brad had left me. I'm just rolling with it. I've learned the hard way that even the most meticulously planned things can go really, really wrong. So, I'm just going with what feels good.

Like me and Liam.

Things between us are so easy. As always. Even with these added extras. Like admitting we're in love.

His declaration was surprising, and I still get butterflies when I think about it, but I wasn't *shocked*. It felt right. It felt like something I'd been waiting for somehow.

It was also very easy to say it back to him.

And now, three hours into our trip, Liam is driving and we've had absolutely no argument over the radio, or snacks, he's stopped every time I've asked, and even the sweet and casual PDA—a kiss on the top of my head, a hand on my lower back, our fingers linked as we walked to and from the car—has already felt second nature.

We are like we've always been, but with hand-holding and kissing.

I really like it.

I steal a look at Liam.

I've known him for so long that his face, his body, the way he moves and sits, his gestures and expressions, are so familiar that it's funny and thrilling to me that looking at him now makes butterflies swoop in my stomach.

He glances at me and catches me watching him.

The corner of his mouth curls. "What?" he asks.

"I was just thinking about how much I like looking at you. You're pretty hot."

He laughs. "Thanks. You're pretty hot too."

I reach out and he takes my hand, linking our fingers. "No, it's just funny. I've always thought you were attractive. But I guess it became just an objective fact rather than something I let affect me. Probably because I felt like we couldn't act on it. But it was really easy to throw that switch."

He looks very interested in that answer. "Threw that switch, huh?"

"Yeah. I am loving the idea that you're my boyfriend. And that I can reach out and touch you whenever I want." I run a hand up and down his arm. He's not as bulky as Ford but he's trim and muscular, and I love the tattoos on his arms.

I quickly shake off the thought of Ford. Ford is not here. He chose to leave. And how I feel about him doesn't matter. I am with Liam now.

Except that was an abrupt ending to something that seemed to be just beginning, and I hate that. I really feel like I want to talk to

Ford, have some kind of closure, but I'm not sure if that's the right thing to do or not.

Because of both Ford and Liam.

Right now I'm with Liam, though, so I focus on him.

"And I know tonight we'll be sleeping in the same bed. And not with pillows stuffed between us or you fully clothed on top of the covers. Or any of the other ways we've shared the bed before."

His fingers curl against mine, and he glances away from the road. There is heat in his eyes. "I've had a few sleepless nights because of you. You owe me."

I can't help my smile. Or the tingles spreading through my body. "I *owe* you?"

"Yeah, I think you should have to repay me somehow for all that torture."

I lean closer. "It was torture? You poor thing."

"Sleeping next to you? Thinking about how you would look naked? Thinking about how you would feel if I pulled you up against me? My cock hard and aching all night? Yeah, torture."

His words have heat and some aching happening between my legs.

"What about last night?" I venture to ask. I shouldn't bring it up. We should forget about last night. We should probably try to forget about Ford and Harrison completely.

Still, I want his answer.

His fingers grip me tighter. "You mean, when you were naked, grinding against another man, his fingers buried in your pussy, you coming apart, just a few feet away from me?"

He's not looking at me. He's studying the road, concentrating on driving. I feel my breathing speed up. "Yeah. When you were naked with another man in the bed next to mine. When you had another man's cock pressed up against you. When you were coming in another man's fist."

I see him grip the steering wheel tighter. "It was hot as fuck," he says huskily.

It was. It really was.

It's also reassuring that I don't have to be guarded with Liam about my confused feelings for Ford.

"Did you picture me at all?" I ask. "When Harrison was touching you?"

"Of course. I was seconds away from turning on the bedside lamp. I wanted to see you so badly."

I swallow hard. "I wanted to see you, too. I was picturing everything you were doing."

He looks over at me. "Hearing you come was so fucking hot."

I lick my lips and nod. "Same."

Suddenly, he mutters, "Fuck it." He looks in the rearview mirror, then turns the wheel to the right.

I reach out and brace my hand on the dash. "Liam!"

"I know we still have a long way to drive, but I can't wait any longer," he tells me.

"Wait for—" But I don't need to ask the question. There's a motel just off this exit.

At least this one is in a national chain that I recognize the name of.

My stomach swoops and I grin. "We're making a stop?"

He pulls up in front of the motel and throws the car into park. He leans across the seat and cups the back of my head, pulling me in and kissing me deeply. Hotly. He pulls back and looks into my eyes. "We're making a stop. I need you. Right now."

Heat sizzles through me and I simply nod.

He's out of the car and in the lobby of the motel a minute later.

I press my hand against my stomach, trying to calm myself, but the adrenaline is pumping hard.

I can't think about Brad or my wedding disaster right now. Or Ford. Or Harrison. None of them matter. Well, they do to the extent that they are part of our experience, and part of how we got here.

But right now, it's just me and Liam.

He comes striding back out to the car a few minutes later, and slides behind the wheel. He drives us around to the back of the motel and then parks, gets out, and comes around my door.

This is a much nicer place than where we were last night.

He grabs my hand and pulls me up out of the seat. But rather than start for the door of the motel, he presses me against the side of the car.

He takes my face in both hands. "I love you."

I smile. "I love you too."

"Good. I just needed you to know that before I take you into that room."

My brows arch. "Why is that?"

"Because this is probably not going to be sweet and romantic. I'm not going to make love to you. Not this first time. I'm going to fuck you. Fuck three years of pent up lust and emotion into you. Fuck the I-almost-lost-this-chance into you."

I laugh, even as every inch of my body feels like it's on fire. I wouldn't expect sweet and romantic from Liam, even if we didn't have feelings building between us for years. But I say, "Well, believe it or not, that is kind of romantic. And perfect for us. And I'm all in."

He gives me a delicious growl, then kisses me quickly before taking my hand and practically dragging me into the motel, up the flight of stairs to the second floor and down the hallway to room two seventeen, then through the door.

I expect to be spun and pressed against the door or wall, but instead he pushes me toward the bed.

"Stay right there," he commands.

He goes around the room, opening the curtains fully so the sunlight spills in, then turning on every light. Then he grabs the armchair near the window and drags it over.

He positions the chair so there are a few feet between the chair and the foot of the bed. He drops into the chair, props one ankle on his opposite knee, sits back, then says, "Okay."

"You're not going to undress or even get on the bed?"

"I have been waiting for this moment for three years. I intend to savor every single moment, study every single inch, *touch* and taste every single inch of you."

I shiver as desire ripples through me.

"Well," I say, my voice breathless. "Just tell me what you want me to do."

He grips the arms of the chair, but says, "Strip."

This won't take long. I'm wearing a simple summer dress. Underneath, I am wearing a bra and panties, though.

When I pulled them on this morning, I remembered what Ford had said about the jumpsuit I wore months ago that he still remembered.

You have to stop thinking about Ford.

It's not like I'm not focused on Liam. I am. I am so happy to be here with him. I feel like my entire body is buzzing with excitement and I very much want to do this with him.

I kick my sandals off to the side, then start unbuttoning the tiny buttons that run down the front of the dress. I wouldn't have to. I can slip the dress on and off over my head, but there's something about unbuttoning for him that makes me feel sexy. And the way he grips the arms of the chair tighter, and the flare of heat in his eyes tells me this is the right choice.

I unbutton to my waist and he growls, "Enough."

I smirk as I let the dress drop to the floor. I pause, letting him study me in my bra and panties. I don't have huge breasts, but they are enough to fill his hands, and I can't wait to feel his touch. My nipples are very hard, and I'm sure he can see them through the thin silk of my bra.

"Bra and panties. Off."

Liam is a man of few words anyway, but the gruffness in his voice tells me that some of his short commands have to do with his tightly wound desire. That gives me a heady thrill.

I reach behind me and unfasten my bra, tossing it to the side. He sucks in a sharp breath as my bare breasts are revealed for the first time. Then I hook my thumbs in the top of my panties and push them down.

I can feel his gaze on me as if he's touching me. I stand, waiting for my next command. There's something about letting him lead this that makes my pussy flutter.

Liam does not coddle me. He's always there for me. If I need a ride home, if I need someone to bounce ideas off of, the time I was sick with strep throat and Brad was out of town and I needed someone to bring me soup and more cough drops. But Liam doesn't assume I need to be taken care of. He'll help me with anything if I ask, but he doesn't take over. Usually, I like that. He fully respects me and admires my independence.

But now? Here in the bedroom? With sex? It's very hot to be taking orders.

"Turn around," he tells me.

I do, intending to turn a full three-sixty. But he stops me when I'm facing away. He leans forward and I feel his hands on my waist. I shiver. "I love having your hands on me."

"Good thing. I'm going to be doing a lot of touching for a long time."

I smile, but then he drags his hands down the outside of my thighs, and my smile dies. His touch sends sparks along all of my nerve endings.

He runs his hands back up my thighs, then to my ass, where he kneads and squeezes before running them up my back, then around to my stomach, then back to my hips.

"Your skin is like silk," he says roughly.

"Thank you," I manage.

"Turn."

I do and I hold my breath as his gaze scans me from head to toe, right up close. He drags his hands from my hips down to my knees again. Then he slides them back up over my hips to my ribs and then up to cup my breasts. I suck in a sharp breath. My nipples pull even tighter and he runs his thumbs over both at once.

"Liam," I say breathlessly.

"You're so fucking beautiful," he says, rubbing my nipples, then plucking at them.

Heat hits my pussy and I give a little moan.

"Yeah, that's a pretty sound."

He's watching his hands and fingers on my breasts. I run my hands along his arms, needing to touch him somehow.

His hands glide down over my belly to my hips and he sets me back slightly. "I need to see this pretty pussy."

It hits me that it should maybe be awkward that my best friend is talking about my pussy and looking at me completely naked while he sits fully clothed.

Instead, it's hot as hell.

He nudges me back to the bed. "Spread your legs for me, Ivy."

I never thought I'd hear those words from Liam. But I wanted them. I'd shoved my attraction to him deep down, it seems, but it's all rushing to the forefront now.

I sit on the end of the bed and part my knees.

He leans forward, resting his forearm on his thighs, studying me. He wasn't lying. It seems he truly does intend to see every inch.

"Lie back," he tells me.

I do, spreading my legs for him. My hands go to my breasts, playing with my aching nipples.

"Fuck," he mutters, rubbing a hand over his jaw.

"Touch me," I beg.

I feel more exposed than I ever have been. But I don't feel vulnerable. I am completely safe with Liam. Instead, I am incredibly turned on. I need his touch. I need him to help with this deep growing ache.

He runs both hands up my inner thighs, his thumbs coming together at my center and brushing over my folds. I am incredibly wet and maybe should be embarrassed. But his groan and, "Fuck you're perfect," makes me feel sexy and gorgeous and empowered.

I think at this moment, I could get him to do anything I

wanted him to. I might be spread out, completely naked, but I'm in control here.

"Liam, touch me. Please."

He runs his thumbs over my pussy, dragging wetness from my slit to my clit.

I moan. "*Yes.*"

He circles and presses and I feel the tightness of an orgasm gathering already.

"God, I've thought of you so many times like this," he says almost reverently.

I lift my hips, trying to get closer to his touch. "More," I urge.

He slips a finger into me, sliding deep, then dragging it out before circling my clit again.

I whimper.

"How did—" He cuts himself off.

"How did what?" I ask.

He lifts his gaze from my pussy to my face. He shakes his head. "Never mind. I don't need to know. It's me getting you off this time."

I realize he was going to ask about Ford. And last night.

So all of that is not only on my mind.

It was hot. It was very intimate sharing that with Liam. In a way, that was more intimate than I've ever been with anyone else, even the people I've slept with. He got to hear me with someone else. That's...unusual. But I don't want anyone else with us here at this very moment.

"I only want you right now," I tell him.

I hear a low rumble from the back of his throat and he slides another finger into me, circling over my clit with his thumb.

My orgasm begins to coil tighter, and I squeeze one nipple.

"God, I love feeling your pussy around my fingers," he tells me. He stands and leans over me, keeping his fingers deep inside me, curling them against my G-spot. He lowers his head and takes a nipple into his mouth, sucking hard as he fucks me faster with his fingers.

"Let me hear you come again. But *loud*. No whispering in here. Let me hear my name come from this pretty mouth."

The way he's looking at me is so intense, the way he's braced over me, the way he's touching me, firmly, fully, deeply—not tenderly or sweetly, but like he knows I can take everything he's giving me, combines to make my orgasm suddenly pull tight, and then release, pleasure rushing over me.

"Liam!" I call out loudly.

"That's my girl," he praises, his fingers still moving between my thighs. "That's my sweet fucking girl."

Then he stands, pulling his fingers from my body and lifting them to his lips. He licks them clean, his gaze locked on mine. I start to move my knees together, instinctively I suppose, but he steps close, blocking the motion with his own knee. "Oh no. I'm not done with that pussy yet."

I'm breathing fast. I let my legs part again. Then I watch as he unbuttons his jeans and pulls the zipper down.

"Shirt off too," I tell him.

He grasps the shirt between his shoulder blades and yanks it over his head, tossing it to the side.

I've seen Liam shirtless before, but again, I must have suppressed my true reaction to the sight. Now, I notice the muscle definition, the ink, all of the places that I want to lick and bite him.

My breath shudders out. "God, I want you."

He pushes his jeans over his hips, kicking his shoes off, then stepping out of the jeans. He's left in only his underwear, and I catch my lower lip between my teeth as I watch him slowly strip them off.

This is definitely new. I have never seen Liam naked before.

But holy shit. He's gorgeous. His cock is long and thick and... "You're *pierced*?" I prop up on my elbows. "How did I not know you're pierced *there*?"

"Despite the fact that I've wanted you up close and personal with my cock many times over the years, it hasn't actually come up as a topic of conversation much between us," he says wryly.

I sit up and lean forward, running my hands down his sides to his hips, studying his cock and the piercing.

I look up at him. "Can I touch it?"

He gives a short laugh, but it sounds pained. "Jesus. Fuck yes."

I do, tentatively, running my finger over the ball.

"It's called a Prince Albert."

"It's so sexy," I tell him.

"You're going to love it." Then he grasps my thighs and tips me back. He leans over me, his expression full of heat but also affection. "You wet and ready for me, Ivy?"

I nod quickly. "So ready."

"There are so many fun things we're going to do, but right now I just need to be inside you."

I nod again. "Yes. Please."

He doesn't climb up on the bed. He pulls me until my ass is at the end of the mattress, spreads my legs, then asks, "You still have your IUD?"

I laugh. "See? We have talked about some pretty private things." He actually drove me to that appointment. That was pre-Brad. "You could have told me about the piercing."

He grins. "Not exactly the same. But I love knowing intimate details about you." He strokes his hands up and down my thighs. "I'll go get a condom if you want me to. But I haven't fucked anyone without a condom. Not in years. And I get tested regularly."

I nod. I know this about him. "I trust you. We don't need a condom."

Heat flashes in his eyes, then he takes his cock in hand, stroking up and down the length once with a firm grip. He's looking at me with an intense mix of desire and affection. "God, you're so beautiful. I can't believe we're here."

"Careful," I tell him. "I feel like you're on the verge of saying something sweet or romantic."

He narrows his eyes, then says, "You're right. Spread your legs and take this dick like a good girl."

He runs a finger over my clit and I've barely gasped before he's at my entrance, then sliding deep.

It's a tighter fit than I expected, but I love it. This is Liam. Probably the person I love most in the world. And fuck, his cock is amazing. Even without the piercing. But damn, if women knew what this felt like, they would insist all men get these.

"Oh my God, Liam," I moan, arching my neck.

"That's my girl, take me. Take every. Fucking. Inch." He says each of those words with another thrust.

Then he's all the way in, and I have never felt this full.

"Perfect," he breathes. "Fucking perfect."

Then he starts moving.

And I'm right with him. I love unleashed Liam. He fucks me into that mattress like it is his entire mission in life.

He showers praise on me the entire time, telling me how amazing I feel, how perfect I am, how long he's wanted me, how this is everything he dreamed of.

The idea that Liam has wanted me like this for so long adds to everything else I'm feeling and I'm quickly climbing toward the pinnacle.

"Fucking come for me, Ivy. Let me feel this sweet cunt squeeze me. I'm going to fill you up so good. I want you to feel me the rest of the day."

I'm suddenly there, pleasure bursting through me, crying out his name again.

And then he lets himself go. "Fuck, Ivy!"

He hammers into me, and I can only hold on.

Then he shouts my name, "Ivy!" And comes even as my orgasm is still rippling.

He drops forward, bracing his hands on either side of me, sucking in air, still buried deep.

I lift my hands and run them through his hair. "That was amazing," I tell him. "God, we're so good together."

He lifts his head and pins me with an intense look. "Yes. We are. Forever."

I can only nod. Forever. It makes so much sense.

How did I not see that this man was who I wanted and needed all along?

And to think I almost screwed this up.

I am definitely not going to do that again.

CHAPTER 15

Liam

"WELCOME TO SOUTH CAROLINA," I tell Ivy as we pass the big sign on the side of the highway.

"Thank fucking God," she declares.

That makes me laugh. "What, you're not having fun driving endlessly in your ridiculously small car with me?"

I'm driving and it's late afternoon. Most of today has been an oxymoron of both the amazing haze of intoxicating pheromones hovering between us and then just endless fucking pavement stretching out in front of us.

"I love spending time with you," she says, her knees up on the glove box of the passenger seat. "It's using public toilets that I object to. I'm ready to be in the same hotel for multiple nights, too."

I'm a little worried about how we're going to pay for this extended stay but I am not leaving Ivy alone to handle getting the house listed for sale. Now that we're officially together, I don't want to spend even one day away from her and I need to help her clean up Brad's mess.

"Me too. It will be a good opportunity to plan what comes next, too."

She has her phone in her hand and she waggles it at me as I

drive. "I'm already looking at job postings in L.A. Even if I hadn't quit *Southern Charm*, I wouldn't be able to work with Brad, anyway. That's so gross and awkward. And why would I stay in South Carolina when I never wanted to move here in the first place?" She gives me a smile. "Especially with you back home."

I smile back. "Why *did* Brad want to move? I never understood that."

"Honestly? I have no idea. He said it was to help his mom now that she's older, but they never struck me as all that close and she doesn't have any health issues that I'm aware of. Also, she's all of sixty-five. Now I have to wonder if he has a secret girlfriend in L.A. or something."

That's my fear too. "On set?" That would definitely make sense, but what a painful revelation for Ivy. "Have I mentioned today that Brad is a total prick?"

"That's actually the first time today. You're slipping."

"And here I thought my rage would never abate. Turns out there is one thing that makes me feel better."

"Tacos?" she asks with a grin, referencing our lunch choice.

"Yes. Obviously tacos. But more importantly, you," I say simply.

"Aw, you're so cute when you're being romantic."

"Was that romantic to you? Damn, the bar is set low. I can work with this."

She smacks my thigh. "Hey!"

I laugh. I glance over at her. She's back on her phone, typing. "Any promising job leads?"

Ivy makes a face. "I actually just texted Ford. I wanted to make sure he and Harrison got home safely. Is that weird?"

"No." My own thoughts have been jumbled and confused surrounding Harrison and his sudden departure with Ford. "I don't like the way all of that went down. It doesn't take away from you and me to feel bad about that."

She sighs in relief. "Oh my God, I'm so glad you feel that way. I can't stop thinking about Ford and yet feeling guilty that I am."

"It's unfinished business." I wish I wasn't driving so I could be looking directly at her while we're having this conversation because I want to be able to reassure her with eye contact, but we're already in it, so I have to just roll with it. "I'm attracted to Harrison. You're attracted to Ford."

Ivy sighs again. "Yes, I am. What do we do about that?"

"I don't know right now. That's a separate thing from what you and I have. What we've always had. I want you to move in with me when we get back to Los Angeles."

A glance over shows she is just nodding. "I assumed I would be."

I give a crack of surprised laughter. "Why, because you don't have a place to live?"

"Yes, there's that. But also, we've been friends for years. Why would we just, I don't know, *date*? That doesn't seem like enough for us. We're already beyond that."

My heart feels like it's about to burst out of my damn chest. "I agree. I just want to be with you. Always."

"Same." Ivy leans over and kisses my cheek. "I love you."

"I love you too."

"Besides, you already offered to let me stay with you." She gives me a sassy smile. "Now it's just permanent."

"*Permanent.* God, I love the sound of that."

We drive another couple of hours, our vibe relaxed and easy and comfortable with each other.

I'm very aware we didn't really resolve the dilemma of Harrison and Ford. I've been trying to decipher what my feelings are and what they mean. All I can land on is that I'm still very much attracted to Harrison, and not just sexually. The way he approaches life is so confident, so carefree. I admire that about him and I don't like that he basically blew me off. Again.

I want him to admit that we have a connection that goes beyond sex.

That he felt it, and got scared, and ran.

Would I have enjoyed seeing him kissing someone else? No.

But I would have talked to him about it. Or tried to anyway. He just…left.

That doesn't stop me from thinking about him, though.

Ivy keeps looking at her phone. I suspect she's checking to see if she's gotten a response from Ford. I had zero expectation of hearing from Harrison and yet I still want to. The frown and the wrinkle of her nose suggest Ford hasn't answered her. It's a bizarre feeling that I'm one hundred percent in love with her and yet I'm sad for her that she's not getting the attention she wants from another guy.

I honestly don't know what the fuck that even means.

Or what to do about it.

"Are we there yet?" I joke to Ivy to distract her.

She looks at her GPS. "We actually are. ETA only fifteen minutes, woo-hoo!"

"Excellent." Even with good company, I'm more than a little sick of being in the car.

Ivy rolls down her window and sticks her head out a little. "I smell the ocean!"

"It's very…quaint here."

We're driving through a town that looks like a retro movie set. Colorful shops, an ice cream parlor, a barber with the spiral pole, and people leisurely riding bikes with woven baskets perched on the front of them. Back home, biking is a fitness lifestyle, not a sightseeing excursion. They'll run your ass over if you're walking too slow.

"Liam, this is actually so cute. A little touristy, but everyone looks…happy."

"That's because there's no traffic."

She laughs. "Right? Does that mean you could actually run a quick errand here and it would actually be, you know, *quick*?"

It seems that way, which is a foreign concept to me. "Do you want to eat dinner or check out your house first?"

I still can't figure out why Brad gave Ivy a house. Or why he bought it in the first place.

"The house. I need reassurance that it is real and not a figment of my imagination, like my relationship with Brad."

Ivy puts the address in her phone and we're only two minutes out.

Then we're parked in front of the infamous wedding-that-wasn't-gift.

"Huh," I say, staring at it. "It's bigger than I expected."

"It's really big." Ivy blinks. "Twenty of my first apartment in L.A. could fit in here. Thirty even."

It's a cool fucking house. It's on the water, so it's up on stilts, with a porch that wraps entirely around it. The siding is mint green, and there are white shutters on all the windows and ferns hanging from the porch roof. It's exactly what I would picture for a Carolina beach house. The peek of the beach behind it is a visual reminder that we just traversed the entire country in Ivy's tiny car.

"Coast to coast," I murmur as we open our car doors. "Delivered right to your door."

"Let's make out in it," she says, jogging up the steps to the front deck.

That makes me grin. "We're going to do a whole lot more than make out. There has to be a kitchen island that I can spread you out on."

"Oh." Ivy glances back at me over her shoulder. "You have such good ideas."

"Do you have a key?" I ask once we're at the door. I peer through the windows and see a fireplace and soaring ceilings. The movers delivered everything yesterday, and it's just furniture and boxes everywhere with no rhyme or reason.

That is going to pose a logistical problem, since Ivy doesn't plan to unpack. Though maybe she will have to stage the house for sale. I have concerns over how much work this will be and the timeframe we're dealing with. I can work on the road for a week, but much beyond that and I'll need to be back in the writer's room.

I don't want to overwhelm Ivy, though, so I keep my mouth shut for now.

"No key." Ivy tries the doorknob. "But there's a keypad with a code. Who let the movers in? Brad?"

"I think the code was in the paperwork."

"Where is that?"

"I have no idea. The trunk? Ford's bag?"

Ivy groans. "Ford hasn't even answered me. Let's look in the trunk. If it's not there, then you can call Ford. I don't think he's going to answer me."

"Speaking of Ford..." I sit down in a rocking chair on the porch. "Come sit down with me." I pat my lap.

"You want me to sit on your lap? I never knew you were a girl-on-your-lap guy. This is a whole new side of you."

But she gives me a sweet smile and slips her arms around my neck and perches on my thighs. The feel of her tight ass resting on my cock gives me an instant hard on. I wrap an arm around her back and kiss her.

"We need to get a hotel tonight. This house isn't habitable right now, and I need you naked, Ivy. Now that I've seen you and tasted you, I want you naked all the fucking time."

"That can be arranged." She wiggles a little under the guise of balancing herself.

I groan a little. "But first, let's talk about Ford and Harrison."

"What about them?" Ivy flicks her tongue over my ear, which is very distracting.

I've been thinking about this all day. "We need to fuck them. Together."

Ivy freezes. "What?" she asks, and her voice has dropped two octaves. Her chest is rising and falling rapidly, but otherwise she's completely still.

"The four of us, in one bed together, having sex. I know you want Ford to fuck you and I want to watch him get you off, see how you scream when his cock is inside you."

She's staring at me.

"What?"

"Isn't that…complicated?" she asks. "We're in love. In a relationship. It's new. But you want me to sleep with someone else. While you watch. Does that mean that what we're feeling maybe isn't what we think it is?"

I lift a hand and push her hair away from her face. "Do you think it means I don't really love you? Trust you? Know you? Respect you and like you and would choose to spend time with you whenever I'm given the chance?"

She sits, thinking, her bottom lip between her teeth. Finally she answers, "No."

"And why do you believe that?"

"Because I want to see you with Harrison, and I still feel all those things for you. I love you, trust you, consider you my best friend. I just…want you to be happy. Fully, completely happy. And I want you to have *everything* you want. All the pleasure. All the love."

I nod. "Exactly."

"So…you think the four of us could have sex together?"

"I really do."

"With no jealousy?"

"I didn't feel jealous that night in the motel. Did you?"

She shakes her head. "I was just really turned on. You and Harrison being there just made it even hotter. But I also loved being with Ford."

"I loved that he was good to you. That you had all of that pleasure. That he could make you feel like that," I tell her honestly. "I've never had this before, Ivy. I think I would typically feel jealous. But I think it's because we're already so close. Because of our friendship, I want everything for you, and I also completely trust you and believe it when you say you love me."

She nods. "Yeah. I get that. It's how I feel too." She takes a breath. "But I have to be honest. I think I could fall for Ford."

I smile. "I think you already have."

She laughs. "And that's okay with you?"

"That my favorite person in the world is getting all the love she deserves? Absolutely. Ford is different from me. He's not a replacement for me. He's…additional."

Again she nods. "You're different with Harrison than you are with me. But it's like, together we help you be your full self."

I pull her close, hugging her. "Exactly."

She hugs me back. Then says, "So…the four of us together. And you would fuck Harrison? And I would be there too."

"Yes." I nuzzle her neck. "And I'd fuck you. I can't get enough of your sweet cunt, beautiful. What do you think?"

"I mean…I don't know. It could get messy."

"Not if we all are on the same page."

"What page is that?"

"That we're adults who want to fuck each other."

Ivy gives a soft moan.

"Are your nipples hard right now thinking about it?"

"Yes."

I run my hand down over her thigh and between her legs, teasing over the center of her panties. "Is your pussy wet imagining both Ford and I touching you, kissing you, fucking you?" I can already feel that it is.

She gives a soft moan and leans into me. "*Yes.*"

Now that the idea has formed in my head, I can't get rid of it. Seeing Ivy getting fucked by Ford is a hot as hell visual that is going to make it impossible to sleep tonight.

"Then you do know what you want. Let's do this. Let's go get our guys."

"*Yes.*"

CHAPTER 16

Harrison

I WAS NEVER ACTUALLY GOING to text Cara for a date. I would have if Ford agreed to go out on a double date, but he didn't, because Ford never fakes anything.

He has feelings for Ivy and he isn't going to pretend he doesn't.

I'm a different story.

My house is on a golf course. Do I golf? No. I pretend to golf because everyone thinks I should want to golf.

Like just about everything in my life.

I pretend that I'm not lonely.

I pretend that I don't worry that if I wasn't gifted with the privilege of my family's money, I wouldn't be all that successful.

I pretend that it doesn't bother me that people have treated me like a superficial playboy to the point that I've just allowed that perception to be real.

And I pretend that when I date I don't hold back because I don't trust that someone cares about me for me, and not for my money.

I'm pretending that I'm not in love with Liam.

That's gotten under my skin and rubbed me raw.

I'm in love with Liam and I've been a total dick to him.

Using my phone, I unlock the gate to the private community I live in and drive down the winding streets, past the perfectly manicured mansions. When I first got access to my trust fund at twenty-one, I bought a beach house, but then I quickly realized that most of my neighbor's houses were vacation properties and used as short-term rentals when they weren't in residence. It never felt like a true neighborhood, so I turned my own into a rental and moved into this golf course community.

Which also doesn't feel like a neighborhood because no one walks or bikes in it. Everyone stays in their own tricked out back-yards and when they do venture out onto the streets, it's in a golf cart zipping past the other houses with barely a wave in anyone else's direction.

This isn't what I want either.

That's why I enjoy being at the restaurant—I like being around people. I love the hustle and bustle and the energy of both the staff and the people dining. Raw has become known as a place to celebrate milestones in life and the joy that surrounds birthdays, baby showers, retirements, and engagements is cool to watch. I like that we're contributing to relationships.

Brad always likes to say food is love, but Brad is a bigger dick than me, so where the hell does that leave me and my under-standing of life?

Alone.

That's where it leaves me.

I pull my Porsche 911 into my three-car garage and enter the house through the mudroom.

When I first bought this house, I envisioned using this mudroom as storage for sports equipment but I keep the big items like my kayak and my clubs in the garage. This mudroom is like a mockery of my single life, with its individual locker-style cubbies. It's meant for backpacks and beach bags and floppy hats and most of the hooks just stick out forlornly, serving no purpose.

I had said something to my family about the wasted space

once and my father had grinned. "So get married," was his response.

My grandfather wasn't even remotely kind about it. "No one wants to hear your first world problems."

"Sell the house," my mother—who is a real estate agent—said. "The market is hot. You'll make a twenty percent profit."

In the end, I had taken my grandfather's advice and made sure not to complain to anyone anymore. I am fortunate. I know that.

No one wants to hear the rich guy complain about being lonely, especially when he shoves everyone he meets away with jokes and unanswered texts.

Dumping my phone onto the charging pad in my kitchen, I turn and almost have a fucking heart attack. My housekeeper, Clarissa, is standing in the doorway with a mop in her hand.

"Harrison! I didn't think you'd be home so soon. I'm sorry. I'm almost done here."

"You're fine. I forgot you were coming today." I like Clarissa a lot. She has five adult children, including a daughter who Ford, Brad, and I went to high school with, and six grandkids that she is constantly showing me photos of. She's sixty-something, slight, and capable of making every surface shine without even breaking a sweat.

I used to feel guilty as hell for having a woman twice my age cleaning my ridiculously large house but when I said something to that effect as a joke, she had turned pale and explained how much she needed this job because her husband is a diabetic and the medication is expensive. Which made me feel even worse, so I gave her a hefty raise. So now I have probably the highest paid housekeeper in the entire Low Country.

"Any weekend plans?" she asks, taking her bucket to the laundry room and dumping it.

Not a one. "Nope. You?"

"I've got the youngest grandkids so my Katie can work her shift at the hospital. By the way, she told me Brad's wedding got canceled." She comes back out of the laundry room. "That's such a shame."

Was it?

I picture Ivy, eager to indulge in my roadside stops, laughing at the honky-tonk while dancing with Liam. I remember her eager cries of pleasure in the bed next to me and Liam as Ford stroked her pussy to an orgasm.

I don't think it was a shame at all that Brad let a woman as free and fully herself as Ivy go.

Holy shit.

I have feelings for Ivy, too.

Immediately, I open the refrigerator, even though I have no interest in anything inside it. I just need the flat-paneled door to hide my heated face from Clarissa.

"I don't think people should get married unless they're very sure they want to get married," I say to the eggs. All the contents of the fridge start to blur together, as it feels like my entire world has just shifted beneath my feet.

I don't know what to do with this new information.

Ford would kill me if I told him. I think. Would he? Probably.

Then there's Liam. With him it's real. He likes me for who I am.

Fuck.

Complicated, adorable, easily ruffled William.

Who is now with Ivy, if that kiss outside the motel room was any indication.

"I don't think that's true at all. I threw up the morning I married Sam because I was so nervous. I thought I was making the biggest mistake of my life. Turns out it was the best decision I ever made."

I close the refrigerator. "So I should marry the first person who makes me throw up?"

Clarissa laughs. "No! Just the person who makes you feel so much that it feels like your heart is in your throat every time you think about them."

Like Liam.

"I pity whoever that person is," I joke. "Getting stuck with me is no picnic."

Clarissa reaches up from her barely five feet tall height and pats my cheek. "Hush. You're a good man, Harrison, even if you don't believe it yourself." She steps back. "Now pick up the phone and call whoever it is that has put that look on your face. Love is risky business, but you're up for it."

Maybe I could be.

"Sam's a lucky man," I tell her.

"Damn right he is." She gives me a grin.

That makes me laugh.

"Okay, I'm heading out." She gives me a wave and picks up her purse off the kitchen counter. "Your phone is dinging."

"Thanks. Have a great weekend."

I walk to my phone and pick it up.

It's a text from Liam. I have his name in my phone as William the Cock Conqueror. He probably wouldn't appreciate knowing that. But it's a well-earned label.

My heart is pounding hard as I grab the phone and open the text. It's actually a group text thread. I hit info and see it's Liam, Ivy, Ford, and me.

> Ivy and I are in Honeysuckle Harbor. The four of us need to talk.

I text back immediately.

> Agreed. Want to meet at Raw? Glad you made it here safely.

Ivy responds.

> Somewhere more private.

I *really* like the sound of that. We have unfinished business.

This is my chance to pry open my mouth and actually admit how I feel—about both of them.

Love is risky business.

I'm not going to blow this opportunity.

> Come to my house. 354 Worthington Way. I'm home now.

Liam answers.

> On our way.

> Great. See you soon.

Then I pick up the phone and call Ford.

He answers with, "I'm not coming over so don't ask."

I go into my wine cellar and pull out a couple of bottles of different white wines, since I don't know what they like. I pop them in the fridge to chill as I tell Ford, "Get your ass over here now or be miserable for the rest of your life."

"No."

"I'll stop being your friend."

It's an empty threat, and he knows it.

"No, you won't. Harrison, I can't. I'm in love with Ivy. I can't watch her hanging all over Liam." He sounds miserable and tortured.

"You need to come over *because* you're in love with her. What if she wants to come over to tell you they're just friends after all? Or that she's in love with you, too?"

"You sound excited," he complains. "Why are you excited?"

"Because they didn't say we need to talk because they want to settle up the minibar bill. They have a *reason* and I'm convinced it will result in all of us very naked and very happy."

"You think?"

He sounds doubtful, but with a glimmer of hope.

"I know so," I say confidently, even though I have no idea if I'm right or not.

But we can't deny that something was simmering on that road trip and it was between *all* of us. I'm going to do my best to make it happen, even if it means letting my mask slip a little. I'll be vulnerable as fuck if it means I can have Liam and Ivy in my life.

"But what if…"

"Fuck the what ifs," I tell him. "You'll what if the rest of your life if you don't at least hear Ivy out."

I can practically hear him nod.

"Fuck it. You're right. Let me finish up here and I'll be over."

CHAPTER 17

Ford

I HAVE no idea what I'm feeling as I make the drive to Harrison's.

I didn't need to be at the restaurant tonight. It was an attempt to distract myself from thinking about the very people I'm now driving to meet. So that was a huge waste of time.

I think the staff were actually happy when I told them I was leaving. I know our night manager was getting sick of me.

I'll admit I was hovering. Over the reservations up front, over the wait staff, over the kitchen. I was making unnecessary changes and confusing everyone, and Lucille had suggested nicely that maybe I could find something to do in my office. Then she'd suggested much less nicely that the olives needed to be counted. One by one. *All* of the olives.

I didn't inventory the olives. Obviously. But she made her point.

When Harrison called I was actually doing dishes. The two high school boys who were on dish duty tonight had been shocked when I'd told them to take a break, with permission to eat oysters, grilled asparagus and French bread, and that I'd do dishes for the next hour. But they'd quickly taken me up on it.

And scrubbing the pots and pans had definitely let me work

off a little tension. And had kept me out of the staff's way. And kept me from going home and moping around.

It hadn't, however, kept me from thinking about Ivy and Liam.

I park in Harrison's driveway and stare at Ivy's car.

I'm the last one to arrive.

I should go back to Raw.

They have a reason and I'm convinced it will result in all of us very naked and very happy.

Harrison's words come back to me.

Ivy and Liam are here for a reason. This isn't just a social call. And they're not here to rub their new relationship in our faces. They wouldn't do that. They're good people. Very good people.

That's why Harrison and I have fallen in love with them.

I sigh and shut my car off. I'm going in. For better or worse.

I let myself in through the front door and kick off my shoes and shed my jacket, tossing it over the coat tree. Then I follow the sounds of their voices to the kitchen.

My gaze lands on Ivy as soon as I step into the room. Like a fucking magnet.

She looks gorgeous. She's in a pink top with straps that leaves her shoulders bare and white shorts with sandals. Her long blonde hair is up in a twisted ponytail thing. And she's glowing.

Because she's in love.

And being well fucked by the man standing right next to her with his hand resting on her hip.

I suck in a deep breath, then step into the room.

Ivy seems to sense me and her gaze meets mine immediately. She straightens and her pretty smile fades.

Harrison is the first one to speak to me, though.

"Ford!"

"Hey."

"How's Raw?"

"Fine." I haven't looked away from Ivy. "We have plenty of olives."

"O-k-a-y," Harrison says slowly. Then he turns to the refrigerator and pulls out a bottle of wine. He pours a glass and brings it to me. "You need to relax," he tells me in a low voice.

"Do I?"

"Yes. The woman you're in love with is right there. That's a *good* thing. Relax." He presses the glass into my hand.

I tip it back, gulping half of it down in one drink.

He rolls his eyes. "Yeah. Just like that. I said relax, not get drunk."

I blow out a breath and step past him to walk the rest of the way into the kitchen.

I face Ivy across the wide marble-topped center island.

And Liam. He's right there, beside her. He's a part of this. He's her boyfriend. Apparently. Okay, then. Let's see why they're here.

"Hi," I say.

"Hi."

Her voice saying *one* word punches me in the gut.

I've missed her. It hasn't even been forty-eight hours, but I've missed her so fucking much. I know it's not the actual time we've been apart, but the fact that I've felt like I've lost her.

I've felt it before. The times I've left her behind with Brad. But this is so much worse. Because for a while I thought she could be mine. For a brief while, she *was* mine. For those hot, amazing moments in my bed two nights ago.

"Are you together?" I ask.

She wets her lips, then nods. "Yes."

"*Together?*" I press.

"Yes. We're having sex," she says.

"And we're in love," Liam interjects.

She nods. "Right. Yes, of course." She looks from him to me, then to Harrison. "We're in love. And having sex."

I really didn't need to have that repeated. "So why are you here?" I ask. Bluntly. But this is a blunt sort of situation.

She takes a deep breath. Then Liam nudges her forward. She rounds the island and stops directly in front of me. "We're here because I want you too."

"And I want Harrison," Liam says.

Out of the corner of my eye, I see Harrison straighten. His gaze is locked on Liam.

"What?" Harrison's voice is gruff.

My best friend is charming, funny, and usually articulate.

The fact that Liam can knock him off his game like this is always amusing to me.

I actually feel myself smile.

"That's *not* a surprise to you," Liam says. "Jesus, Harrison."

"That you *want* me? No." Harrison takes a step toward Liam. "But that you would make a declaration about it in front of your girlfriend, yeah. A little."

Liam gives a short laugh. "My girlfriend probably realized how I felt about you before I did."

"And how's that?" Harrison asks.

I brace myself for some reason. This moment feels big.

"I'm falling in love with you," Liam says simply.

I finally pull my eyes from Ivy to look at my friend. He's staring at Liam as if the other man had just slapped him across the face.

"Well, say something," Liam tells him. "Fuck, you never shut up when I want you to and now you've got nothing?"

"You're *falling* in love with me?" Harrison asks.

Liam frowns. "Yes."

"You haven't *already* fallen in love with me?"

"Why? Because people just can't help but fall in love with you?"

"No, because...fuck. We've been doing this for a year, Liam. You know me. It probably won't get better than this. So if you haven't fallen by now, it's not going to happen."

I can't read Harrison's expression. He looks frustrated. Or sad. Or something I've never seen on his face before—defeated. My friend never looks defeated. Harrison never believes he's down and out.

Liam frowns and takes a step forward. "I mean...I've just realized this. You ghosted me, remember? So we really haven't been doing anything for a year but avoid each other when our paths have crossed until this week. You're a huge pain in my ass, Harrison. You live half-way across the country. You don't take anything seriously, especially relationships. So, telling you this is a huge risk. But yes, I'm falling in love with you. Despite everything."

Harrison folds his arms. "And you feel like you can say this now because you have Ivy to fall back on? Like it's safe to put yourself out there for me, because you're going home with a gorgeous, sweet, sassy, amazing woman no matter what I say or do?"

Ivy looks from me to Liam to Harrison. "Um, thank you?"

But Harrison just gives her a little nod and then turns right back to Liam. "Tell me, Liam. Is *she* why you're telling me this now?"

Liam draws himself up taller. "I guess maybe so. She's opened me up. Made me realize that I can't wait around and keep everything bottled up anymore because I could miss out on the opportunity to tell the people how I feel and they might fucking walk down an aisle and say 'I do' to someone else because I was chicken."

"Well, I guess I'm the better man then," Harrison says.

"How so?" Liam asks, also crossing his arms.

"Because I'm willing to see you, date you, fuck you, whatever, and I don't have anyone else waiting in my bed to make me feel more secure about the risk of rejection."

"Now. What about a year ago? How fucking willing were you then?"

Ivy moves closer to me. "Are they *fighting* about falling in love with each other?" she whispers.

I can't help it, I laugh. "Of course they are." They can't even do this without annoying each other.

"Oh my God," she says. "Sex with them is going to be wild, isn't it?"

I feel shock and lust pound through me. I take her upper arms and turn her to face me. "*What?*"

She sucks in a breath, but then nods. "Yeah. I, well, *we,* think we should all...be together. We have all these feelings, all of *this,* going on between all of us and Liam and I want both you and Harrison. We all need to be together and get it out of our system, and get some closure. We didn't like how things ended."

Out of our system.

Right. Because she and Liam are together for the long haul. But they have feelings for us, and there's unfinished business here.

"Out of our systems in bed?" I ask, needing to know exactly what she's saying.

"Yes."

"How long?"

"While we're in town. However long it takes for me to sell the house," she says. "And..." She glances at Liam. "If you guys want to see us when you come to L.A., we'd love that."

"So an ongoing friends-with-benefits, fuck-buddies kind of thing?"

She doesn't look *happy.* She's chewing on the inside of her cheek. But she nods.

I blow out a breath.

Fuck. I'm in love with her and she wants me to fuck around with her and her boyfriend, the man she's probably going to marry.

But...I guess that's a step-up from her marrying Brad, and me never, ever having the chance to kiss her, hold her, make her laugh, make her come.

"I'm in," I say.

She looks surprised. But then she smiles. "Oh. Okay. Good."

"Let's go," Liam says. He starts out of the kitchen. Then he stops in the doorway. Sighs. Then turns back. He glares at Harrison. "I don't know the way to the bedroom."

Harrison growls, but stomps across the floor. He shoves Liam in the direction of the bedroom. "Come on."

I start in that direction as well, but realize Ivy is hanging back. I turn to her. "You okay?"

"I um…" She sighs. "Sex with Liam and Harrison sounds really hot, but…should we wear helmets or football pads or something? It suddenly seems dangerous to get between them."

And that makes the tightness in my chest loosen slightly. I grin and extend my hand. "I'll keep you safe."

She hesitates, but then gives me a smile and takes my hand. "Well…not *too* safe. I don't mind things a little rough."

Which makes *me* growl, then bend and throw her over my shoulder and head in the direction of Harrison's bedroom.

CHAPTER 18

Liam

I SHOULD HAVE KNOWN Harrison would piss me off and turn me on all at the same time.

Even as I was trying to tell him I want to be with him, he was fighting with me about it.

Standing in the hallway of his giant house with a throbbing dick and staring at a literal sea of doors, I glare at him. "How many fucking bedrooms does one man need?"

I thought he would just jump at the chance to fuck me, but he caught me off guard by probing into my feelings. I also thought I was being pretty damn clear about where my head and heart are at, but he wanted more. Nothing shocking there—Harrison wants more of something.

He's going to get more. He will get all the more he can fucking handle.

Harrison stops in front of a door and throws it open. "We'll start here tonight and then fuck our way down the hall until we run out of rooms."

My cock immediately jumps in my jeans. "Then start all over again?"

"Depends on how many days you plan on staying."

If he keeps looking at me the way he is, it's going to be really damn hard to go back to L.A. any time soon.

Just to keep the upper hand, I lean in and kiss Harrison, hard. Right when he's growling and reaching to tug me against him, I step back. "Get in there," I growl, slapping his tight ass.

His nostrils flare, but he obeys.

I love this dynamic between us. I love bringing such a tall, sexy, confident man to his knees.

Literally.

But this isn't just about us. As Harrison enters the bedroom, I turn and reach for Ivy's hand. She takes it but she glances back at Ford. I know this is an important moment. This is about all four of us enjoying ourselves. I'm sharing Ivy, not staking a claim.

I know what we have.

Having Ford give her pleasure doesn't take away from my relationship with Ivy. Giving her what she wants—hell, needs—is part of loving her. This is an enhancement.

Ford needs to understand that clearly.

So I tell him, "Give Ivy a kiss."

He doesn't hesitate.

Ford cups her cheek and takes her mouth in a hot press of his lips to hers. Ivy's fingers tighten on mine and it makes my body tense with lust. I've seen Ford kiss her, but never like this, watching, yet still touching her.

Her free hand wraps around his neck and I shift in behind her, dropping my hands to her waist. I briefly press my hard cock into the curve of her ass just to let her know how this is going to go. She's going to be surrounded by her men all night.

Knotting my free fingers into the loose strands of her ponytail, I tug, which takes her mouth off of Ford's mouth. Ivy gasps.

Ford understands the assignment. He drops his lips to trail kisses over her neck and down to the swell of her breasts. When she dips her head back on her own to give him further access, I'm satisfied.

Turning, I see Harrison is on the bed, and completely naked already, ankles crossed, hands behind his head.

"That was fast," I say to him, taking my hand behind my head to yank my T-shirt off.

Harrison shrugs. "I was getting bored. Figured I'd speed things up."

"You getting bored? Shocker. Maybe you should learn about delayed gratification."

His eyebrows lift. "You'll be the one to teach me?"

"Yes," I say simply. I stalk toward the bed, but then I deliberately turn my back to Harrison and sit facing outward, spreading my legs apart. "Bring Ivy to me, Ford."

Ford looks to Ivy for confirmation this is what she wants. She gives permission with a nod. He's definitely the protector. Ivy's always been really damn independent, but I can see how it makes her feel cherished, taken care of.

It's not my strength, so I can appreciate what he does for her.

Harrison's feet are close enough for me to reach back and tickle the arch of one, just so he knows I haven't forgotten about him, but that in this bedroom foursome, he isn't the star.

Ivy is.

She steps between my legs and puts her hands on my shoulders. She bends down to give me a light kiss and a soft smile.

"Take her dress off, Ford," I say, caressing over her nipples and cupping her breasts.

Ford locks eyes with me over Ivy's shoulder. His expression is stormy. "I didn't agree for you to be the director."

I was expecting pushback. With a raised eyebrow, I say, "Oh, you want her dress to stay on?"

He makes a sound of impatience.

But before he can do anything, Ivy takes matters into her own hands and lifts her dress off over her head and tosses it to the side.

"You're not going to bicker with everyone," she tells me

sternly. But she ruins the force of it by smiling at me, wearing just her bra and panties.

All that bronze skin and tight curves has me running my hands all over her, easing her panties down to expose her pussy to me. I can never get enough of seeing Ivy naked.

"I'm not bickering, Ford is." I push her panties past her hips and down to her knees.

"I'm about to *bicker* big time," Harrison says from behind me. "William, you suck at this. Let Ford take over."

His insults don't bother or fluster me. It only ramps up the lust I feel for him. I can't help it—the way he baits me constantly is so fucking hot, for whatever messed up reason. We're definitely the fight and fuck types when we're together.

"You're good just watching, right?" I ask him.

"I can watch all fucking night."

A glance back does show Harrison looks content to just lie there, but I know half of that is because he wants Ford to get his time with Ivy, and half of it is because I got under his skin with the comment about delayed gratification.

He wants to prove to me he can wait, even with a rock solid dick and tight balls.

Tense need is coiled up inside me, this crazy, unexpected concoction of lust for Harrison *and* Ivy. I want my girlfriend to be well fucked by this man she is deeply attracted to, yet I also want to exert my alpha dominance over Ford, which is not the right approach.

I can't fuck this up so that she feels weird or doesn't have a great time. She won't be able to get him out of her system if I don't give him equal playing time, nor will we be able to do this again if I make any of the three of them uncomfortable.

Hell, I've never done this before. I've had several menages with a man and a woman, and once with two guys, but never when there was this much emotionally on the line.

Not with the woman I love. Not with *Ivy*, who deserves everything she wants and more, especially after what Brad did to her.

And not with Harrison, who, even when he's poking at me, makes me feel lighter, brighter. More alive.

There's one shot to get this right. So even as I'm brushing my thumbs over Ivy's soft folds, I swallow hard and tell Ford, "Ivy's center stage. That's all that matters to me. I don't need to be in charge."

Ford has been running his hands over her back, down over the curve of her ass while I tease at her tight clit. Her eyes have drifted closed and she's starting to lightly rock her hips forward into my touch.

She's in charge.

That's the message here, whether she means to be giving it or not.

"Ivy's center stage," he says. "I one hundred percent fucking agree. So tell us, pretty girl, would you like it if I finger fuck you while Liam sucks your nipples?"

"Yes, I would definitely like that," she breathes.

Ford looks to me and understanding passes between us.

We're in this together. For her.

I drop my hand away from her clit and she gives a sigh of disappointment.

But then I reach around her back to undo her bra at the same time Ford slides his palm across her hip and eases his finger into her pussy. Ivy moans and digs her nails into my bare shoulders. Hearing her pleasure at Ford's touch as I slide the straps of her bra down her arms has my mouth hot with need.

God, she's so sexy and uninhibited. She's arching her ass backward and leaning forward so that her nipples are at the perfect position for me to draw one of the tight buds between my lips and suck lightly.

"She's so wet, boys," Ford says. "Very, very ready already."

"Have you been thinking about this all day, Ivy?" Harrison drawls from behind me. "Picturing yourself the perfect sexy little sandwich between two hot guys?"

"Yes," she murmurs, as I continue to lick and suck and tease at first one nipple, then the other. "This feels so good."

Her voice catches at the end of her sentence and I look up to see her eyes are wide. She's watching Harrison. When I glance back, I see he's roughly stroking his cock.

Ivy obviously enjoys the view. I do too.

Now who the fuck is suffering delayed gratification?

I'm painfully hard as Ivy pumps herself onto Ford's fingers harder and Ford swears harshly under his breath. Squeezing her breasts, I push them together so I take both nipples into my mouth at once.

"Oh, God!" she exclaims.

"That's it," Harrison tells her. "Let yourself come, Ivy. You're right there on the edge, I can see it on your face. Ford, slap her ass."

"Is that what you want?" Ford asks. "My hand on your ass?"

I'm buried in her chest, my legs surrounding her, and I revel in the taste and touch of my sexy girlfriend. She's giving tiny cries of pleasure now, the movement of her hips more frantic as she fucks Ford's fingers.

"Do something," she begs. "Please, Ford. Oh, God, Liam, that feels so good."

Ford smacks her ass, and she jumps a little on a low gasp. "Like that?" he asks.

"*More*."

"That's it," Harrison says. "Tell him what you want."

Ford complies, rhythmically smacking the soft curve of her ass as I suck her nipples.

It registers that I'm definitely not the one in charge here, but I don't mind. If anything, it's only enhancing the experience for me —to see how this combination of three men involved in pleasuring her has Ivy losing herself in the moment.

She's a golden goddess right now, head back, lips parted as I glance up the length of her graceful neck.

When she shatters, our groans join hers.

"That's it," Harrison says. "Damn, you're beautiful."

"Keep soaking me," Ford demands. "Ride it out."

I don't say anything. My mouth is still wrapped around her nipples.

I'm not sure I would know what to say anyway.

I'm overwhelmed with love and pure raw lust that Ivy is getting to experience being with Ford exactly the way she wants to.

This is the hottest thing I've ever experienced.

And we've barely gotten started.

Once she settles back down, I pull back and release her breasts, breathing hard. She eases her grip on my shoulders and tumbles forward into my arms when Ford steps back away from her, sucking on his fingers. I kiss her softly, then shift her down on my lap.

"Look and see what you do to Ford," I tell her, tilting her chin so she can see the man she can't stop thinking about lapping up her essence.

Heat blooms on her cheeks, staining them a pretty flushed pink. "Oh, wow." Then she leans against me, her voice a little shy. "What do we do now?"

I pet her hair, stroking down the golden strands, and easing her hair tie out so it can flow freely down over her shoulders.

"Ford is going to get undressed."

"On it." He's instantly unbuttoning his shirt.

He was clearly dressed to be in front of diners, because he has on black pants and a button up shirt.

"Then once he's ready, I'm going to put your mouth over his cock. You haven't gotten to taste him yet, have you?"

Okay, so maybe I am making demands and ordering them around.

But it feels right, easy, a natural ebb and flow of the three of us focusing on Ivy.

"No. Not yet." She wiggles a little on my lap.

"Would you like that?"

"Yes."

Ford is unzipping his pants now.

"What else would you like?" I lazily play with her nipples and spread her knees so I can tease at her pussy. She's soaking and still quivering from her orgasm. It's unreal how hot that is. "Damn, beautiful. Ford got you very wet, didn't he?"

"He did. I need to be fucked, Liam. Soon."

"Soon," I agree. I look over at Ford. "You get first fuck, Ford. If that's what you want."

"Jesus fucking Christ," Ford spits out. He pumps his fist over his cock. "Hell, yes, that's what I want."

"On your knees," I tell Ivy, setting her off of me. "Suck him until he's ready."

"I'm ready now," Ford says.

"Where's the fun in that?" I drawl, borrowing some of Harrison's nonchalance.

Once Ivy is on her knees in front of Ford, I slip my finger around her chin and push it into her mouth, thrusting in and out to get wet. Ivy sucks eagerly. Then I drag her saliva over her lips and guide her head forward until she's wrapped around Ford's cock.

He groans, eyes drifting shut.

I turn and study Harrison. I'm still wearing my jeans, which is the only thing keeping me sane right now. My mouth is thick with desire and it feels like every nerve ending in my body is pulled taut, ready to snap. The view of Harrison's muscular frame, that delicious dick rising high from his narrow hips, doesn't help my situation.

I want him. "Get over here," I demand, gaze shifting between him and the incredible view of Ivy taking Ford in and out of her mouth while he grips the back of her hair.

"Such a fucking bully, William," Harrison complains.

But I note he does exactly what I tell him to.
"You love it. You love me."
His eyes darken. "I do. But I also hate you a little."
"Then you're really going to hate what I'm going to do next."
I unsnap my jeans and shove them down.

CHAPTER 19

THREE MEN.

I'm in bed with three men, and each of them brings with them their own personality, and it's *very* sexy.

This was never a fantasy of mine. I didn't sit around and wish for an experience like this—until this week. I had fantasized about being with Liam at various points and then when Ford was comforting me in the first hotel room, but my thoughts never even imagined something like all four of us in one bed together until Liam suggested it.

Now that I'm here, my mouth gliding over Ford's satin cock, while Harrison does the same to Liam, I'm overwhelmed with how absolutely hot this is. When they discussed who would take off my dress, I felt so appreciated, so damn sexy.

I actually regret taking it off myself. I need to be more patient, because I have a feeling if I let them be in charge, they're going to take me to a whole different sexual level. The out-in-orbit-on-another-planet kind of level.

"That's it," Ford tells me, his hands smoothing over the back of my hair. "Take me deep, sweetness."

Ford's voice always makes my toes curl. He has a deep but gentle voice, even when he's being commanding. He also feels incredible, his muscular thighs the perfect place to rest my palms as I open my throat and take him as fully as I can because I want to please him.

I want to please them all.

Liam is swearing under his breath. A glance over shows him shoving Harrison off of his cock, indicating he can't take anymore or he'll be done.

Harrison wipes his mouth in triumph. Then he leans down and eases me off of Ford long enough to give me a searing kiss. It's unexpected and the plunging of his thick tongue sends heat shooting through me.

"Just a taste," Harrison says. "You mixed with Liam."

My breath catches as I lick my lips. "And mixed with Ford. All of us."

Harrison nods. "Exactly."

I can distinguish the taste and touch of each of them and I'm certain I could even with my eyes closed. That thought makes my stomach swoop. *My* three men. Excited, a frenetic energy rushing through me, I return to Ford eagerly, but he holds me at bay.

His grip on my head is firm, and he shakes his head even as I open my mouth and try to flick my tongue over the tip of his shaft.

"That's enough, Ivy." His voice is tight, strained. "Get on the bed before I come in your mouth."

"That sounds fun," I tell him, even as I obey.

Ford shakes his head. "No. I need your cunt."

That makes me shiver. I love that I can bring Ford to brutal need, given how calm he normally is. He's the consummate gentleman out of the bedroom and loves to take care of me. Seeing his control shatter is a powerful feeling.

I don't know how any of this is going to work, and while I don't consider myself submissive, in this case I'm happy to let the guys boss me around. It's a genuine relief to be able to let go and know that they'll take care of me and my needs.

They've been doing that all week and it's been amazing.

Liam reaches his hand out to help me onto the bed, and I smile. "You're overdressed," I tell him, tugging his unzipped pants further down his hips.

"My thoughts exactly," Harrison comments, even as he shifts in behind me and plays with my nipples, rolling them between his thumbs.

The unexpected contact has me sucking in a quick breath.

Harrison is unexpected. I never anticipated he would make my pulse quicken the way he does, but there is something about his casual cockiness that does just that. Harrison takes up space in the bedroom and doesn't apologize for that. He's always up for a good time, and I love it.

Leaning back against Harrison's hard chest, into his embrace, I stroke Liam's hard cock while he kisses me. His kisses and taste are familiar to me already and I will never get tired of how his lips on mine make my pulse leap.

Now fully undressed, Ford climbs on the bed beside us.

"Switch with me?" Liam asks him through gritted teeth. "If you want."

But Ford shakes his head, rubbing his palm down over his mouth. "I need a minute to recover."

"Then pull her back, Harrison," Liam says, without hesitation. "Ivy, spread your legs."

"What—

I'm not sure what he means, but then suddenly I'm on my back, head in Harrison's lap, Liam over me. "Oh!"

Harrison obviously understood.

Being surrounded by this much *man* is…interesting. In the best fucking way.

Harrison eases his finger into my mouth and I suck on it eagerly, desperate for more contact. For all of it, for all of them. My whole body feels tense and sensitive, and when Liam raises my knees up to rest against his forearms, I'm begging him, "Please, Liam. Inside me. Now."

For a split second, Liam gives me a look I can't decipher. "Is this what you want?" he asks, voice rough with desire.

"Yes. So much." I wiggle on the bed, wanting more. Wanting *all* of them.

Harrison holds me down. "Stay still for William so he can fuck you nice and tight."

Liam's eyes darken, and he spares a glance at Harrison. I can feel the sizzle between them but they make no move to touch each other. It only adds to the beautiful sexual tension in the room.

Then Liam is inside me with one powerful push and I'm deliciously full, his piercing teasing my inner walls. "*Yes.*"

"Jesus, Ivy," Liam breathes, resting deep inside my aching heat. "Your pussy is so fucking wet." He turns to Ford. "Thank you for that."

Ford smirks. "You're welcome. Any fucking time."

The interaction makes my nipples tighten and my inner muscles involuntarily clamp tighter around Liam's cock.

"Do something," I tell him. "Please."

"Yeah, do something," Harrison echoes. He reaches around between me and Liam and squeezes the base of Liam's cock.

Liam emits a pleasure-filled groan.

Then Harrison swirls his thumb over my clit.

"Oh, my God!"

Harrison is touching both of us at the same time as Liam starts to stroke in and out of me. It feels incredible. My senses are on overload but I still want more. I turn and reach for Ford, who's watching with a hooded gaze.

"I want you too." I want to say more, but I'm not sure what exactly. I just want to be connected to all three of them.

Ford stays back a little, but he entwines my fingers with his and lifts our hands to his mouth. He sucks on my fingers, slowly, dragging his tongue down the length of each one with agonizing slowness. My eyes flutter shut, so I can just enjoy the intensity building in my body.

The room is filled with my soft moans, the hard slap of Liam against me, and the murmurs of encouragement from each of them.

It's intoxicating to hear their voices mingling in awe and arousal.

"Your fucking tight pussy, Ivy, Jesus," Liam grinds out.

"That's it, pretty girl," Ford encourages.

"This little clit is so tight and ready to let go," Harrison says, his voice gravelly and raw. "God, I can't wait to see you come all over me and Liam."

The rhythm of Ford's fingers in my mouth is off from the quick, deep thrusts of Liam inside my aching pussy, which is also off the pace of Harrison strumming one of my nipples and my clit.

The chaotic assault is overwhelming in the best way possible.

It reminds me that they're everywhere, surrounding me, fucking me, pleasuring me.

Tight need grows and swells until I'm writhing and crying out, arms held down by Harrison, Liam squeezing my thighs. It's sensation overload and I break.

When I shatter, I bite down on Ford's fingers.

"God, you're so fucking sexy," he tells me. "Bite me harder."

It's the only thing holding me down on earth.

Well, that and Harrison gripping me and Liam fucking me.

I can't believe I get to do this, feel this.

My orgasm rips through me like a cyclone, wave after wave of pleasure drowning out every thought in my head besides *I love this.*

"She's milking my cock so hard," Liam pants. "It's killing me."

"Come inside her," Harrison urges. "Let me see you fill her so good."

He does, his throbbing cock pausing inside me before he takes one final thrust on a deep throaty groan. The look on his face…I'm enamored. I want to see that expression every single day for the rest of my life.

Easing my teeth off of Ford, I inhale deeply, desperate for air. "I think I forgot to breathe," I murmur. "Jesus, Liam. I love your dick so, so much."

Liam chuckles softly. "Get ready to love Ford's dick. He really, really wants you, sweetheart."

I turn toward Ford, running my finger down his muscular torso. "Is that right?" I purr.

Yep. I fucking purr. I am strangely satisfied and yet...I want Ford. I need him.

Especially since he looks ready to devour me.

"That is a fucking understatement. Come here." Ford yanks me by my thighs toward him. "On your knees."

Harrison helps me up, brushing my hair off of my face and giving me a deep kiss that makes my nipples tighten all over again. "Show Ford that tight little ass, Ivy."

Liam has stepped back off of the bed, but he's still watching with hooded lids and running a hand through his disheveled hair. "Do what they say," he tells me. "Now."

Goosebumps rise on my skin as I climb onto my knees. I've never felt so commanded and yet so safe in my entire life.

None of these men would hurt me.

They've driven across the country to protect me.

So when Harrison reaches around and smacks my ass, it makes me moan in approval. "Yes. I really like that." I wiggle in open invitation, wanting to feel his palm on me again.

"I think our girl loves that, actually," Harrison says, the corner of his mouth turning up.

Now that I'm on my knees, he does the same so that his hard cock is bobbing in front of me. I'm not the only one extending an invitation.

As Ford moves behind me, reaching between my legs to tease at my pussy, Liam tells me, "Open up for Harrison."

Thick heat settles low in my pussy at his words. I immediately comply, opening my mouth for Harrison. He swirls the tip of his cock over my lips and in and out, just a tiny bit, while Ford starts up a steady smacking of my ass. It's making me hot and wet and very desperate.

"Ford, fuck me," I breathe, even as Harrison's fingers curl in my hair and tug, preventing me from turning around.

"Shh. Do you trust us?" Harrison asks.

His voice is whiskey smooth, sending shivers down my spine. Right now I will do anything they ask, if Ford would just get inside me. I nod, though, because I absolutely trust them with all of me.

Liam cups my pussy, even as the light blows Ford is delivering to my ass sends a stinging vibration through my whole body. I groan and slide my mouth further down over Harrison, sucking in my cheeks to hold him there.

My body is throbbing and I'm shaking.

It's then that Ford pushes deep inside me without warning.

I cry out around Harrison's length, right as he starts to pull in and out, holding my hair tightly still.

"Take it," he tells me. "Suck that cock like the dirty little girl you are."

Liam continues to swirl the pad of his finger over my clit. "Make Harrison come, gorgeous. I want to see him spill all over your lips."

Ford pulls my cheeks apart so he can drive deeper into my pussy. The movement pushes me further onto Harrison, who is gasping now.

"I'm so close. Just like that."

"Hold off," Ford growls. "You're going to want this pussy. This sweet, tight, juicy little pussy wants all three of us."

Liam pinches my clit.

I come hard, choking on Harrison's cock, clamping down hard on Ford's.

Ford lets out a growl and I feel his hot cum spurting deep inside me and I convulse in total abandonment. Sweet oblivion.

Harrison is suddenly gone from my mouth.

Ford pulls out of me with a sigh and runs his hand down the curve of my ass. I barely have time to register they're switching positions when Harrison is pressed against my entrance.

"Still want more?" he asks casually, even as I can feel the rock solid hardness of him stroking against my thighs.

The sticky damp of both Liam and Ford has them slick and warm but it only seems to turn Harrison on more. Which turns me on even more. I lift my hand—to do what—I have no idea, but Liam is there to entwine his fingers with me and take my palm back to the mattress.

"Hold still."

When Harrison thrusts inside me, it's a firm, tight fit. He's thick and relentless and I close my eyes, drowning. He slides his hand up my spine and eases me forward so my backside is tipped fully up for him.

"So. Fucking. Good," he spits out through gritted teeth.

My hair is in my eyes, so all I can see are Ford's and Liam's bare thighs on either side, but I know they're watching intently. I'm on display and I love it.

I'm center stage.

They said it and I feel it.

The thought has me reeling off into another orgasm, tighter and more electric than the last, a careening cry ripping from my lips.

Harrison comes with a roar.

"Oh my God," Ford says. "Ivy, you're incredible."

"This is what you do to us," Liam says. "Drive us all fucking crazy."

Harrison squeezes my ass. "God, I love being the closer. You're wrecked, aren't you, beautiful?"

I can barely nod, sinking to the mattress as Harrison eases out of me.

Hands brush my hair off of my face, and even though my eyes are closed, I know it's Ford touching me.

I know the feel, the smell, the taste of each of them.
Liam has a warm washcloth between my legs.
Harrison is tracing a line down my shoulder.
And I'm hooked on this. On them.
That's my final thought before I drift off to sleep.

CHAPTER 20

Harrison

"DON'T EAT THAT."

I look up with my bagel halfway to my mouth.

Ford strides across the kitchen floor.

"Why?" I ask. It's nearly ten and I'm starving. I never sleep this late. Of course, I've never had a night quite like last night. I grin as heat seeps through me. Damn, last night was amazing. I've been replaying it all morning.

I left Ford, Ivy, and Liam asleep in my bed about thirty minutes ago. They all looked as worn out as I felt. But they all looked happy. Ivy was sandwiched between Liam and Ford, both of them with their hands on her, and all of them fast asleep, looking like they'd been sleeping that way for thirty years.

I'd been on Liam's other side, spooning the shit out of him.

I love that asshole and if he's not in love with me yet, then… well, I don't know what I'm going to do. He said he's falling but what the hell does that mean? How long does that take? And that probably means I can still fuck it up.

"We need to get them to fall in love with us."

I look up at Ford. Was he reading my mind?

He's across the breakfast bar, arms crossed, staring at me, determination in his steely gray eyes.

I set my bagel down.

I am definitely interested in this. "I'm listening."

"Last night was amazing."

I nod. "It was."

"I want more of that."

"Me too."

He frowns. "*A lot* more of it."

"Same."

"I'm talking long term. For good. That's all I want."

"Same."

"Harrison," he says carefully. "I'm in love with Ivy. I want her forever. And I'm good with sharing her with Liam. And you. For *good*. I want a relationship with all four of us. Committed. Monogamous." He frowns. "Or whatever. No one else. Just the four of us."

I sit up straighter and brush my hands together. My best friend doesn't believe I mean it when I say 'same' and 'me too.' Fair enough. I've never had a serious, fully committed, lasting relationship with anyone.

If I don't take anything too seriously, then I can't be upset when it doesn't work out. I haven't given too much of myself away. I haven't put too much time or emotion or energy into anything, so when I screw it up, it doesn't hurt as much.

This is different.

"I understand what you're saying, Ford," I tell him, meeting his gaze directly. "I want that too."

"Really? You're into having a poly-relationship with us?"

"Yes." Fuck, that sounds perfect, really. Three other people in the mix means less pressure on me. If Ivy and Ford are a part of this, they can help fill in the gaps for Liam that I leave, right?

Ford studies me for a long moment. "You really are in love with him."

I nod. "And I have feelings for Ivy, too. She's amazing. I could easily fall for her. Now that I know that's okay."

Ford looks mildly surprised. But not upset. "Yeah?"

"Of course. What's not to love? I haven't let myself go there because of Brad, and you, and Liam. But absolutely. We have chemistry too. And I need *someone* to laugh at my jokes and go to armadillo circuses with me."

Finally, Ford smiles. His shoulders relax. "In that case, she's your girl. For some reason, she finds you amusing."

I grin. "She does, doesn't she?"

His smile grows softer. "She does. And she needs you. Liam is an introvert. I'm over-protective. She needs someone who can be free and fun, more adventurous than either of us."

I feel a warmth in my chest. That all feels really good. I can definitely be that for Ivy, and I love the idea of it.

I also love that Ford is essentially encouraging this. I've never seen him like this over a woman before, and the idea that he *wants* me to also be involved with her is, frankly, humbling.

"Thanks," I tell him sincerely. Then it really hits me what we're saying. "I guess it shouldn't really surprise us that when it comes to long-term real love that we are going to be bound together, sharing our people."

He nods. "We've shared just about everything else."

"And I can't imagine living without you. Or actually having a family unit that doesn't include you."

That seems to surprise and touch him. "Yeah. Same."

"So, you'll all stay here while they're in town," I say decisively. "And we'll work on convincing them that they want and need us forever, too."

"Exactly," he agrees. "We need to date the hell out of them."

I laugh. "Okay. How do we do that?"

"I'm not completely sure. But I think we need to show them Honeysuckle Harbor. Show them this place we love. Get them to fall for the town, our families and friends, and kind of go from there?"

It's not a terrible idea. Honeysuckle Harbor is so much a part of both of us that Liam and Ivy really do need to love it.

I'm not sure how it will work out with Liam's job in L.A., but I want them both here with us permanently. We can make trips to the west coast as often as needed, but I want this to be home.

"So what are you thinking?" I ask.

"Let's take them to breakfast at Mabel's," Ford says. "Introduce them to the town and some of the people."

I'm already nodding and standing, tossing my bagel. I'll take breakfast at my aunt's cafe any day of the week.

"Let's go wake them up," I say with a grin, starting down the hall, anticipating how to wake my boyfriend—he's my boyfriend, whether he likes it or not—and *our* girlfriend.

Ford is right behind me as I enter the room and crawl up the bed from the foot. I wiggle myself in between Liam and Ivy. Liam is spooning her and it's a wonder the poor girl can breathe the way he has himself wrapped around her.

But he's probably just as amazed to have her in his arms now as Ford and I are about this whole thing.

"Okay sleepyheads, I know we fucked you into comas, but it's time to wake up. You gotta build up your stamina because that's just the first night of many."

Liam grumbles, but actually makes room for me between them, rolling slightly and lifting his arm. "Just when I thought I'd seen you at your most annoying."

Ivy just snuggles up against me with a little smile, her eyes still shut.

I'm surprised by how easily she gets close but I don't mind it at all. I roll to face her and wrap my arms around her. Yes, I'm very aware the other men in the room have very much staked a claim on her. That just makes it even more fun to nuzzle my face against her neck. "'Morning, sweet thing." I run my hand down her back to her ass. "Is your pussy nice and sore this morning? Does it need a kiss?"

She giggles and opens her eyes. "Wow, you're just right at it, even first thing in the morning?"

"It's hardly first thing," I tell her, feeling myself get hard as her soft curves move against me. "It's after ten. We really wore you out." Flashes of last night go through my mind, and my cock reacts. "But yes, I'm right at it. With my bed this full of hot people, how can I not be?"

I didn't let myself think about it too hard when I first got up, but waking with these three in my bed was the most contented I've felt in a very long time. And it wasn't about the sex. It was about not being alone. Being with my people. It felt really fucking good. Right even.

"You did wear me out," she says, clearly not minding my hands all over her. "And yes, I'm a little sore."

I squeeze her ass. "Clearly, we need to get you in shape."

"Okay." Now Ford's at the side of the bed and he leans over, wrapping an arm around her waist and dragging her out of my arms. "Let's feed her first."

She goes into his arms easily as he lifts her off the bed. She wraps her arms around his neck and her legs around his waist.

"Morning, Ford," she says against his neck.

"Morning, Princess," he says, his voice a little husky. He starts toward my en suite bathroom. "Why don't you shower, and we'll take you and Liam out for breakfast at our favorite place."

"That sounds nice."

They step into the bathroom and I suspect Ford might be busy for a few minutes "helping" Ivy shower.

I roll toward Liam and prop up on my elbow. He's on his back, eyes still shut.

Fuck, he's gorgeous.

"Want to mess around until they're done in there?" I ask.

"Yes," he says.

I'm surprised. I reach for him, running my hand down his abs. "Really?"

"I want to mess around with your coffee pot," he says, opening one eye and trapping my hand before it gets to anything really good. "And the biggest mug you've got."

I laugh. "Mabel has coffee."

"Is Mabel in your kitchen? Because Ivy and Ford might be a while and I'm several hours past needing caffeine."

He's got a point. "Fine." I give him a grin. "You owe me a blow job."

He quirks an eyebrow. "Oh, you thought *I* was going to give *you* a blow job?"

I push up off the bed. "Well, in that case, you can lean back against the counter, drink your coffee, and let me do all the work." I pause on my way to the bedroom door. "As usual."

That gets me the growl I'm expecting *and* gets his ass up out of bed.

It's an hour before we leave the house, but everyone is even more satisfied than we were when we woke up, and when we walk into Mabel's for lunch instead of breakfast, my aunt stops halfway across the cafe to stare at us.

"What?" I ask her on our way to the corner booth.

"What happened?" she asked.

"What do you mean?"

"You haven't smiled that big since the opening night of Raw."

I open my mouth to protest, but quickly shut it again. That actually sounds about right. I have a great life. Full of good things. Easy. Privileged. But I'm restless. My life feels stupidly empty.

The night Ford and I opened Raw, I was so fucking happy. It felt like a huge accomplishment. I felt like I was doing something tangible. Something *I* had worked at and could point to and say, "I helped create that."

Everyone was impressed. My family told me how proud they were. I saw how happy and proud my best friend was. Raw was the start of the business that was going to keep Ford and me tied together permanently. That really mattered to me.

It was a great night. Probably the best of my life to date.

I glance at the three people who have slid into the blue vinyl booth a few feet away. It's in the "corner" of the cafe but it's perfectly positioned so that every person in the cafe and anyone coming into the building can see it clearly.

Wow. They make me smile as big as Raw's opening night. That's...huge.

"I'm really happy," I tell Mabel.

"Did you win the lottery or something?" she asks. Mabel is my grandmother's youngest sister. Her gray hair with blonde streaks is pulled into a bun. She's wearing her usual yellow ruffled apron, and carrying a coffee pot, obviously on her way to offer refills around the room.

The cafe has thirty white wooden tables. Twenty-three of them are filled. All have little glass vases full of yellow and white flowers. The windows have ruffled yellow curtains that match the staff's aprons.

It's cozy and quaint. Everyone who comes in knows the menu by heart, and has their go-to favorites. And Mabel knows everyone's usual order.

The fare is simple breakfast and lunch offerings, and while the food is extremely good, people also come for the camaraderie. The usuals know each other and chat from table to table about everything from the weather to what the city council is currently considering to the latest Hollywood scandal.

During tourist season, visitors do wander in, but Mabel's is one of the places that stays full with more locals than tourists. The tourist area is closer to the water and, well, we like it that way. We certainly appreciate the boost to the economy and are friendly and welcoming, but it's also nice to have some places that aren't infiltrated—not my word, since I love meeting new people.

"I did kind of win the lottery," I tell my aunt, glancing from Ivy, Liam, and Ford back to her. "I'm in love."

Her eyes widen. "No shit."

I laugh. "No shit. So make a good impression, okay?"

She studies the booth. "Which one?"

"How about you be nice to both of them?"

Ford already loves Mabel, and it's reciprocal. She also already knows that he's going to order her Everything Omelet and extra toast.

She swats my arm. "Well, of course I'll make a good impression on them both. But which one are you in love with?"

I grin down at her. "How about both?"

She shakes her head. "So selfish. How about you let Ford have one of 'em?"

I laugh even harder. "You're right. Maybe I'll share the pretty blonde with him."

Mabel nods. "There you go." She gestures toward the booth with her coffee pot. "Go sit. Coffee for all of you?"

"Yes. And a *big* mug for the surly one," I say, watching Liam say something that makes Ford laugh.

"Got it. Soup bowl of coffee for the hot guy."

"You don't think Ford's hot?"

She wrinkles her nose. "I changed his diapers. Yuck."

Fair enough.

I make my way to the booth and slide in next to Liam, putting Ivy and Liam between me and Ford.

Perfect. Now we just have to keep them there, metaphorically if not literally, until they fall in love with Honeysuckle Harbor.

And both of us.

CHAPTER 21

Liam

"IT MIGHT SURPRISE you to know I'm not really a boardwalk kind of guy."

Ford looks over at me. "Oh, I'm totally shocked." He grins. "Me either."

"Really? I would've thought you'd love it like everyone else here."

We're down along the boardwalk that runs the length of the beach in Honeysuckle Harbor. It's clearly a favorite spot for locals as well as tourists. It's also obviously been here for a very long time. There are shops and snack carts, an actual boardwalk and an area with rides and games.

That's where we are now. Harrison and Ford wanted to show us around town after breakfast. It didn't take long since the town is so small, but when Harrison drove us down here, and Ivy saw the Ferris wheel and let out a little squeal that got a huge grin out of Harrison, Ford and I exchanged a look. We both knew then that we were going to be here for a while.

We are standing back, watching Harrison and Ivy at the ring toss.

Ivy *really* wants a gigantic pink stuffed bunny.

But she is terrible at this game. They've been playing for

fifteen minutes. Harrison told her that he would win her a giant stuffed animal, but she'd have to get on her knees later. Or she could try to win her own. Despite the fact that she's gone eight rounds without winning, Harrison just keeps handing money to the guy in the booth. Despite it also means no blow job. Ivy is smiling up at Harrison as if he's her hero. I'm not sure who is having more fun.

I am a little surprised, however, that Harrison didn't push the blow job angle a little harder. Ivy is damned good at that. But I think maybe my boyfriend is starting to have more than just a small soft spot for the girl in our foursome. I suspect the reason she's tossing rings instead of getting on her knees is because Harrison is enjoying watching her have a good time.

I know I am. And it's very clear looking at Ford that he is too.

"Oh, when I was a kid, it was awesome to come down here," he says. "But I guess I've become a little bit more of a curmudgeon about crowds and strangers."

I snort. "Curmudgeon? Yeah, you must have. I think only curmudgeons actually use that word."

He chuckles. "See what I mean?"

Though I've never actually used that C word, I can relate. Crowds and strangers are overrated.

Just then Ivy throws both arms up in the air and yells, "Yes!"

Harrison scoops her up in his arms and twirls her around, laughing. "You did it!"

No one says *finally*. Though I'm thinking it. And I'm sure the guy running the game is as well.

She chooses a bright pink rabbit that is nearly half her size and comes practically skipping over to us.

And officially she is the cure for curmudgeon-itis. I feel myself smiling and see the huge grin on Ford's face.

Clearly, we would do, or put up with, anything for her.

She thrusts the rabbit at me. "Look what I won!"

I laugh. "Honey, Harrison *bought* this. The money he forked over on that game could've bought you *two* of these."

She leans in, squishing the bunny between us and presses a kiss to my lips. "This was way more fun, though."

See? It's all about fun with her and Harrison. But I have to admit that it's contagious.

"Okay, Ferris wheel next," Harrison announces.

Small correction—I would do *almost* anything for Ivy.

I shake my head. "Nope."

Ivy tries pouting. "Come on, we *have* to go on the Ferris wheel."

"I don't think that thing has passed a maintenance inspection in at least a decade," Ford says, eyeing the rickety thing that's half a football field away.

Ivy laughs and looks up at Harrison. "You only live once."

"Exactly." He looks at Ford. "Seriously? You're not riding either?"

"Very much a fan of my feet being on the ground," Ford tells them.

"Fine," Harrison says with a shrug. "Guess it's just me and Ivy. Again."

Ivy grabs his hand and starts tugging him away. "Come on. Maybe we'll ride twice to make up for them."

Harrison gives Ford and I a grin. "Just so you know, I'm going to finger fuck your girlfriend on that Ferris wheel just because you won't be there to stop me."

Ivy stops and looks back at him. "*Just* because they won't be there?"

Harrison put his arm around her, his hand right on her ass. "Well, and because you have a *very* nice pussy."

She smiles up at him, sliding her arm around his waist. "Thank you very much. And you have very nice fingers."

They walk off together looking very much like a couple.

"Tell me I'm not alone in being a little turned on watching another guy take Ivy on the Ferris wheel with that promise," Ford says, watching them go.

I look at Ford. "You are definitely not alone. And I'm not a little turned on. I'm a lot turned on."

He blows out a breath. "Well, at least we're in this together." He turns toward the stand selling kettle corn, cotton candy, and other treats. "I'll buy you soda."

"Sounds good."

We approach the stand and wait in line behind a dad and his kid, who's about twelve.

When they turn to leave, I notice the kid's shirt.

It's from *My Fellow Aliens*, my TV show. I grin. "Like your shirt," I tell him.

The kid grins. "Thanks."

We place our orders and Ford hands me a cola, then we turn and start to stroll toward the Ferris wheel.

"That must be really cool," Ford comments.

I take a pull on my straw. I'm not sure what he's talking about. "What?"

"Seeing people wearing the merch out and about. Or hearing people talk about the show. I assume you're probably on forums and stuff, though, right?"

I stop walking and turn to look at him. "You know my show?" I'm completely surprised by that. I'm aware that Ford and Harrison know that I'm a writer for a TV show, but I honestly had no idea Ford knew the name of the show.

Ford's eyes widen. "Are you kidding? I'm a huge fan."

"Are you serious?" I ask. "You watch *My Fellow Aliens*?"

"I've watched it since season one. Before I knew who you were. But that's how I knew your name when we were introduced."

I shake my head. "I didn't know you knew my name when we were introduced. Or I guess maybe I thought you knew my name because of Ivy? That Brad told you my name?"

"I think he might've mentioned you, probably by your first name, but when we actually met in person, Ivy said your first and last name. I immediately put it together."

I peer at him. "You know the name of a writer on the TV show?" No one ever knows that.

"What can I say? I'm thorough when I get into something. I love the show and the writers are the biggest part of anything like that. So I looked you all up. I know you're one of the head writers."

I'm actually shocked. Ivy knows the name of the show and she knows I've been with it since the beginning, but she doesn't know much about what I actually do on the show. Harrison might know the name of the show, but I sincerely doubt it. "That's amazing. I'm so glad you like it."

"No, Liam," Ford says sincerely. "I don't like it. I *love* it. It's so well done. The world building is outstanding. The layers to all of the relationships are so compelling. And the humor's top-notch."

I'm stunned. We start walking again. "I guess I don't see you as a sci-fi guy."

"Well, in fairness, there's a lot about me you don't know," he says with a chuckle. "And vice versa. Though I feel like I have a little insight into you because of the show. But yeah, we haven't gotten to know each other that well."

"I guess that's true. This is a very welcome surprise."

Ford smiles. "Well, I'm glad. If you ever need a pep talk about how the show is going, I'm your guy."

"That's amazing to hear."

"And considering our...situation..." He nods toward the Ferris wheel. "If you wanted to share anything with me about what's coming up for Captain Daniels and Princess Daria..."

I laugh. "Oh, very smooth. Very subtle."

He chuckles. "Well, it was worth a try."

We walk a little further until we find a bench to wait for Harrison and Ivy. They're still going around but as we watch, suddenly it stops at the top. They're the only people on it and I narrow my eyes.

"He totally paid them to stop it at the top, didn't he?" I ask.

"Yup."

I sip more of my soda, thinking. But what the hell? "So Captain Daniels is actually one of my main characters. I'm in charge of his character arc." Daniels, the captain of the primary spaceship, has been on the show from the very beginning.

Ford turns to look at me. "No shit? That's incredible. He's by far one of my favorite characters."

I was hoping he would say that. "Yeah. And as you just alluded to, everyone's kind of thinking he should end up with Princess Daria."

I've actually been stuck on this point for about a week. I haven't been able to work through it.

Ford nods. "That's been pretty obvious."

"Yeah. That's what the other writers and the showrunner have been pushing for. It's actually something I'm supposed to be working on right now. But I've been a little stuck," I confess.

Ford squares up to me. He looks very serious. "You don't think they should end up together?"

I shake my head. "I really don't. I think that's why it's so hard to write."

"Because he needs someone softer," Ford says. It's not a question.

My eyebrows lift. "Yeah. Daria is amazing. She's kick ass. A born leader. There's no question they have a ton in common. But she doesn't offer him anything that he doesn't already have, you know?"

Ford's head is nodding up and down before I even finish. "I do know. I get it. I mean, they have chemistry. They're hot together. And clearly they're both fighting for the same thing. But yeah, she doesn't ever let him kind of...I don't know, let down?"

I jab a finger toward him. "Exactly. It's like he's got all these hard edges. And they're there for good reason. But he needs somebody who can get past that. Not someone who just reinforces those, right? I mean, Daria is a fantastic warrior. She's a great like...co-worker for him. A good friend. But to be in love, doesn't he need someone who can go a little deeper with him?"

Ford looks at me for a long moment, then toward the Ferris wheel. He smiles. "Yeah. I think he does. He needs someone who can smooth out some of those rough edges. Someone who will encourage him, and support him, but who also lets him be softer, and has a softer side for him to lean on."

I take a deep breath and blow it out. Okay, yeah, this is probably all just me writing about me and Ivy. But still, I feel it in my bones. This is what's right for this character. "I'd be lying if I said there wasn't a big piece of me inside Captain Daniels," I say.

"Well then, lead writer, take him on the journey he needs to go on," Ford says. "I can promise you the fans are gonna be there for you."

I can't even describe how that makes me feel. Pride, relief, and a sense of rightness. I know what I'm doing. I need to go in this new direction.

"Thanks Ford."

"Anytime. And I promise I'll keep my lips zipped about anything you spill to me. I go on the fan forums, but I just lurk. I never post." He pauses. "Okay, I do post and comment, but I swear I won't say anything about this. I am here for you if you need to talk about the show."

I laugh, but actually, I love that idea. Having someone outside of the show itself, but who's still knowledgeable and passionate about it, could be the most amazing thing for my creative process. I am really gonna need to get this guy some merch.

Finally, Ivy and Harrison come strolling back over to us.

Our girl is smiling widely, and her cheeks are flushed. I shake my head. I should probably feel jealous or something that my friend fingered my girlfriend on the Ferris wheel and clearly got her off, but I don't. I just grin at both of them.

"How was the ride?" Ford asks.

Harrison tucks something into Ford's front pocket. Ford frowns and pulls on the edge of it. It's clearly Ivy's panties.

I lift a brow at first Harrison, then Ivy.

"So, you had a good time?"

Harrison steps close to me and lifts his hand to my mouth. He slides his index and middle finger over my lips and into my mouth. "Taste for yourself."

With my gaze locked on his, I swirl my tongue over the end of his two digits.

I don't think I'm just imagining the taste of Ivy on his fingers.

I suck hard, watching Harrison's eyes darken, then pull back and look at my girl. "Delicious."

Her cheeks are dark pink, but she's grinning.

Fuck, I actually *love* that she and Harrison are getting along and having fun—even sexy fun—together. I love that Ford and I had a moment.

Yes, Ivy is definitely going to be my muse for the sweet tavern wench on the far-off planet of Nestia who Captain Daniels is going to fall head over heels for.

She's been in the back of my mind for almost a year.

But dang, now I kind of have an urge to give her a couple more boyfriends.

Captain Daniels maybe needs more than just one person to really figure his life out.

CHAPTER 22

Ivy

I'VE BEEN to Brad's offshoot of Raw in L.A. a few times for obvious reasons, but it's in Malibu and I hate the traffic on a good day, despise it on a bad day. It's also what I consider a typical restaurant, pleasant and upscale, with excellent food, but it's lacking in any sort of distinctive atmosphere.

Not that I ever told Brad that.

Raw in Charleston is a totally different vibe.

Maybe it's the diners, who are in general, older and yet more boisterous than the L.A. crowd that frequents the Malibu location. Everyone seems to know everyone and there are a lot of diners stopping at other tables to chat and miraculously that doesn't seem to piss off the wait staff. That behavior in L.A. would garner death stares from the staff, and fair enough. L.A. isn't the kind of city that generates a lot of patience. Sunshine, great shopping, celebrity spotting, and fantastic hillside housing with views it has in abundance, but patience? Not so much.

Or maybe it's watching Ford and Harrison in their element that gives Raw such a personal atmosphere.

Liam and I are seated at the large circular bar so that we don't steal a table from a regular and so that the guys can pop over and chat whenever they have a free minute.

"This is my kind of place," Liam says with appreciation as he runs his hand over the walnut bartop. "You know I like wood."

I laugh. "Good thing I wasn't drinking anything when you said that. Because yes, I know how much you like wood." I squeeze his forearm and smile at him.

Liam grins back. "You've seen all the ways I appreciate wood, haven't you? But I actually meant I like the decor. I'm so tired of everything being designed for a social media moment. This place is built around the concept of conversation. Great acoustics, comfortable chairs, ample spacing between tables. I like it."

"I do too. You know what else I like? Being here with you."

Liam is different in South Carolina. He's more relaxed, more chatty.

Maybe it's all the sex he's getting or maybe it's the slow pace of life in Honeysuckle Harbor.

Maybe it's how fun and easy it has been being with Harrison and Ford. It's been amazing to watch him find common ground with Ford and to see his relationship with Harrison deepen, whether he realizes it has or not.

Whatever it is, I like this for him. He's clearly happy.

Liam's gaze softens. "I like that too. This has been incredible, Ivy. I'm so damn in love with you."

"And me," Harrison says, walking up to us.

The corner of Liam's mouth turns up ever so slightly. "Almost. Not quite. But I'm considering it."

Harrison chucks Liam on the chin. "You're so fucking cute when you're in denial, William."

I don't always understand their teasing—it definitely wouldn't work for me—but they have their own thing and it clearly *is* working for them. Watching the passion they share is sexy as hell to me and I'm learning they enjoy what I think of as a fake hate fuck.

The real surprise?

My own spark with Harrison.

I didn't anticipate that at all.

But over these last few days of hanging out, he's made me laugh so hard I've snorted. He's much smarter than even he gives himself credit for, and he barely touched me on the Ferris wheel and I was having an orgasm.

Okay, so not *barely* touched me.

It didn't take long, though.

Harrison turns and gives me a smile, flipping my hair over my shoulder and massaging my neck lightly. "Did you order a drink? They make an excellent martini here, and I know how much you like your vodka."

"We haven't ordered anything yet."

"This menu was developed by our new Head Chef after Brad left for the show," Harrison says. "Don't tell him, but I think it's better." He gives me a wink.

"As if I'll be telling Brad anything," I say wryly. "We've been studying the menu and taking in the atmosphere. You guys should be very proud of Raw, Harrison. It's really relaxed and elegant in here. Like you."

He's wearing a tailored blue suit that fits him to perfection and while he's always crisp and tidy, he's in his element at the restaurant, talking to all the patrons and encouraging the staff and building them up.

Harrison almost looks embarrassed by the compliment. He leans in, crowding us both with his muscular frame. "I'm going to make you call me elegant later. 'That's an elegant way to suck Liam's cock, Harrison. You look so elegant fucking me, Harrison. You have incredibly elegant orgasms, Harrison.'"

The image makes me laugh, a high full laugh that is definitely *not* elegant. "I cannot say any of that with a straight face."

"Sex is no time for laughing," Liam says.

"Well said, William."

Harrison acknowledges someone who is trying to get his attention with a lift of his chin. "Gotta go. Daddy needs to keep the lights on."

With that, he's gone and Liam watches him stroll away, confident and damn it, elegant. Whether he likes it or not.

"You get it, don't you?" Liam asks, turning to face me, his knee bumping mine. "Why I'm so…enamored."

"I do. He's fun, but much more than that. He's smart, socially adept, arrogant yet vulnerable. He cares deeply about his people. He's the full package."

Liam rubs his jaw. "Full package, indeed. God, what the fuck are we doing, Ivy?"

"I don't know," I say, happily. "But I don't care. I just want to enjoy our time here. Now let's order a cocktail."

Liam nods and raises his hand for the bartender. We request two martinis, and the bartender tells us Ford has ordered a sampling of the restaurant's signature dishes to be sent out to us.

Ford.

I have no idea what I'm going to do about Ford, who is sweet and caring and oh-so-attentive. If he's any more attentive, my vagina is going to implode.

Just the thought of what he can do to me with his tongue has me wanting to fan myself with a cocktail napkin. Plus, he's the most protective and competent man I've ever met.

Case in point, two small bowls appear in front of us. "Blue crab bisque," the bartender says, sliding two black cloth napkins with soup spoons tucked in them toward us. "Ford wanted you to start with this."

Maybe Liam is right. What are we doing? We might be in over our heads.

It's a question I can't answer. All I know is that I'm falling in love with Ford.

It's the first time I'm acknowledging that to myself and as I take my spoon and dip it into the bisque, I marvel that it's possible to love two guys at once. I would have never thought that could be real, but I can't deny it's happening.

But it's complicated. For so many reasons. I'm with Liam. We live in L.A. How would any of that work? I don't even know how Ford and Harrison feel beyond we're all having fun.

"Holy shit, this is really good," Liam says, sinking his spoon back into his bowl for another taste.

I take a spoonful in and immediately relax my shoulders. "Mmm, oh my God." I'm not a person who normally gets orgasmic over food, but it's creamy and salty and absolutely delicious.

"I could eat a gallon of this," Liam says.

"Save room," Ford says, appearing behind us as I take a sip of my martini. "I asked Chef to make you fried green tomatoes, a low-country bouillabaisse, braised short ribs, and bourbon butter oysters."

"Holy shit," Liam repeats, immediately putting his spoon down on his saucer. "I want everything you just mentioned twice."

The menu is different from the Malibu Raw, which is almost exclusively seafood and salads. "I've never had fried green tomatoes," I say.

"What?" Ford looks scandalized. "And you being a food stylist. I'm shocked and appalled, Ivy." He gives me a smile to let me know he's teasing. "Prepare to be blown away."

"I already am," I say, softly.

He stills and his eyes darken. His jaw tenses and his nostrils flare. He wants to kiss me.

But he doesn't.

A little disappointed, I add, "I don't *eat* the food. I make it look pretty."

"They're going to miss you on the show."

That makes me shrug. "They've already replaced me." Then, because I don't want to think about my current unemployed status, I add, "So Harrison is front of house and you're back of house? What's your favorite part of what you do?"

"Having happy staff and diners. That's what I love. Knowing we've created a well-oiled machine but one that has the highest food standards and an exemplary customer experience. People come here to celebrate and share time with friends and family, as well as to enjoy the food. I love when they leave full and happy." He grins. "And maybe even a little drunk. We have great cocktails."

"You do." I lift my glass in salute. "Cheers."

A woman comes out of the kitchen wearing a pastry coat. "Don't get too drunk," she says. "I want you to try my famous coconut cake."

Her smile looks familiar and I'm wracking my brain trying to remember where I met her. The diner? The boardwalk?

"This is my sister, Frannie," Ford says. "And she does indeed make amazing coconut cake. Frannie, this is Ivy and Liam."

That's why her smile sparked something in me. It's a carbon copy of Ford's. "Oh, it's so nice to meet you! I see the resemblance between you and your brother."

"God help her," Ford jokes.

"Seriously." Frannie gives her brother a faux wince. "But I look more like my sisters."

"Well, two of you are identical," Ford points out.

Frannie laughs. "Exactly."

"Wait, triplets?" Liam exclaims. "Wow. That's...wow. I'm an only child."

"It's actually awesome," Frannie says. "I always had clothes to borrow and someone to play with. My twin, Fiona, is a pastry chef here too. I'm sure you'll meet her sooner or later if you're in town for a while." She turns back to me. "I hear you have a house to sell?"

That gives me a weird pang. "Yes."

"Good luck with that. Nice to meet you both." She waves and heads back to the kitchen.

She's sweet, like Ford. His parents must be good people.

"Here are the tomatoes." Ford claps Liam on the shoulder. "What's with the face?"

"I don't like tomatoes," Liam says, eyeing our two appetizer plates with trepidation. "I had a childhood incident with tomatoes."

Ford laughs. "That sounds like a story for never." He pulls his phone out of his pocket and frowns when he reads whatever is on the screen.

"What's wrong?" I ask.

He hesitates, then he asks, "Has anyone from the FBI contacted you asking questions about Brad?"

I set my martini glass down so hard vodka splashes over the rim onto my hand. Liam hands me a napkin as I sputter, "What? No. Why? Are they contacting you?"

Brad is not someone I want to actually think about. All week I've assumed he's sitting on a beach somewhere doing yoga and feeling intense relief that he didn't marry me. A feeling I share.

The FBI and Brad are not two things I would put together in one sentence. I don't even know what to think about that.

"Yes. This is the second message. This one sounds more urgent. They don't give any details. They just ask me to call them back."

"You probably should," Liam says, edging the tomatoes away from him and pulling the bisque back in front. "Ivy, are you sure they haven't reached out to you?"

"I think so." But I've also been studiously avoiding my phone for huge chunks of time, not wanting to deal with the flurry of texts and social media messages asking if I'm okay after being jilted on the day of my wedding.

Not just because it's embarrassing to have been publicly dumped, but because how do I adequately explain to everyone that I'm more than fine? That I'm actually quite fucking awesome, thank you very much, in love with two guys, and getting well fucked by three?

That won't go over well in a text to literally anyone I know except Patrice.

So I've been avoiding. And if I get one more inspirational quote from my mother, I might toss my phone into the Atlantic.

Digging it out of my purse, my frown immediately matches Ford's. "Oh wait, I have a voicemail." I open it to read it as a text and yep, it's the FBI. "Why the hell is the FBI asking about Brad?"

"That's what I would really like to know. I'll return the call tomorrow." He tucks his phone away. "Liam, if I give you first dibs on eating Ivy's pussy, will you try the tomatoes?"

I don't even blush. I love having them talk about me like this.

Liam scoffs. "You act like I wasn't going to have her pussy first, anyway."

"We'll just have to see who gets there first." Then Ford runs a hand over my knee and, ever-so-slightly and very briefly, brushes his fingers between my thighs.

I gasp.

But then he's gone with a wave. "Make sure you feed each other the oysters. Give me and Harrison a real show."

Forgetting all about Brad, I shiver. "Ooh, I *love* that idea."

CHAPTER 23

Ford

"SO BEAUTIFUL," Ivy says, wrapping her arms around her chest.

She means the view of the shoreline.

But I only have eyes for her. Her hair is shifting in the soft summer breeze as we stroll down the beach. The setting sun has cast the right side of her face is in shadow as she hugs the edge of the water, occasionally dipping her toe into the surf.

"You sure are," I murmur.

Ivy glances over and catches me staring at her. The corner of her mouth lifts up. "You're not so bad yourself," she says lightly. "But I meant the water." She breathes deeply. "God, there's nothing like that ocean breeze. I could never live away from the ocean."

Good thing we have an ocean.

I don't say it though, because I don't know where Ivy's head is and I don't want to pressure her or come on too strong.

I'm trying to live in the moment and as far as moments go, this is an incredible one. Liam and Harrison are back at the house and I'm savoring the opportunity to have Ivy to myself.

I don't mind when the guys are around—hell, I enjoy it—and all of us together in the bedroom is actually really damn hot, but

Ivy is the draw for me. Her pleasure, her happiness, gives me pleasure. I want to enjoy having a few minutes with her by myself without the constant banter with the other two guys.

"What's your favorite thing about California?" I ask, because I want to get to know Ivy better, hear her story, but also there's nothing wrong with trying to replicate *here* what she loves about *there*.

"Oh, wow, that's a broad question." She bends down and slips her shoes off to carry them in one hand. "I don't know—California is special. I've never lived anywhere else, so it's home, but it's also a vibe. Sure, there's traffic and it's expensive, but it's sunny and beautiful and I love that so much of life can happen both inside and outdoors. Whether it's dining alfresco or taking a hike in the hills, you're experiencing being outside. There's also a hope and optimism that people have. Dreams can come true. I love that."

Ivy shrugs. "I don't know if any of that makes sense. I'm not sure anyone has ever asked me that before."

"It does. Loving where you live is important."

Ivy stretches her free hand out and slips her fingers through mine. "What do you love about Honeysuckle Harbor? Could you imagine living anywhere else?"

My chest tightens a little but I need to be honest with her. "No," I admit. "Not really. I love that my family and friends are here. Community is important. Continuing traditions, helping out your neighbors. That matters to me."

Even now, seeing various other people on the beach, families and couples, and one man throwing a stick to his dog, I probably know half of them. From childhood, or high school, or through my family, or because they dine at Raw. I'm invested here.

But I'm also invested in Ivy, even if most people would find it too soon to even contemplate a future together. I've been crazy about her since the minute I laid eyes on her and I want this to work, in whatever form it takes.

"That's because you're a good man." She squeezes my hand tighter. "Do you know what I love about Honeysuckle Harbor?"

"Tell me."

She dips her toe into the water and grins. "The water is warmer."

I laugh, even though I'm a little disappointed by her answer. "It is."

But then she leans in, bumping her shoulder against mine. "And *you're* here. I like seeing you in your world."

"I like seeing you in my world," I tell her.

"I like being here."

She drops a light kiss on my shoulder, which makes my heart just about jump out of my chest. God, this woman. I want so much to have her with me like this every single day.

Ivy stops walking and stares up at me. "Ford, I want you to know that I've loved this week with you."

That sounds like a breakup line. I clear my throat a little, trying not to tense up. "I've loved it too."

"I can't just go back to California and not see you again," she says in a rush, biting her lip. "I need...I want..." She sighs and glances down at the sand. "I don't know right now how any of this will work. I just want you. Is that selfish?"

I'm so relieved that I cup her cheeks and kiss her softly on the lips. "I want you too. I want you to be happy. I'm here for whatever this is going to be. Let's just have fun and get to know each other even better. I want to know everything about you."

Ivy wraps her arms around my neck and kisses me, her lips trembling and I draw her closer, wanting to inhale her scent, her essence, her pure *Ivy-ness*.

She breaks off the soft kiss and smiles up at me. "You know what's fun?"

"Me getting you naked?"

She laughs. "Well, yes. But guess again."

"Road trips?" I joke.

Ivy reaches down and scoops up a handful of water and tosses it in my direction. "Getting the man walking on the beach in a suit wet."

Given that most of the water slips between her fingers she barely gets any of it on me. I don't care anyway. It *is* ridiculous that I'm in suit pants and a dress shirt. But after we left Raw she said she wanted to walk on the beach and I didn't want to take the time to change. I don't want to waste a single second I have with her. So I left my jacket and tie on the deck at Harrison's. I ditched my shoes and socks at the bottom of the stairs.

"This isn't a full suit," I protest, grinning back at her. "And you're going to have to try harder than that."

She sees the gleam in my eyes and backs up, shaking her head and laughing. "Ford. Don't. That's not a good idea."

But I'm already scooping her up in my arms and running into the surf. She's shrieking but I persist, and once I'm in water up to my waist, I drop down so we're submerged to our chests.

My pants and shirt are clinging to me, but I don't care. It's worth it to see the delight on her face. Her own top is plastered against her chest, giving me an incredible view. I settle her on my waist and she wraps her legs around me. We bob, her pussy bumping up against my sudden erection.

"Now what?" she asks.

I kiss her, dragging my tongue across her bottom lip. "Whatever we want, Ivy."

She grips the lapels of my dress shirt. "I love that. Whatever we want. Take me back to the house and fuck me, Ford. Just you."

My cock swells. "Gladly."

CHAPTER 24

Harrison

PAUSING in the doorway to my bathroom, I lean on the frame and just watch Liam for a minute before he realizes I'm here.

He's naked, in the shower, eyes closed, running his hands through his damp hair.

God, he's gorgeous.

I'm so in love with him.

Have been for a while now.

But damn, that's scary as hell.

Yet I knew when he and Ivy showed up in Honeysuckle Harbor, I couldn't fuck up this second chance to be with him. I'm going to do everything in my power to make him happy and to make him see that we can be together. Forever.

The four of us having sex was incredible. I know Liam loves Ivy and I understand why. She's smart and sexy and the total package. I don't know a lot of women who could weather being stood up on her wedding day with such class—aside from her highly entertaining reception speech—whether Brad was the love of her life or not.

I'm very attracted to Ivy as well, which is a bit of a surprise to me, but all of this feels so damn right.

Now Ivy and Ford are taking a stroll on the beach because Ford is a romantic motherfucker and Liam is in the shower.

There is no way I'm letting an opportunity like this pass me by.

Stripping my T-shirt off over my head, I quickly drop my shorts to the floor and step into the bathroom. It's a modest size, given this is one of my guest rooms. Liam is keeping his clothes in here because my closet is packed full. I'm surprised he hasn't spotted me yet. Hell, maybe he has, and that's why he's taking so much time soaping up his chest.

The room is steamy though, given its size, and when I pull the glass door open, Liam actually jumps.

"For fuck's sake," he says. "You almost gave me a heart attack. I thought you were a serial killer."

He doesn't sound even remotely scared. His eyes are drifting down over my body, the corner of his mouth turning up in a smirk when he spots my hard dick.

"You should lock the door if you don't want visitors." I step into the shower.

"Who says I don't want visitors?" Liam turns and lets the spray hit his chest.

His tight ass is covered in water droplets and I run my hands over him, squeezing, before shifting in behind him. I like being taller than him. It feels right to wrap my arms around him and tug him back against the hard plane of my body. The spray hits us both.

Liam instantly protests. "The water is in my eyes." His hand reaches up to swipe his face.

I lean down and suck lightly on his earlobe before murmuring, "Quit your complaining, William. Do you want me to get you off or not?"

He likes to be in charge. I know he hates this position—me encapsulating him in the small shower, my arms holding him, hot water running down over his face.

Hates it and loves it at the same time.

Because even when he's always trying to pick a fucking fight with me, Liam also can't resist me.

I ease my hands down over his abs and fist his warm cock. I slide my palm up and down over his length, thrilling at the way his breath hitches.

"How are you going to do that?" he asks. "This shower is too small to do anything in."

"You underestimate me, as usual." Lacing my fingers through his, I kiss his neck, trailing kisses over his damp skin.

Liam turns his head, offering me his mouth.

We kiss, a hot tangle of tongues, but the position is awkward, so I break away and I lift his hands. I press his palms flat against the shower wall.

"Harrison…" Liam growls.

The movement pushes his ass further into my cock and while I really, really love the way that feels, I know that's not what he wants.

"William," I tease back as I run my hands down his firm thighs as I descend into a squat.

He groans when I run a finger down between his ass and swirl it around his entrance. "Like this?" I ask.

"More," he pants, arching his back to give me better access.

"Happy to," I grind out, enraptured by the steam and the feel of his skin and him.

He's mine.

Slicking my finger up by sliding it into my mouth, I return to teasing at his tight hole until he's swearing and makes a move like he's going to stand up straighter. That's when I ease my finger into his tightness and pump in and out while he moans in approval. I take it deep, the way he likes, and he says, "Yes, Harrison, like that."

Hearing my name on his lips in that throaty tone of ecstasy makes my dick harden even more. Thick need is settling in every inch of my body and as I stroke inside him I run my lips over his hip, his waist, his ass. I lightly nip at him, and he jerks a little.

"*Fuck,*" he exclaims.

The excitement in his voice has me pumping my own cock a couple of times, just to ease the ache.

But my main focus is him.

Holding him in a firm grip, I ease my finger out and replace it with my tongue. I love the way his thighs start to tremble as the pleasure floods over him.

"Harrison," he says. "Jesus fuck."

Pulling back, I run my thumb over his entrance, applying pressure with the pad. "That feel good, baby?"

"Yes." His voice sounds strangled.

Water is sluicing down his ass and all over me, droplets pinging onto my arms. Someone could drop a bucket of ice water over my head and I still wouldn't stop. I love being with him like this, I love giving him pleasure.

I dip my tongue back inside his ass and pull him back onto me by his hips, a rhythmic pumping that has us both breathing hard. My thrusts are getting harder and more desperate, the throb in my dick painful, my balls tight and drawn. I'm pounding him onto me and his voice is louder now, a repeated chant of my name over and over.

God, that's so fucking good. I want my name on his lips all the fucking time.

When I'm about out of my mind with want, I stand up quickly, and slide my hands around the front of him. I grip his cock, bury my head in his hair, and stroke him with a hard, fast rhythm. He's trembling, leaning against my weight, his eyes closed.

I yank his hair roughly with my free hand. "Look at me," I demand.

He tilts his head, his eyes glazed over with pleasure, his lips parted.

"I'm yours," I tell him, even as I tighten my grip on the base of his cock. "I'm all fucking yours. Tell me you know that."

"I know that," he whispers, and the look in his eyes almost undoes me.

He loves me.

He hasn't said it, but he does. I can read it in the depths of his hazel eyes.

I give him a long hard stroke and his eyes roll back.

"Oh, god, damn!"

He spills out onto my hand in several shudders.

Liam's shoulders relax and I ease my grip on him, feeling about as triumphant as I ever have. State lacrosse champions in high school was nothing compared to the way I feel when I bring Liam to his knees.

"Did you come?" I joke, running my lips over his temple.

Liam laughs softly. "Fuck you."

I tighten my grip, drawing another shudder from Liam. "Does this count?"

He nudges me off of him. "Yes, I suppose it does. Now let's go to the bed and I'll return the favor."

"William the Brilliant." I run my hand under the water and open the shower door. "You always have the best ideas."

CHAPTER 25

Ford

I'VE JUST STARTED the coffee when I hear knocking on Harrison's back kitchen door.

I frown and glance down the hall. I heard someone get up and go into the bathroom, but I'm not sure who it is.

Do I answer the door at Harrison's?

There is a ninety percent chance that I'll know whoever it is. But explaining why I had a sleepover at Harrison's—which is obvious, considering I'm wearing my sweatpants and a T-shirt, my hair is still mussed from bed, I haven't shaved, and…

I sigh as the knock sounds again. It's nine a.m. and my car is out front. Everyone here knows my car. Hell, everyone in this town knows what brand of cold medicine I prefer when I'm sick, how much I paid for my car, and that I cheated on a chemistry test junior year of high school.

I'll never live that down.

So everyone will know soon enough that I spent the night at Harrison's. Might as well get it over with.

I pull the back door open and am nearly plowed over by Harrison's father, Bill.

Followed immediately by *my* father.

"Dad?"

"Morning, son!" my father greets, pulling me into a one-armed hug.

Bill hands me a plate. It's filled with muffins. "You baked for us?" I ask him.

Bill's a fantastic baker. It's been one of his hobbies since he retired. That and frisbee golf. And regular golf.

My father's hobbies since *he* retired—because he couldn't handle Bill being retired and having fun free time without him—include canning pickles, canning jam, making his own salsa, frisbee golf, and regular golf.

Judging by how they're dressed this morning, they're heading out for regular golf.

"I did," Bill says. "I hope I made enough. There are only four of you, right?"

He and my dad both laugh as if that's the funniest thing they've heard in days.

I roll my eyes. Now I know why they're here.

"Mom and Daphne sent you?" I set the plate on the counter and cross to the coffee maker, grabbing the first cup and *not* offering it to our 'guests'. But I put another cup on the little platform and add a new pod, then start a new mug brewing.

"Well, they had to go to work," dad says.

"And we were heading out to golf," Bill says. "So she figured we should stop by and…" He looks at my dad. "What were the words?"

"What were what words?" Harrison strolls into the kitchen, pulling a T-shirt on, his hair wet.

It must have been him in the shower. Thank God. Our dads are a lot, even with both of us handling them, but Harrison can match their energy a little better than I can. Especially pre-coffee.

"Your mom said, 'Tell those boys that parading their new girlfriends around at the cafe and all along the boardwalk and even at Raw, but not bringing them over to meet us is unacceptable and we *will* be coming over for dinner'," my dad recites. "She said she'd really like Harrison to make fajitas."

I open my mouth to respond, but Bill interjects, "Girlfriends? I thought Harrison had a boyfriend? Isn't that what Daphne said Mabel said? Or maybe it was Britney?"

My dad turns to him—instead of to the two other people in the room who would actually know the answer to the question—and says, "But Travis said Harrison was playing games and going on rides with a beautiful blonde. And that they got frisky on the Ferris wheel."

I shoot Harrison a look. He grins at me as he snags a muffin from the plate and takes a big bite, clearly unconcerned about the inaccurate gossip.

Except that it is, actually, accurate.

I sigh.

"But Bruce was at Raw and he said they came in with two other people. I swore one was a man and one was a woman," Bill says.

"But Mabel said Ford was dating the blonde," my dad says.

Bill nods. "Yeah, he did." He finally looks at his son. "Is your boyfriend blonde?"

Harrison shakes his head as he chews, then swallows. "Nope. Dark hair."

"So who's the blonde?" Bill asks.

Harrison points his muffin at me. "Ford's girlfriend."

"She's not officially my—" I start.

"Was Travis drunk while he was running the Ferris wheel?" my dad asks, looking alarmed.

Harrison grins. "Nope."

"But he said you and the blonde rode together, you paid him to get you stuck at the top, and you had your hand under her skirt," Dad says to Harrison.

Harrison nods. "Ivy. She's awesome. Very sweet. Fun. Beautiful."

My dad looks at me. Then takes in my bed head, then the coffee cup I'm holding, then my bare feet. Then he smiles. "Oh."

I quirk a brow, but Bill asks, "What?" before I can.

"The gossips got it wrong," Dad says, seeming pleased by that. "There's just one girl. They're sharing her."

Bill looks at me, then to Harrison. "Oh." He shrugs. "That makes sense."

They are not scandalized. Or concerned. Seemingly.

Bill crosses to the coffee pot and grabs the freshly brewed cup.

"Start me one," Dad says, settling on a stool at the breakfast bar. "So," he says to me. "You need to bring Ivy to the house, you realize."

I'm resigned to the ridiculousness at this point. "Yes, I realize that."

"What about Liam?" Harrison asks, grabbing another muffin.

"Who's Liam?" Bill asks.

I lean back against the counter, settling in. See? Harrison matches their energy.

"Liam is Ivy's boyfriend," Harrison tells them.

My dad sits up straighter. Bill turns.

"What?" they ask at the same time.

Harrison just nods. "Ivy and Liam are dating."

"And Harrison is in love with Liam," I add, lifting my mug in a little salute.

Harrison nods again. "Right. The dark-haired guy with us at the cafe, on the boardwalk, and at Raw. And Ford is falling in love with Ivy. And I *really* like her too."

Bill frowns. "So you're sleeping with...Liam." He looks very confused. "But you're—" He looks at me. "Sleeping with Ivy?"

Harrison and I look at one another, grin, and then nod. "Right," we say simultaneously.

"But Liam and Ivy are sleeping together?" my dad asks.

"Yes. And Harrison has slept with Ivy too," I say.

Bill and my dad exchange a look.

Then they both start grinning.

"Finally," Bill says.

"Thank goodness," my dad agrees.

Harrison and I frown. "Finally?" I ask.

"Thank goodness we're both sleeping with Liam and Ivy?" Harrison asks. "That's kind of an extreme reaction, considering you don't even know them. They could be psychopaths."

They ignore that.

"Thank goodness *you* two are finally together," my dad says. He crosses to me and pulls me into a hug. "You know we've hoped for this for so long."

Oh. This.

Again.

When Harrison came out to our families, both at once over brunch one Sunday by the way, they immediately started hoping for the same from me and that Harrison and I would be a couple forever.

I pull back. "Sorry Dad, I'm still totally straight."

He looks so disappointed, I actually feel bad.

"Are you *sure*?" Bill asks. Not for the first time.

I nod. "I am. But the four of us are…" I look at Harrison. He gives me an encouraging smile. "We've got something special. We just kind of fit really well together and Harrison and I are hoping that we can convince Ivy and Liam to make this a permanent situation."

"A polycule," my dad says.

I give him a surprised, but pleased, look. "Yes. How do you know about polycules?"

He scoffs. "I don't just play golf all day, you know."

Harrison snorts.

My dad grins. "I *read*," he says. "I haven't participated in a polycule myself, but I know what they are."

I laugh. "Well, great. Then you can explain it to mom."

"Your brilliant pediatrician mother?" he asks. "I think she'll be able to keep up."

I nod. "You're right."

"And we can keep hoping that you and Harrison…" Bill says, trailing off suggestively.

Harrison shakes his head and throws an arm around his dad's

shoulders. "If Ford and I are in a committed relationship with Liam and Ivy, then you'll have everything you want out of wanting us to be together. Us living together, all the family occasions, grandkids."

I straighten quickly. So do Bill and my dad.

"Kids?" we all say at once.

Harrison looks at us like we're all *very* slow. "Of course. Eventually. Somehow." He gives me a questioning look. "Right?"

For fuck's sake. This is so Harrison's style. We have been doing 'this thing' with Ivy and Liam for two days.

But…

I can't say no. That would actually be the dream situation.

Of course, we haven't even talked to Liam and Ivy about our actual feelings. Or about them staying. Or about…anything other than fucking while they're here.

I sigh. I am in love with her, and I do want them to stay. This is Harrison and our fathers. I'm not going to lie and say I *don't* want those things.

I shrug. "Sure. Maybe. Eventually."

Our dads are grinning.

"Daphne is going to be *thrilled*," Bill says.

My dad is nodding. "And you know they're going to show up on this porch tonight. So, *fajitas*. I'll bring a few kinds of salsa."

"No!" I say quickly.

My dad looks mildly insulted.

Harrison, thankfully, jumps in. "Jesus, we're trying to get Liam and Ivy to fall in love with us. And this town."

"We are offended that you think meeting our family would be a detriment to that," Bill says haughtily.

A beat passes, then we all start laughing.

Okay, maybe *detriment* is a strong word, but it would be overwhelming for them.

It's not as if they'd be simply meeting our parents. Between the two of us, we're related to most of the town. And our families not only get along within our family units, but they also like *each other*. Our dads are best friends, our moms are very close, our aunts, our grandmothers…

"Okay, listen," I say as an idea occurs. "Tell mom and Daphne to plan a bonfire for tonight. That way we can have everyone show up at the beach and it will just seem like a party, a town event. Liam and Ivy don't have to know that it's *all* family. They don't have to know they're the reason for it. Just have everyone come down and be *cool* about it."

Bill nods. "Great idea."

"Agreed," Dad says. "Except for the cool part. I don't think they can all pull that off."

Yeah, I'm pretty sure he's right.

But maybe Liam and Ivy will think the town of Honeysuckle Harbor is just *very, very* friendly. And nosy. And maybe they'll think it's quirky that a tiny coastal town in South Carolina happens to know a lot about polycules. Because I'm certain that piece of information is going to get passed around with the invitation and the search engines are going to be humming before tonight.

CHAPTER 26

Liam

"WILLIAM! CATCH!" Harrison throws me a football without warning from ten feet down the beach.

I drop the towel in my hand so I can jump a foot to the right and reach for the ball.

Sports weren't really my thing as a kid but I'll do just about anything to look good in front of Harrison.

It's a problem.

Or is it?

I don't know.

"Yes!" he calls out with a fist pump when I manage to catch the ball. "I knew you had it in you!"

I smile in spite of myself. Harrison might drive me fucking insane, but he also makes me feel lighter. I'm starting to figure him out more, too. He presents himself to the world as a carefree fuck boy, but the truth is he cares deeply about the people in his life, Raw, and this town.

Even though I grew up in California, my family was working class, and we lived far enough away from the beach that I haven't attended a lot of beach bonfires.

None, as a matter of fact.

This is my first.

The fire hasn't been lit yet because the sun's still out, but it seems like half of Honeysuckle Harbor has shown up today. We've been swimming and kayaking and picking at a massive picnic spread all day with a dizzying number of Harrison's and Ford's friends and relatives.

"I'm full of surprises," I call back. I toss the football a foot in the air and twirl it in my hands, enjoying the view of Harrison shirtless in swim trunks and Ivy sprawled out on the sand to my right in a bikini.

I wasn't the quintessential California teen partying on the beach that you see in movies. I started working at sixteen as a busboy in an Indian restaurant across from our apartment building to save up to go to community college and studying around the clock for my AP exams.

It was the total opposite of Harrison's high school experience but I don't resent him for that or wish my own was any different. I'm grateful for my parents and for the work ethic they instilled in me. I'm thrilled I have my dream job—as long as the show continues, anyway—and I'm damn proud of the life I've built for myself.

Harrison has a lot to be proud of as well. Sure, he was given a trust fund, but he's leveraged it into multiple businesses. He has rental property, the restaurant, and has Raw's bourbon butter sauce in production for distribution by the new year. He works hard, and he's generous. I've seen how he tips excessively, how he treats his housekeeper like family, and how he's respectful to his parents and grandparents.

He's way more than a fuckboy.

In general and to me.

I've fallen in love with him.

There's no denying it anymore.

He jogs over to me. "You're supposed to throw the ball back. That's how catch works." He holds his hand out.

I let the corner of my mouth turn up. "Maybe I just wanted you to come over here."

"Ah. And why is that?"

"So I can tell you I can't stop thinking about the expression on your face when you were fucking Ivy last night."

His eyebrows raise. "Jealous?"

I shake my head slowly. "Watching the two people I care about get each other off is my new favorite thing."

"You care about me?" His voice is husky and his hand drops onto my waist.

He's going to kiss me.

But I shove the football into his chest because my emotions are too close to the surface to allow him to touch me. I'm not a fan of making out in public, and if he lays one fucking finger on me, that's going to happen. "Yes. Told you I'm full of surprises."

"I've loved you since that first night. Why do you think I ghosted you?"

That makes me snort. "You're ridiculous."

But I understand Harrison now.

I'm actually not that much different from him.

I've been holding back from him just as much as he's been holding back from me.

Partly because I was angry and hurt he didn't return my calls after our first night together. And then partly now because of both Ivy and the fact that Harrison lives here in South Carolina.

I wasn't sure it would be possible to have a relationship with both Ivy and Harrison at the same time, and the physical distance was daunting.

But now Ivy has proven herself to be the perfect girlfriend— she doesn't care if I'm with Harrison, too. In fact, she's encouraging it. She knows how I feel about Harrison and she's enjoying Ford.

The four of us are having a great time together and I'm not going to worry about the fact that we live on different coasts.

"I'm ridiculous? You tell me you care about me and that I'm ridiculous ten seconds later. You're ridiculous."

"You knew I care about you. Otherwise, I wouldn't have been so angry with you."

"Yep." He grins and turns. "Now have a seat and look pretty while you watch me kick Ford's team's ass in football. My family versus his."

He doesn't wait for a response but I don't have one, anyway.

I'm just amused. At him. At myself.

At fucking fate.

A week ago, I was grumpy as hell, convinced Ivy was lost to me forever and that Harrison was an asshole who didn't know a connection when it hit him in the face.

But now I have…this. Whatever this is and whether it can be anything long-term, I don't know. Right now, I'm just enjoying the hell out of myself.

I plop down on the sand beside Ivy. She looks a little pink. "You need more sunscreen. Where's the bottle?"

"In my bag." She rolls onto her side, which gives me a great view of her chest spilling out of her black bikini top.

"Can you do that again?" I joke.

"What?" Then she realizes where I'm staring. She makes a sound of approval and preens a little. "I love when you look at me like that."

The look shoots straight to my cock. I clear my throat and adjust myself in my trunks that I just purchased at a local shop. I'm trying not to think about my bank account or the fact that the lead writer on *My Fellow Aliens* emailed me, asking when I'll be back in the writer's room.

Fortunately, being surrounded by three dozen people serves as a distraction.

"How's that?" I tease, reaching out for the sunscreen.

Ivy slaps it in my hand. "Like you want to suck on my nipples."

"You're very good at reading my expressions because that's exactly what I was thinking."

"It doesn't take an instructional manual to figure you out," she says, laughing. "Even if that wasn't totally obvious, I know you too well."

"Better than anyone." I squirt some sunscreen into my palm and tell her, "Lay flat on your stomach."

She folds her arms in front of her head like a pillow and rests her face on them. "This is nice, isn't it?"

I smooth sunscreen over Ivy's shoulders, massaging the muscles as I go. She sighs contentedly.

"Laying in the sun or being in Honeysuckle Harbor?" I still have a hard time saying the name of this town without a healthy dose of big city cynicism. It's just so foreign to me, the southern charm, the fact that everyone knows everyone, and that people look after and out for each other.

I've lived in my apartment building for three years and I've never spoken to a single neighbor except for the woman who is always drunk at the pool and thinks I'm Timothee Chalamet. Three years ago, I would have loved to be him. Now? I'm fucking thrilled to be me.

"Both," Ivy says. "This is so relaxing and I love the vibe here. The pace is slow and everyone is so damn nice."

"They are, aren't they? I haven't had anyone cut me off or swear at me yet."

As if to prove our point, a young girl runs up as I'm massaging down Ivy's back, dipping my fingers under the string of her bikini top.

"Hi, are you Liam?" she asks, putting her hands behind her back and rolling her shoulders back and forth. She's wearing a one-piece swimsuit and a cover up, the hood flipped up over her damp hair.

"Yes, I'm Liam. Can I help you?"

"I just wanted to tell you that the episode of *My Fellow Aliens* that you were lead writer on, Season Three, Episode Eleven, was my favorite episode of all time. The character development was extraordinary. You brought Sante to a whole new level."

I'm impressed with her understanding of what I was aiming

for. "Wow, thank you. That's exactly what I was trying to convey, so thank you for recognizing that. And I can't believe you know which episode I wrote."

"Ford is my cousin. Sometimes we watch the show together and he knows that's my favorite episode, and he told me you wrote it and I honestly can't believe it." She gives me a grin, flashing braces. "I want to be a writer someday, too. I'm Emily, by the way. I'm ten."

"It's very nice to meet you Emily. This is Ivy." I gesture to my girlfriend. "She's worked on the cooking show *Southern Charm* as a stylist, so she's in the TV business too."

"Hi, Emily," Ivy says. "It's lovely to meet you. Liam is a great writer, isn't he?"

"Yes, ma'am." Emily nods eagerly. "I've watched your show, too. I prefer adult programming because I'm a 'miracle baby.'" She uses air quotes. "My parents are fifty-five and fifty-seven."

That explains her aura of mini-adult. "You said Ford's your cousin?"

"Yes, sir. His father and mine are brothers. Okay, bye!" She runs off, kicking a little bit of sand over Ivy's back.

I shake my head, amused. "I don't think I've ever been called sir in my life."

"She called me ma'am. That was definitely a first. It's charming, though it makes me feel old."

Sliding my hands down her thighs, I lean forward and murmur, "You're not old, but even when you are, you'll still be gorgeous."

"You must be Liam and Ivy."

The unexpected woman's voice startles me. I jerk back guiltily, since I was dangerously close to squeezing Ivy's ass. I turn and see a tall woman wearing a floppy hat, a flowing dress, and a lightweight sweater. She's nailed the coastal grandma fashion look.

She elegantly drops into one of the four beach chairs Harrison set up. "I'm Daphne, Harrison's mother." She drapes her hand out for me to take.

I scramble to my feet, wiping my hands on my trunks.

My heart is beating unnaturally fast and I feel like I'm seventeen, for whatever reason.

Then I realize I know exactly the reason—I want Harrison's mother to like me because Harrison is important to me. Really damn important.

After I lightly shake her hand and say something I hope is polite, I turn and help Ivy into a sitting position.

"Are you enjoying Honeysuckle Harbor?" she asks, eyes masked with giant sunglasses so that I can't read them. She does smile though and her voice sounds friendly, so I relax a little.

"Yes, we are, very much, thank you. Great food, even better people."

She nods in approval. "Excellent. I understand you're staying with Harrison. Is he being an adequate host?"

The image of Harrison naked in the shower sucking my cock leaps into my mind and I can't get rid of it. "Excuse me." I cough into my hand and turn and reach for a water bottle.

Ivy raises her eyebrows at me and assures Daphne, "Yes, of course. He's been very *accommodating*."

My cheeks feel like they're on fire. For fuck's sake, I think I'm *blushing*.

Oh, Ivy's getting my hand on her sweet little ass for that later.

I clear my throat and face Harrison's mother again. "Yes, especially on such short notice. We're appreciative of his hospitality."

She lowers her sunglasses a hair and gives me a wicked grin. "I bet. I have eyes and ears. Anyway, Ivy, I just wanted to let you know that we have an offer on your house for twenty-five thousand over asking price, no inspection and no other contingencies. Cash, with a seven day close."

Ivy blinks. "Oh. Wow. That was fast."

That was fast.

I know the market is hot, but it was only listed two days ago.

"You don't have to be here for the closing. Everything is electronic, so you can return to L.A. whenever you'd like." She rises to her feet. "In the meantime, enjoy your time here. I look forward to having more time to chat with you both."

Then she's walking away, and Ivy and I are left staring at each other.

"I guess you sold the house," I tell her, surprised that I'm not more excited by that news than I am.

It was Brad's stupid wedding gift that she didn't even want.

I should be thrilled that it's being taken off of her hands and she's going to receive a large amount of money.

But she doesn't look any more excited than I feel. "That was fast," she repeats.

Her gaze drifts to the right, and I follow it.

Harrison and Ford are giving each other a one-armed friendly hug, the football tucked under Ford's arm.

"You don't want to leave, do you?" I ask.

"Not yet," she admits. "What about you?"

"No. Not yet." I sit down next to her on the towel and pull her into my embrace. "We don't have to leave right away. We were planning to stay another week anyway, right?"

"Right." She's watching Ford and Harrison intently.

The guys are lining up with various relatives in a football play. The center passes the ball to Ford and yells out, "Go long, go long!"

Go long.

I wonder if our foursome could do just that.

CHAPTER 27

I DON'T WANT this day to end.

I'm sitting around a bonfire, sipping a vodka seltzer and listening to the stories being exchanged by a dozen people who are either related or who have known each other forever. There's laughter and good-natured finger-pointing as three or four of them are insisting that Harrison was behind the senior prank, while he's laughing and denying it.

"I swear, it wasn't me. If it was, I would take credit, trust me."

"That's true," Ford's sister says with a nod. "Harrison will never let us forget his accomplishments."

Ford is sitting next to me and he leans in and brushes a quick kiss against my earlobe, causing me to shiver. "I have a confession," he murmurs. "I was the mastermind behind the senior prank."

I pull back and eye him. "What? Are you serious? Though I can see that relocating the principal's entire office to the football field would be just your style. They say not a paperclip was out of place."

Ford nods. "And yet, no one believes me, even though I've tried to take credit. I have a spotless reputation."

That makes me grin. "That's because they didn't see you last night. That's a whole different side of you."

He nudges my knee. "You bring out the growly in me."

I lean against his arm. "I like that side of you."

"I'm going to show you yet another side."

At first I assume it's a sexual innuendo—which I'm all for—but Ford jumps up off the log we're sitting on and maneuvers through the crowd, heading back toward the nylon gazebo he and Harrison popped up earlier to give us relief from the sun.

I turn my attention to Harrison and Liam, who are bantering about the s'mores they're making.

"You're toasting your marshmallow wrong," Harrison tells him.

"I want to do it this way." Liam has four or five stacked on his metal skewer and is turning it over the fire like it's a spit.

"They'll never cook that way." Harrison only has one on his skewer and has it buried in the flames. "You have to really get in there."

"I don't want to burn it."

"How many bonfires have you been to?"

"Uh…one?" Liam says.

"So none, since you posed it as a question."

Crossing my arms across my chest, I hug myself a little. I'm wearing Ford's sweatshirt since it got chilly when the sun went down. I wasn't really cold, but I wanted to wear his shirt. I raise a sleeve to my nose and take a subtle sniff. Sandalwood and burning wood. I love it. I'm not cold now either, I just am ridiculously happy.

Watching Liam and Harrison with each other makes my heart full. Being here with them, and Ford, makes it feel almost impossible to imagine my regular life back in California.

Harrison is trying to shove Liam's skewer into the fire.

"Stop. You're so annoying," Liam tells him, even as he leans closer into Harrison's personal space.

Harrison removes his own marshmallow, and it's charred to within an inch of its life.

"Perfect," he declares. Then he pulls it off and holds it up to Liam's lips. "Taste."

"No." Liam pulls away.

Harrison taps Liam's bottom lip with the marshmallow anyway, leaving a sticky smear behind. Then he leans in and licks it off of Liam. "Definitely perfect."

Liam grips the front of Harrison's T-shirt.

I shift on the log, suddenly warm. God, I just love watching them fuck each other. Even this, where they're just eyeing each other with naked desire, turns me on.

Harrison turns and presses his marshmallow between two graham crackers and two blocks of chocolate. "Ivy, try my creamy center."

I laugh while Liam rolls his eyes. I oblige Harrison and take a tiny bite, pulling away when the sweetness hits my palate. "Mmm, I love your creamy center."

A woman sits down next to me and gives me a smile. "I see Harrison is up to his usual tricks. I'm Celeste. I was his date to prom, but just as friends."

"I'm Ivy, it's nice to meet you. We'd love to hear all of Harrison's tricks, wouldn't we, Liam?"

"I think I know them all," Liam says.

"He flirts with food," Celeste tells us. "He's always trying to shove something in your mouth when he likes you."

For a split second, we just freeze. But then Celeste realizes what she's said, and we all burst out laughing.

"That didn't sound right."

"But very, very true." Harrison puts the s'more to Liam's lips. "There's more where this came from."

"I can't, I'm laughing too much." Liam waves the s'more away and meets my eye. He's grinning.

I've never seen Liam so light and carefree as he is here in Honeysuckle Harbor, and it's not because he isn't going to work.

He loves his writing career, and he loves the show he's been such an integral part of creating.

It's *us*.

All four of us. Together.

And this town, with its beautiful beach, quirky residences, and adorable shops.

The pace here suits him.

Since we decamped to Harrison's beach house this morning, Liam went out for coffee in the morning and to play chess with the retired guys. He spent a few hours writing in Harrison's home office or on the back deck facing the ocean, then helped the Ford put together our burgeoning picnic basket for our beach dinner. He even agreed to play golf with Harrison's and Ford's dads tomorrow.

Liam's grumpiness has been nonexistent and when we found out my jilted-bride-house sold, he didn't look pleased about it either.

I'm not ready to go home.

Not even when I get up for another vodka seltzer and I practically run into Brad's father.

It's been pretty damn easy to forget that Brad's from here and his family lives here, even with the house sale looming over me.

There's no forgetting it now. "Oh, hi!" I say, a little flustered.

"Ivy! I heard you were in town." Doug Richardson holds his arms out for a hug.

I return it awkwardly, but grateful he's not upset with me for invading Honeysuckle Harbor. "Yes, I'm here to sell the house Brad bought."

"I, uh, I have to say I'm sorry that Brad ran out on you the way he did. That wasn't right and I've told my son that."

"Thank you. I'm sorry you came all the way to California for a wedding that didn't happen. Honestly, that's on both of us. We should have called the wedding off months ago, but I didn't really realize that." Or I did, and didn't want to admit that.

"I hear you've been running around town with Ford. Did that

have anything to do with things falling apart?" Doug doesn't look angry, just curious. He also looks a little drunk, swaying a bit on his feet in his parrot T-shirt and swim trunks.

I'm still wary. I'm not surprised he's heard some gossip though, given everyone seems to know everyone here.

"No, not at all. That wasn't on my radar at all. Ford has been there to…comfort me."

"That's what we're calling it these days?" Brad's father laughs jovially.

"I'm going to blame the beer for that sounding a tad insulting, Doug," Ford says from behind me.

"Oh, hey, Ford."

I should have known the guys would notice where I was and who I was talking to.

Ford slips an arm around me, his hand splaying possessively over my stomach as he pulls me back against his body. Clearly he's trying to make a point.

"You didn't mean to insinuate that Ivy cheated on Brad, did you, Doug? Or that I messed around with a friend's fiancée? That *we* might have been the problem when clearly it was Brad who walked away." There's a steely tone in his voice.

I look up at him. He's staring Brad's father down.

"No. That's not what I meant," Doug says.

Then Ford kisses the top of my head. "Not that I'm not thrilled with how it turned out. But you should know that Ivy and I are simply moving forward now that Brad made this decision."

Doug is nodding earnestly. "Yeah, yeah, of course. I didn't mean anything else."

"I know you're sorry for making Ivy uncomfortable," Ford says.

"Oh, I'm—" I start, but Ford squeezes me and I press my lips together.

Doug focuses on me. "I'm sorry, Ivy. You've always been very good to Brad and you didn't deserve what he did. But Ford is a good man. I'm glad you're happy."

I nod, squeezing Ford's arm. "Thank you, Doug. I am."

"So, how are you?" Ford asks Doug.

"I'm fine. Considering the FBI is swarming our house and accusing my son of some shady bullshit."

I feel Ford's body tense. "They've been at your house?"

"Yes, the whole investigation into Brad allegedly misappropriating funds or whatever. Barking up the wrong tree, I'm sure of it, but yep, they're crawling all over our house. The Mrs. is worried about her Waterford crystal getting broken. I'm just worried they'll find my weed. Haven't they talked to you yet?" he asks me.

I shake my head vigorously. "No. They left a voicemail but I haven't called them back."

"Better do that tomorrow. I expect they'll want in your house with a search warrant."

I nod absently. "Okay. Thanks for the warning. Take care."

I forget all about getting another seltzer as Ford turns me toward the bonfire, and we walk back.

This information about Brad clears up the FBI calls and I decide not to say anything to the guys right now. It doesn't matter. I didn't share any bank accounts with Brad, and the house here is fully in my name. I don't know anything so I don't feel like I have anything to actually worry about.

"You okay?" he asks.

I look up. "Yes." He looks unsure. I squeeze his hand. "I'm fine. He's drunk. And he didn't really say anything that bothered me."

"I don't like the suggestion that you and I were messing around before your breakup."

I smile up at him. "Just in our imaginations."

He grins. "Right."

"*We* know the truth. It doesn't really matter what other people think."

"You're sure?"

"Of course." I squeeze his hand. "And everyone who *really*

knows you knows that you're not the type to do something like that."

He lifts my hand and presses a kiss to the knuckles. "You're right. But my imagination got *very* inappropriate."

"Promise to give me a demonstration of a few of those imaginings later."

His gaze is hot, but also full of affection, when he says, "Any time, anywhere."

We claim seats on a log near the fire and Ford reaches behind the log and pulls out a guitar. To my complete delight, he starts strumming it as if he does it all the time.

I put my arm around him and give him a side hug. "You play the guitar? You get sexier by the minute."

He gives me a slow smile. "That's what I was aiming for."

Harrison sits down on the opposite side of me. "Play her a song and get her sexy ass all turned on for us."

Ford plays a few chords, then he starts singing.

Instantly, I'm transfixed. He has a warm smooth voice as he sings, "Hey there Delilah," alternating between looking at me and the guitar strings.

"Damn, he's good," Liam murmurs, sitting down beside Harrison.

Harrison slips a hand over my knee and puts his other arm around Liam.

Wanting all of us connected in a chain, I ease my hand into Ford's pocket so I don't disturb his playing but I'm still touching him.

Not many people seem to be taking much notice of us, and those who do are smiling or look amused.

I wouldn't care if they were glaring.

Nothing can ruin this moment.

Because I realize without a single doubt that I'm in love with all three of these men.

CHAPTER 28

Harrison

IVY WAS ABSOLUTELY FANTASTIC TONIGHT. As was Liam.

I'm not surprised, but I'm thrilled.

They fit in with our family and friends so easily, and they seemed to actually enjoy themselves.

I haven't stopped smiling.

As we walk up the path to my house, Ivy and Ford lead the way, holding hands, her laughing at something Liam just said from behind them. I realize that everything is going according to plan.

I mean, I shouldn't be surprised. Things usually work out for me. But I realize at this moment that I've been worried about this.

Worried that Liam and Ivy wouldn't be comfortable here. That Honeysuckle Harbor is too small for them. That our families would be too much for them.

Okay, I've been worried that *I* would be too much for them.

For Liam.

It's not the first time that I've been at risk of overwhelming or annoying someone to the point they bail. But it's the first time I've really cared.

I love him. And I need him.

I'm happier when he's around. I feel like I can be more myself. I'm an even better version of myself.

I also think *he's* better when he's with me.

Ford stops at the front door and punches the code into the keypad. Liam crowds close to Ivy and presses a kiss to her temple.

Or hell, maybe it's Ivy that makes him so happy.

"I had a really great time tonight," Liam says to no one in particular as Ford pushes the door open.

Or maybe it's Honeysuckle Harbor, I think with a sigh as I follow them inside the house.

Whatever it is, I can make all of that happen. Long term.

Liam is more relaxed than I've ever seen him. Tonight he was laughing and talking and genuinely seemed comfortable and happy. I want that for him. I want to be a part of making that happen for him.

I know he and Ford have been talking about *My Fellow Aliens*. He's, of course, head over heels for Ivy.

So, all of *this*—the four of us—needs to keep happening.

I know Ford's in.

I know Honeysuckle Harbor is in.

So I have to do whatever I can to be sure Ivy is all in.

All in on the four of us being together. Here in this town. For good.

She's the Queen. Our Queen.

If she wants to stay here long-term, then Liam will stay.

I can so work with this.

Ford moves ahead of us, flipping on lights.

Ivy and Liam are still in the entryway. She's bracing a hand on the wall as she slips her shoes off. Liam's saying something to Ford. I can't even concentrate on the words.

All that's going through my head is my plan.

Blow Ivy's mind. Show her how fucking good this can be. Always. Show her that she wants this. For good.

It's already been good. So damned good. But I need to make

sure she knows that she can have all of this all the time. She's calling the shots. She holds the future in her hands.

The future for all of us.

I move swiftly as she drops her foot to the floor. I step in front of her, cup her face in my hands and turn her back to the wall.

"Hey pretty girl," I say, pressing close.

"Hey," she says, surprise flickering through her eyes, her voice breathless.

"Everyone loved you tonight."

A smile tips her lips. "It was so fun."

"Honeysuckle Harbor is enamored with you," I tell her honestly, studying her up close.

"Do you think so?" she asks softly, almost hopefully.

She's so fucking gorgeous. And sweet and funny and bright and brave.

I can absolutely spend my life as one of her best friends, helping her make my best friend and the love of my life happy. If we team up, it will be the easiest, most fun gig ever.

"Of course," I tell her. "Like we all are." I meet her gaze directly, stroking my thumb over her jaw, and repeat, "Like we *all* are."

One side of her mouth curls. "I like you a lot too, Harrison."

I give a soft laugh. "I know you do."

She grins at my clearly expected cocky reply.

It's quiet behind me. I don't know what her two other men are doing, but they're not pulling me away from her or stepping between us.

"What do you think about coming to the bedroom with me?" I ask her, running my other hand over her hip.

"Just us?" she asks.

I smile. "We could have a lot of fun."

She nods. "We could."

"But I won't be mad if it's *not* just the two of us."

"Me either."

"So why don't we go down there and see what happens?"

Her gaze flickers to something over my shoulder.

Okay, someone. Or two.

Then she gives me a sly smile. "Sounds good."

I lean in, nuzzling against her neck and putting my mouth to her ear. "Let's make our guys crazy."

"Yes," she whispers.

I turn her face and take her mouth. The kiss is not quick. Not sweet. I kiss her deeply, hotly, fully.

She wraps her arms around my neck, arching close. I drop my hands to her ass and pull her up against me.

Fuck, she feels good.

Doing *this* for the rest of my life seems like a great idea, too.

I lift her, and she wraps her legs around my waist. I turn and start for the bedroom, our mouths still melded together.

I hear footsteps behind us.

Yeah, there's no way Ford and Liam are going to give Ivy and I any time alone.

But hell, forever is a long time. If our girl and I are ever left alone for an hour—okay, twenty minutes—I'm not saying this *won't* happen between just the two of us.

I'm grinning at the thought as I toss her onto my bed.

I start unbuttoning my shirt as she sits up, watching. Her skirt is bunched around her upper thighs, all that smooth creamy skin tempting me despite the fact that Liam has just stomped into the room. She yanks off Ford's sweatshirt and tosses it aside.

"What the hell, Harrison?" he asks. "You're suddenly taking charge here?"

He's so cute when he's riled up.

"I'm just making sure Ivy knows that she's the object of *all* of our desires," I tell him, shrugging out of my shirt and letting it drop.

I haven't looked at Liam yet. I'm enjoying Ivy's eyes on me. But I also feel Liam studying my back and shoulders.

Yes, I like being between these two.

"She was such a good girl tonight, charming everyone,

showing Honeysuckle Harbor what a sweetheart she is, that I think she deserves a *very* big reward," I say.

Liam makes a low humming sound. I feel his hot hand on my back between my shoulder blades. My skin sizzles.

"Is that right?" he asks. "And you're going to take care of that?"

My gaze tracks over her from her pretty head to her cute toes. "Yeah, I think I can handle this."

Liam strokes my back. "What do you think, Ivy?" he asks. "You okay with Harrison taking care of this?"

She gives him a sweet, almost shy smile. "Yeah, of course. Harrison is good at everything he does."

Liam gives a low chuckle. "Yes, he is."

I toe off my shoes. "Yes, I am."

"What do you think, Ford?" Liam asks.

"I think Ivy gets whatever she wants." Ford's voice is low and rough.

I finally glance over. My best friend is leaning against the tall dresser, hands in his pockets, just watching.

I look back at Ivy. "Hear that? You get whatever you want."

She nods. "I heard."

"So," I say, unbuttoning and unzipping my fly. "I guess that puts *you* in charge."

Which is exactly how it's always been. And will always be. And every person in this room knows it.

I just need to be sure that what she wants is all of us, in this town, for as long as we all shall live.

"Tell us what you want," I tell her, stepping forward and grasping her ankle, then slowly pulling her down the bed until I'm standing between her knees. "In graphic detail."

"To be naked," she says.

"Very good."

She's wearing one of the little sundresses that drives us all crazy. She'd pulled it on over the black bikini that had also driven us all crazy all day. The dress is now bunched up around her waist.

I slide my palms up her thighs to her tiny bikini bottoms, hook my index fingers in the top at each hip, and tug them down. She grasps the bottom of her dress and slides it up her body and over her head.

"*Very* good," I tell her as she reaches behind her back to untie her top.

She's gloriously naked, and unabashed about it, a moment later.

I slide my hands up and down her thighs again and she parts them, seemingly almost instinctively. I love that her impulse is to so easily spread her thighs for any of the three of us.

Or all three of us.

"Now what?" I ask, looking up.

Her nipples are nice and tight, her skin is flushed, she's breathing fast.

"I want someone to touch me," she says, her voice soft.

"Where?" I ask, still stroking her thighs.

"My pussy."

"Oh, very, very good," I praise. "Who?"

"You."

Love that. "With what, Ivy? What do you want me to touch this pretty pussy with?" I slide my finger over her slit, then up to circle her clit. "My fingers? My mouth? Or my cock?"

She lifts her hips. "Yes. All of those."

I lean over, bracing one hand next to her hip. My cock is full and throbbing and it's because of this woman. Oh, Liam too. His hand is still on my back and I'm very aware that he's watching me touch his girlfriend. That makes this so much hotter.

But I *want* Ivy. I want to make her come apart. I want to make her scream.

I'm very aware of Ford too, and I feel a fucking *duty* to make her scream with his eyes on us.

Ford is letting me do this. Oh, I know he's letting Ivy call the shots, and this is all happening because it's what Ivy wants, but still, I feel humbled that all three of them are putting me in this position.

I drag my finger through Ivy's very wet, hot pussy. "You're going to let me touch you, and taste you, and fuck you, Ivy?"

She takes a deep breath. "Yes. While Ford watches."

Heat arrows through me, and I hear both of the other men growl softly.

I circle her clit with more pressure. "Oh, that's a little naughty. You want to really tease him? Make him crazy?"

She bites her bottom lip, and one hand grips the duvet. "Yes," she says, her voice a little ragged now as I tease her clit. "And I want Liam to fuck you while you fuck me."

My hand freezes and I feel Liam tense beside me.

"*Fuuuuck*, sweetheart," I breathe out.

"Then—" Her eyes meet Ford's. "I want you to take me hard, however you want to. Do anything you want to me."

"Jesus Christ," he mutters. He shifts off the dresser.

Ivy lifts her hands to her breasts, playing with her nipples. "You all make me feel so sexy. Like I'm being worshiped. Like I make you crazy. I *love* that."

I slide a finger into her, loving the tight, hot grip of her pussy. "You *do* make us crazy. You're a fucking goddess. Of course you deserve worship."

She pinches her nipples, moving her hips restlessly against the duvet as I move my finger in and out. "You all make me wanton." She moans. "God, I just want you *all*. All the time. How can I be with *three* of you and not get enough?"

I add a finger and lean in, kissing her, then say, "Because we're so damned good to you." I finger fuck her a little faster. "So damned good *for* you."

She nods. "I know."

"Because we all love giving you pleasure. Love giving you everything you need and want." I kiss her again. "Just love *you*," I say softer.

Her breath catches, but then I curl my fingers against her G-spot and she moans.

"God, you are gorgeous," Liam says gruffly.

He's gripping my shoulder and I can feel the tension emanating from him.

I bend and take one of her nipples with my mouth, sucking hard, and she shatters.

"Oh, god! Yes!"

Her pussy clenches around my fingers and I immediately slip them from her body. I lift them to Liam's mouth, and he sucks them clean as I drop to my knees. Then I pull Ivy's ass to the edge of the mattress and lean in, licking that sweetness up, circling her clit with my tongue, sucking hard as she cries out again then fucking my tongue into her.

Fuck. She's amazing.

The things the four of us are going to do to and with each other.

The opportunities are endless.

I feel Liam's hand run up my back, his fingers sliding into my hair, then gripping as I eat at Ivy, making her cry and gasp, until she's almost there again. But I don't let her come.

I stand swiftly, shoving my jeans and underwear down and kicking them off. I fist my cock.

"Fuck, Ivy, you're amazing."

Her hair is tousled, her lips swollen and pink, and she's breathing heavily, looking happy and sated—and we're just getting started.

"You still want my cock?" I ask, pumping my fist up and down.

"God yes," she says enthusiastically. She looks at Liam. "And I want you to fuck me with Harrison."

He blows out a breath. "You've adjusted pretty quickly to having three men in your bed, haven't you?"

"It's…incredible," she says.

He laughs. "I think I can speak for all of us when I say we're very happy to hear that." He looks up at me. His smile dies, his eyes heat, and his voice deepens. "Very happy."

I nod. "Yeah."

He reaches back and grasps his shirt, pulling it over his head. Then he strips out of the rest of his clothes.

Out of the corner of my eye, I can see Ivy watching him, but I can't fully take my eyes off of him. The desire I feel for him is as intense as ever.

"Liam—"

He cuts me off by stepping forward, grasping the back of my neck, and pulling me in for a hard kiss.

It's hot and deep, his fingers gripping my neck, our bodies pressed against one another.

He pulls back, still holding my neck and says, "Fuck my girlfriend well, Harrison."

"I intend to."

"And take my cock like a good boy while you do it."

Fuck. "Yes, sir."

He growls again, squeezing my neck. Then he moves behind me, nudging me toward the bed. Ivy is watching us, her gorgeous body spread out for us, her pussy wet—from me, for me—just waiting.

I stroke myself again, taking her in. "God, this is like a dream."

She smiles, stretching like a cat, spreading her thighs wider. "A *very* dirty dream."

I lean over, bracing my hands on either side of her hips. I kiss her as I feel Liam move in behind me.

Then she says, "Love me, Harrison. With Liam."

And I'm one-hundred percent sure I already do.

CHAPTER 29

Ford

I MIGHT LOSE MY MIND.

I don't know how I'm going to survive watching this.

Oh, it's not jealousy eating me from the inside.

It's deep, intense, gnawing *lust*. Unlike I've ever felt before.

These three people are everything to me and watching them like this—pleasuring each other, being so open and vulnerable with each other—is going to undo me.

Harrison takes Ivy with one hard thrust and they gasp each other's names. Ivy grips his shoulders, arching closer as he fills her. His arms bunch as he holds himself over her, staring down at her as if he feels…everything Liam and I feel for her.

Damn.

I'm so glad they are friends. I'm so glad they make each other happy. I'm so glad they want each other like this.

But I didn't realize they'd fall in love.

Or how happy that would make me.

I've always expected Harrison to be in my life forever, but I'd never imagined something like this. I figured our wives, or my wife and his husband, would be friends. We'd have family dinners. Vacations. Our kids would grow up together.

But I never imagined that the wife, the husband, the kids could be *ours*.

And now…fuck I want this *so much*.

I understand what he's doing. He's dedicated to showing Ivy what this can really be. No holding back. Giving her everything.

And I think it's working.

She's clearly in ecstasy. She's moaning, moving under Harrison as he pumps into her.

"Liam!" she cries out. "Please."

"Fuck. Yes, beautiful, I'm right here," he says.

A moment later, he thrusts into Harrison, shoving Harrison deeper into Ivy.

"Oh, God," Ivy cries.

"Fuck," Harrison mutters.

All three pause. Then start moving. Together. Seemingly naturally. It's hot, dirty, and beautiful at the same time.

I've never been this hard, this worked up, and yet this *happy*.

"Ivy, you are so fucking perfect," Harrison tells her, braced on his elbows, his face just above hers.

"This is amazing," she says breathlessly, her fingers gripping his back.

"Is he filling you up?" Liam asks, thrusting into Harrison. "Is he making that greedy pussy happy?"

"Yes, god yes!"

"Can you feel me, Ivy? Do you feel me fucking you too?" Liam demands.

"Yes, fuck us harder, Liam!"

He slams into Harrison. Harrison groans. Ivy cries out.

"Like that? You want more of that?" Liam asks.

"Yes, fuck. Take it, Ivy. I want you to come on my cock before Ford takes you. Get me all wet and sticky with this beautiful pussy," Harrison says. "Let's get you all hot and wet for Ford."

My pulse quickens, and my cock pulses as that seems to take Ivy even closer to coming.

"Oh, God!" Her grip on Harrison tightens but she looks over at me. "Ford," she breathes.

"Right here, Ivy. I'm right here."

"I need you."

"You'll have me."

"Take your clothes off."

I love when she gets a little bossy. She knows she's the center of this little universe. She knows she has all the power. And she's so damned beautiful taking it, because she also gives it.

She's sunshine, and warmth, and laughter, and happiness, and love. For all of us. She gives us her trust, her acceptance, her body, her everything.

And she's going to get it all back. Times three.

I strip out of my clothes as Harrison and Liam fuck her faster and harder.

She's climbing toward her orgasm. I can hear it in her moans and cries, see it in her face.

"Fuck, Ivy, I'm going to come," Harrison groans. "Can I fill you up, pretty girl?"

"Oh, God, yes!"

Harrison thrusts hard, then tenses as he starts to come. Ivy cries out, coming apart. Liam stops, holding Harrison's hips tightly as Harrison buries his face in her neck and Ivy screams out his name.

Harrison kisses her deeply, but then Liam is pulling him off of her, bending him over further, and fucking him hard.

I immediately climb onto the bed between her thighs. I lean in and kiss her, and she wraps herself around me. When I lift my head, I smile down. "Hi."

"Hi."

"You okay?"

She shakes her head. "I need you inside me."

I shift my hips back, then thrust, filling her up.

She gasps, then moans. "Yes. Like that."

I slide one hand under her ass, lifting her hips slightly. Then I pull back and thrust forward. Hard. Fast. Deep.

"This is how I want you," I tell her. "Under me. Around me. Against me. With me. Every. Fucking. Night." I punctuate the last three words with thrusts. "With Liam and Harrison right here with us."

I see her eyes fill with tears, but she's smiling. "Yes. Yes. That's what I want."

I know it's sex. I know it's endorphins and the fact that I'm balls deep in her on the heels of a hard orgasm. I know it's the high and happiness of the night. But I'll take it.

"Need you to come again," I tell her. "Harrison doesn't get all the sweetness."

"I'm so close," she says breathlessly. "How can I be so close again?"

"Because this greedy pussy needs *three* men," I tell her. "Because you deserve more. You deserve *us*."

"God yes. I do. I need you all so much."

I lean in and suck on a nipple.

"Oh, *god*," she moans. Then slides her hand between us, finding her clit.

Her pussy clenches around me and I groan. "Yes. That's it. Just like that."

I move faster, fucking her harder, feeling her pussy responding.

Then she arches into me and calls my name, coming hard. Again. "Yes, Ford!"

God, she's magnificent.

I thrust hard and fast, feeling my climax building. Then I'm pounding it into her.

"Fuck, Ivy, yes! I love you!"

I freeze for a second. Dammit. I didn't mean to say that. At least not like this.

But then she wraps her arms around my neck, puts her face against my throat, and breathes deeply. Contentedly.

She doesn't say it back. But she definitely doesn't seem upset.

"You make me so happy," she says softly long moments later.

"That's all I want," I say, stroking my hand over her hair.

And that's the truth.

I want her to be happy. No matter what.

Unless it means being without me.

I don't know if I can do that.

And we might need to talk about that. Soon.

CHAPTER 30

Ivy

FORD SAID HE LOVES ME.

During sex.

I'm not sure if that counts then, but while I suspect he didn't mean to *say* it, I also believe he means it.

Everything is new and wonderful and sexy.

But confusing.

I have to go back to L.A.

Don't I?

That's where Liam lives and works, and I told him I would move in with him.

But then there's Ford...and interestingly enough, Harrison. Yes, he and Liam are in love, but Harrison is like a best friend with benefits for me. I enjoy being around him.

What the hell do I do?

"Going for a walk!" I call out to Harrison, who is pacing back and forth on the back deck on his phone.

Ford is at Raw because they lost power for a few minutes because of high winds and the generator didn't come on. I know from my own experience working with food that can cause a disastrous domino effect.

Liam walked to the coffee shop to write for an hour, which

leaves me to take a beach stroll by myself. It's much needed solitude. While I've loved every second with the guys, I haven't been alone in a solid week and I need to breathe deep and just…think.

Harrison gives me a wave and calls out, "Don't go in the water. Surf's too high today."

I wave back in acknowledgment.

Dressed in linen pants and a cotton button up, I run down the stairs and kick off my sandals once I hit the sand. It is windy, but I have my hair in a ponytail and sunglasses on, so I don't mind. I grew up in Santa Cruz, California, next to the beach and I miss the waterfront in Los Angeles. Not that it isn't available, but I never seem to have time and the vibe is different. Honeysuckle Harbor having a boardwalk reminds me of childhood.

I used to actually surf as a kid and I find myself wondering if I could do that here. I need to keep up my fitness if I'm going to be twisted and turned around in bed every night by three men.

The thought makes me grin as I walk.

Last night was…wow.

Then immediately I feel confused again.

I could easily live here full time. But I have no idea how that would work and I've just gone and sold my house. Granted, it's a hefty deposit dropping into my bank account—thank you, Brad, truly—which means I have options now.

I've already been rejected immediately for three of the four jobs I've applied for. The rejections came so fast I swear they hit my inbox before my application could have even been glanced at. I'm a little concerned that I've been labeled "drama" given how small the food entertainment world is and my canceled wedding with Brad.

Plus, his legal issues. I tried to call the FBI agent back this morning but I got his voicemail, which is just fine with me. I'll happily avoid that as long as possible because it sounds at best unpleasant, at worst me in handcuffs. I don't know a damn thing about Brad's alleged illegal activities but I've watched Dateline. That doesn't always matter.

I've walked in the opposite direction I usually stroll, away from the boardwalk, and I spot a building up ahead that is hovering on a dune, jutting out over the water. There's an upper deck with nothing on it.

As I get closer, I see the doors are boarded up, but not the windows. It has an abandoned look, the planter boxes empty and the wrap around deck in need of furniture and a coat of paint.

Impulsively, I decide to go up the steps and peek in the windows. It's a restaurant or event center. Or it was, anyway. There is nothing inside but a few dusty chairs and, oddly, a bicycle. Turning back, I draw in a sharp breath.

The view of the beach and the ocean is stunning here, sea grass waving gently left and right, in what would make an incredible wedding aisle down to the water's edge.

Biting my lip, I realize there isn't any other venue that is beachfront here. Not that I've seen, anyway. It's all residential and the boardwalk with its ice cream parlor and french fry stands.

By the time I've walked around the front of the building and seen the large parking lot, asphalt broken through with weed growth and seen the fallen down sign stating, "Morty's Meathouse," an idea is forming.

I'm a stylist. Most of my career has been in food, but lighting and color combinations and presentation are the same across the board.

I could open a wedding venue.

Here, in Honeysuckle Harbor.

I have the money. I have the skills set required. I know a fabulous restaurant for catering, and I've planned a wedding for myself. Ironic and cringey, but true.

I love this idea. It feels like an exciting challenge and a fresh beginning.

Walking back to the house at a crushing pace, I jog up the steps to Harrison, who is drinking coffee and scrolling through his phone. He immediately sets it down and sits forward.

"You okay? What's wrong?"

I'm glad Harrison is home alone. I trust him to be the most objective in discussing a business venture.

"What is Morty's Meathouse?"

"A gross restaurant with health violations that some claim was a front for drug deals."

That sounds about right based on that name.

"That's prime real estate! Why has no one bought it?" I demand, dropping into the chair next to him.

"Locals think it's cursed because nothing that goes in there ever lasts. And the owners won't sell to anyone who isn't local."

That's deflating. Not the curse part. I don't believe in curses. But the second part is annoying.

"Would they sell it to me?" I ask. "Because of you and Ford? If I ask nicely?"

I give him a smile, putting my hands under my chin and fluttering my eyelashes.

"I'll sell you anything you want if you do that naked."

I laugh. "I'm serious, Harrison."

He studies me for a second, head cocked. "Well, I'm very convincing. I'm related to half the town and my family owns most of its commercial property. So yes, I think it could be arranged. We would need to make sure it's structurally sound. What do you want to do with it?"

"It would make an incredible wedding venue."

"We getting married?" Harrison has shifted his knee over and it's brushing mine. "Oh, you mean to rent out? Sorry, I had visions of stripping you out of a wedding gown. What happened to that dress? Can we do that?"

"My sister is selling it online for me. You can rip these pants off of me if you want, but only after you focus on my incredible idea. That view is fantastic, Harrison. It's a great opportunity."

Harrison sits up straighter. "You're actually serious?"

I nod.

"So…you would stay here full time?"

I nod again.

"Then *fuck* yeah." He lifts my hand up and kisses my knuckles. "Let me make some phone calls."

"Thank you." I smile at him and lift his coffee mug and take a sip. "Who is the owner, by the way?"

Harrison gives me a grin. "Oh, it's me. I bought it out of fore-closure six months ago."

My jaw drops. Then I laugh. "So you'll give me a good deal?"

He tugs me onto his lap. "I think we can arrange something."

CHAPTER 31

Liam

I'M on my way down to the boardwalk when my phone rings. I'm still not really a boardwalk guy but I've been playing chess there for the past three mornings and I find myself walking in that direction on purpose now.

The old men who gather there are hilarious and I haven't had a good game of chess in forever. Despite the gossiping and insults and jokes they toss back and forth as they play, they take their chess seriously. Sam's my favorite. He's the one who invited me that first morning, and he's the sneaky one. He seems laid back and friendly, as if he's just there for a good time and doesn't care about the outcome at all. But he'll kick your ass with a grin on his face. And then buy you popcorn while he tells you what's wrong with your game.

I like him.

I haven't asked, but I wouldn't be surprised if Sam was a fisherman back in his working days. It was something blue collar. All of these guys were, I'm sure. They're so down to earth. They've also clearly known each other for years and years. Their friendship reminds me of Ford and Harrison's. Easy and loving, with lots of inside jokes and a clear level of comfort that comes from knowing someone really well and knowing they have your back.

The way the older men have accepted me into their group is a little surprising, honestly. It makes me feel warm as I pick up my pace down the sidewalk.

I really don't want phone calls from L.A. interrupting my mental pre-game prep. But when I don't answer the call, my friend texts.

Pick up! I have news.

Dammit. I stop walking and dial Toby's number. He answers immediately. "What's up?" I ask. "I've only got a minute."

"Well, hello to you too," my friend and fellow writer answers. "I've missed you too. I'm fine, thanks for asking."

I roll my eyes. Tobias Franklin is nothing if not a drama queen. "Hi, Toby. I've missed you. How are you?"

"I'm *panicked*, Liam," he informs me. "When are you coming home?"

I grin, but try to keep it out of my voice. I start toward the boardwalk again. "I'm not sure. Why are you panicked?"

It could be almost anything from a new guy he's seeing that hasn't called in twelve hours to his mother coming to town to stay for a week. The latter is definitely cause for panic.

"Andrew loves the new storyline you've added," Toby says.

I stop. "Really?"

Andrew, our showrunner, actually emailed to tell me that himself. He loves the idea of giving Captain Daniels a new love interest. He even said that he thought changing that up could get us a renewal for another season. I was thrilled, of course. But if he also told Toby and others, that's huge.

"Definitely. They're going to start *casting* soon. You have to get back here or..." Toby trails off dramatically. Then he lowers his voice. "Or he's going to give that storyline to Gwenyth."

I freeze. "*What?*"

One, I had no idea that they'd be casting the part of the love interest so soon. I mean...I should have. Obviously. The storyline really kicks off in four episodes. And we'll need to foreshadow it.

I should have thought of that.

I've been too distracted. I've had too much going on. Ivy. Harrison. Honeysuckle Harbor. I got the pages written and sent off but I haven't really *thought* about it all.

Dammit.

Two, Gwenyth is the worst choice of anyone in the writer's room. But yeah, I can see Andrew giving it to her.

"I *know*! She will *ruin it*," Toby says. "You have to get back here. If you're *here*, you can take the lead in discussions and you'll make Gwenyth look pale in comparison, as always. But if you're not here and you're only emailing or doing it over video call, I'm afraid Andrew will be more impressed with her than he should be."

He's right.

Fuck. By now, Andrew should know that Gwenyth sucks. All of her characters lack depth. She mostly works on very, very side characters so the others cover up their shallowness and how boring they are, but she kisses up to Andrew more than anyone else and she's very pretty. Pretty people get a lot of grace in this world.

And Andrew is very busy. If Gwenyth acts confident enough, he just might give her this storyline.

No. I can't let that happen. This new character will directly impact *my* main character. She cannot be boring and one-dimensional.

I have to get back to L.A.

"Thanks for the heads up," I tell Toby. "I'll...see you soon."

"Oh, holy shit," he breathes out. "Thank the heavens and the hells and everything in between." He pauses, then says, the smile evident in his tone. "Also, I can't wait to see you and Ivy together. *God*, I've been *dying* to see the two of you finally admitting your feelings. You better plan a big dinner party for all of us. No! I'll plan the party. You just bring your gorgeous, sweet girlfriend and prepare for us to all tell her how long you've been pining over her."

I wish I could laugh. I wish I could roll my eyes and then grin, imagining this party. Because yes, Toby and a few others on the show figured out how I felt about Ivy pretty early on. But...

I'm not sure Ivy will be thrilled about going back to L.A. like this. I know this will feel sudden to her. It *is* sudden, even though we've both been planning to go back to California. Now, though, I feel unprepared. I know she will too.

The house sold faster than we expected. I'd really thought I could work remotely longer.

We'd thought we could get Harrison and Ford out of our systems.

But that is clearly not going to happen.

I'm not ready to leave South Carolina.

I'm not ready to leave Harrison.

I don't know if I ever will be.

"Sure. Yeah, I'll let you know when I have more specific plans," I tell Toby, trying to sound normal. "I've got to go right now, though. Thanks again for the call."

"Of course! Talk soon!"

We disconnect and I head for the boardwalk, because I can't even think about going back to Harrison's right now. If I see him, I might decide I don't care about *My Fellow Aliens* or the new character, or...any of it. My *career*, for fuck's sake. I might actually consider giving it all up for a rich and pretty playboy who hasn't committed to anything in his life.

That's not true, and you know it.

He has committed. To Ford, and their business, and this town and his family.

Harrison has roots. More so than I do, if I'm honest. He knows what it's like to be a part of a real community. I've had more long-term romantic relationships, maybe, but Harrison has people who *really* know him. People he can't let down. People who matter on other levels.

He gives money, sure, but he also gives time and energy. He's *here* for these people he loves. He might come off as laid back and fun-loving—and he is definitely both of those things—but watching him with everyone last night at the bonfire, it's clear these people are important to him. And vice versa.

Being someone important to Harrison Reed is actually a big deal. He doesn't take it lightly and being welcomed into his life means being a part of his *entire* life—his town and his family, blood and beyond.

No wonder he keeps things with romantic partners pretty superficial. It would take someone special to really be a part of everything in Harrison's life.

That realization makes my chest feel tight and I have to work to paste on a smile as I approach the table where Sam is sitting, the chess game already set up in front of him. He's chatting with the two men at the table next to his—Walt and Ed.

"'Morning," I greet as I slide into the chair opposite Sam. "Sorry, I'm late. Got a phone call."

"No worries," Sam says. "I've got nowhere to be. Which is glorious."

I grin despite my tangle of thoughts and emotions. "Aren't you the same guy who insists we play speed chess because you're old—your words—and don't have time for classic chess?"

Sam chuckles. "It's just a fact that I'll get more games in if we play speed chess."

I can't argue with that.

He hits the clock and makes his first move.

Ten minutes later, he sits back in his chair. "You're not even trying."

I look up from the board to meet his eyes. He beat me easily. I sigh and sit back as well. "You're right."

"I'm insulted," he says. "I've been bragging about how often I beat you, but if you're not even going to give it an effort, it's not as much fun."

"Sorry, Sam." I study the pawn. "I have a lot on my mind today."

"The phone call you got that made you late?" he guesses.

"That's part of it. But not the entire thing."

"Did Harrison do or say something stupid?"

I chuckle. I'd told the guys that I was here visiting Harrison. They'd known I was staying there. I chalked it up to a small town thing. They knew the next day that Harrison and I are 'dating'. None of them seemed fazed by it at all. In fact, they seemed to approve.

"No, Harrison is…great," I say.

Sam nods. "He is. That doesn't mean he doesn't do and say stupid things sometimes."

I outright laugh at that. "You know him pretty well?"

"Very well."

Honeysuckle Harbor is very small, and Harrison grew up here. I'll bet these guys have some great stories about him, as a matter of fact.

Now I want to hear them all.

"Harrison is making things complicated," I confess. "But only because he's great and I…like him…so much."

Ed snorts and Sam and Walt exchange eye rolls.

"What?"

"You're in love with him," Walt says. "You can say that here. We think it's great."

I like that. I blow out a breath. "Fine. I'm in love with him."

"So what's the problem?" Ed asks. He frowns. "Does he *not* love you?"

Sam sits forward. "I'll talk to him."

That amuses me. And warms me. These three men don't know me that well. They have to know Harrison better than they know me, regardless. But they seem truly offended by the idea that Harrison might not have feelings for me.

"You'll talk to Harrison for me?" I ask Sam. "And what? Demand he fall in love with me?"

Sam nods. "Damn right. Sometimes a boy needs advice from his grandfather. Nothing wrong with that."

I smile. Then frown. Then sit up straighter. Then lean in. I narrow my eyes at Sam. "Excuse me?"

"What?"

"His *grandfather*?"

Sam nods. "Yes, his grandfather. His parents do a pretty good job. God knows Ford is his voice of reason more often than not. But it's not as if I have *nothing* to contribute."

I stare at the man across the table from me. The nice old man I've been playing chess with. The nice old man I've been assuming is just…a nice old man. Who probably used to be a fisherman. Who just happens to know Harrison because it's a small town.

I'm an idiot.

"Sam?" I ask.

"Yes?"

"What's your last name?"

"Reed."

I run a hand over my face. "Your Harrison's grandfather?"

"One of them, yes."

"You were never a fisherman, were you?" I ask.

He chuckles and looks at Walt and Ed. "I've fished plenty."

"But…not for a living."

"Oh. No. I'm rich," he says nonchalantly. "I don't need to fish for a living."

Right. He's rich. He's Harrison's grandfather.

"How about you Walt?" I ask. "You rich too?"

I shouldn't be surprised when Walt nods, but I am.

"Yep. Ed too," Walt says. He holds out a hand. "Walter Ambrose. Ambrose Industries."

I take his hand. Jesus.

"And I'm Edward Parks," Ed says. "Parks Financial Services. I'm not as rich as these two, but I do okay."

I have no idea what to say to that, so I just look back at Sam.

He grins. "Samuel Reed. Reed Investments. And other things. That's what I started with though."

"Were you ever going to tell me that I was playing chess with my boyfriend's grandfather?" I ask.

"You would have figured it out eventually," he says, unapologetically. "At the wedding, if not before."

I groan. "Sam! I mean, *Mr. Reed*—"

He frowns now. "Don't you dare get all 'Mr. Reed' on me. We're friends. It's just Sam to you. I didn't know who you were when I invited you to sit down and we played those first few games. And I didn't tell you who I was because I didn't want you to treat me differently. If you start now, I'm going to be disappointed."

"But you're Harrison's grandfather," I protest.

"So what?"

"So you should have told me," I say, pretty sure that's true. "What if I'd complained about him to you?"

"I'm sure you would have had a good reason," he says. "From your point of view, anyway."

"But wouldn't giving me advice about my relationship with your grandson, without me even knowing who you are, been a conflict of interest or something?" I ask, feeling confused.

Sam scoffs at that. "I would have never given you advice about your relationship with Harrison. I've been in that kind of love with exactly one person in my life. I married her the second she said yes, and never let her go. But that's the only relationship I know anything about. Who am I to tell you what to do in yours?"

I study him. Then I look at Walt and Ed. Excuse me, *Walter and Edward*. But they simply shrug.

"So you don't give business advice either, since you've only ever had the one business?"

Sam laughs. "Oh, hell no. I give business advice all the time. I've done *lots* of business. I also give advice about chess, where to vacation, movies, books, and pizza. Because I've had a lot of all of those."

I nod. "Okay."

"But people aren't pizzas or movies. They're exceedingly complicated and ever-changing and the same one that makes you happier than you've ever been will also have the ability to rip your heart out, so...I'm just grateful to have mostly figured *one* out. I would never try to advise on another."

"That's actually..." I sigh. "Not that helpful right now."

Sam laughs.

"Especially because I'm in love with *two* people. And there are *three* other people in this relationship." I wait for their reactions.

They all just nod.

"Isn't this where one of you says 'love will find a way' or 'if it's meant to be, it will be'?" I ask.

Ed shakes his head and Sam just shrugs.

"Well, that's ridiculous," Walt says. "You have to work at things. Even chess and pizza are crap if you don't *try*. You're going to have to figure it out. You can't just leave it up to chance."

I sigh. Maybe I should have just gone back to Harrison's.

"But," Sam adds. "At least you have three other people to help you. In my experience, chess, vacations, books, movies, and pizza are *all* better when shared with people you care about. A great relationship and the problems that crop up are the same."

That makes sense. At least it *sounds* wise. Finally, something that's a little helpful.

I push my chair back. "Okay, gentlemen, I think I have somewhere I need to be."

"Let me know when you want to get pizza and tell me how smart I am," Sam calls after me as I head up the boardwalk.

I just grin.

I probably shouldn't be surprised to find that I really like Harrison's grandfather.

CHAPTER 32

Ford

"SO THIS MEANS YOU'RE STAYING?" I am staring at Ivy and Harrison, my heart thundering, telling myself not to overreact.

But they've just told me about her idea of turning the old building on the dunes into a wedding venue.

I love seeing them together. They have such a natural friendship. They get each other on a level they both need but don't totally get from Liam or me. A full acceptance of their impulsive, fun natures. It's amazing.

But I'll admit that when I walked into the kitchen to find them huddled at the breakfast bar over a notepad, talking and laughing, clearly colluding on some plan, I had a moment of 'oh shit, what are they getting us into?'.

The idea is amazing, though.

Especially if it means…

"Yes, it means I'm staying," Ivy says, her eyes sparkling. "And I know it's presumptuous. It doesn't have to mean anything changes between us. I'll find a place to live—"

"No, the fuck you won't," Harrison interjects. "You'll stay right here. If Ford thinks that's too fast, he can move back to his place."

Ivy gives him a dazzling smile, then turns back to me. "I promise I have no preconceived notions. This is something Harrison and I have come up with. You can be as involved, or not involved, as you want to be. But I do love this town. It feels like the fresh start that I need and I do want to stay. You and I can keep doing things just like we have been—"

I'm across the floor, around the counter, and have her off her stool and wrapped in my arms before she even finishes her sentence. I bury my face in her hair and take a huge breath.

"I don't want things to stay the same." I hug her tightly and feel her arms come around my neck. "I love you, Ivy. I'm so fucking glad you want to stay."

I hear a little sniff, and I set her on her feet, looking down at her. "Thank God," she says softly. "I'm in love with you, Ford. I know it's fast, and it's crazy and we probably need to slow things down a little, but I want to stay and keep seeing you and...we'll figure things out."

I cup her face. "I'm thrilled with this."

She looks relieved. "I'm so glad."

I look from her to Harrison. "And Liam is staying too, then, right?"

Ivy's smile dims slightly. "I haven't told him yet. All of this just happened. If the building didn't belong to Harrison, this would've been a slower process and I would've talked it over with him. But it's gone so quickly." She takes a breath. "Liam's always been *so* supportive of me and my career and anything I want to do. I know he'll be happy for me, but—" She glances over at Harrison. "I don't know what he's going to say about staying, honestly. I know he's loved our time here."

"But his job is in L.A.," I fill in. Liam's job is huge. It's not as if he can go into Charleston and start writing for a TV show there instead. And even if he could, it wouldn't be *his* show.

We hear the front door open and close.

"Looks like we're about to find out," Harrison says.

If I didn't know my friend as well as I do I would've missed the fact that he looks nervous.

Harrison Reed is very rarely nervous. If I didn't have any other proof, that would be enough to tell me that he is madly in love with Liam.

"Oh, good, you're all here," Liam says, coming into the kitchen. "I have some news."

"Seems like it's the day for it," Harrison says.

Liam focuses on Ivy, still standing in my arms. "I have to go back to L.A. Tonight."

I feel her stiffen. So I guess Liam isn't going to work up to his news.

Ivy pulls away from me, turning to face Liam. "What? Tonight? Why?"

"The show. They're meeting about the new storyline." Liam looks at me. "They love the new stuff."

I smile. I knew they would. That makes me feel strangely proud to think I had a little part in encouraging him in this direction. "That's awesome."

He nods. "It is. But they want to start casting and working on the bigger storyline and everything." He focuses on Ivy again. "I have to go back if I want to lead this. Toby says there's a very strong possibility the character goes to Gwenyth if I don't."

Ivy wrinkles her nose. "Gwenyth is terrible."

"Exactly," Liam agrees.

Ivy sighs. "Well, of course you have to go. This is great. I'm so glad they like your new stuff."

He looks at each of us, his gaze lingering on Harrison. Harrison is still seated at the breakfast bar. His expression is hard to read.

Liam finally says to Ivy. "I know you'll probably want to stay for a few more days. This is really sudden. I'm sure you're not ready to say goodbye. You should stay, finish things up with the house and everything. You can come home next week. Or…whenever."

The words hang in the air, and I'm not sure any of us are breathing.

Ivy needs to be the one to tell him she wants to stay, of course. She needs to tell him about the wedding venue. But I have to bite my tongue not to protest the idea of her leaving.

As it is, the idea of Liam leaving is knotting my stomach. I'll miss him. And it's going to be very painful for the two most important people in my life.

"And how about Ford and me?" Harrison says, before anyone else speaks. "Ivy will come after the house is taken care of and Ford and I will come after we say goodbye to our entire town? Our families? Sell our restaurant and houses?"

Liam turns to him, frowning. "What? Of course not. I don't expect you to move to L.A."

"But you do expect Ivy to move to L.A.," Harrison says.

"Well…yes. Not move. Come back to L.A."

"And why's that?" Harrison asks.

"Because…" Liam sighs, realizing he's walking into a trap.

"Because you're in love with her. Because you want to be with her long term. You want to make a commitment to her and have a *relationship* with her," Harrison fills in. "Right?"

Liam shoves a hand through his hair. "Harrison…"

"So this is it, then. We're done. And Ivy and Ford are done? Just because *you* need to go back to L.A." Harrison is pissed.

Harrison almost never loses his temper. *Almost* never. He has a very long fuse. He lets things roll off. He chooses his battles and finds most not worth the effort.

But from the very beginning, Liam Tate has been getting under Harrison's skin, unlike anyone else ever has.

"We don't have to be done," Liam says. It's clear he's *trying* to hold on to his temper. "We will come back and visit. We love it here. And you guys can come to L.A. Whenever you want. You have a plane, for fuck's sake. Come every weekend if you want to."

"So friends with benefits? Long distance?" Harrison stands from his stool. "I'm not fucking doing that."

"Oh, this isn't worth a little bit of effort?" Liam asks, finally losing his grip and raising his voice. "You can't get on your fucking *private plane* and drink champagne for a few hours to come out and see us?"

Jesus. They're in love with one another, they both know it, but they're hurt and they're going to say something stupid any second now.

Okay, something *stupider*.

I open my mouth to intervene, but Ivy speaks first.

"Hey!" She's stepped in front of Liam and is looking at Harrison. "Stop being such a jerk. You're upsetting *my boyfriend,* too. When you two fight, it affects me too. That's what we all need to realize here. We're in this together and the stupid shit the two of you say to one another and the 'decisions' you make when you're hurt and yelling at one another, affects two other people here."

Harrison shakes his head. "I don't think we need to worry about that, sweetheart. He's just yours. Not mine."

"Harrison," I say, low and firm, trying to be comforting but also trying to keep my friend from fucking this all up. "Take it easy."

Liam pulls in a long breath. "I have to get on a plane in Charleston in an hour and a half. I need to go."

I shake my head. "No. We'll fly you to L.A. tonight. Cancel your flight. Let's take time to talk this out. Ivy's right. This affects all of us."

"I don't know what there is to talk about," Liam says, pulling his eyes from Harrison and focusing on me. "If Harrison doesn't want to keep doing this, then that's it. I'm not going to make him feel bad about it. He has a right to say no to long distance."

"Well, *I'm* going to make him feel bad about it," I snap, looking at Harrison. "He's upsetting *my girlfriend.*"

There are tears tracking down Ivy's cheeks now, and I want to pull her up against my chest. But the truth is, she's not just mine to protect and comfort. These men have to want to protect and comfort her, too. They need to understand how this works.

We're all in this.

Or we're not.

And, we can't *only* protect and comfort her. We need to talk things out and yes, say the things that will sometimes hurt. That's the only way we can make this work long term.

"*I'm* not hurting Ivy," Harrison protests. "It's her other boyfriend who's leaving."

"For fuck's sake!" Liam shouts. "I'm not going out there to surf! It's my fucking job!"

"I'm just saying, I'm probably her favorite right now," Harrison says. "I'm the one giving her the building for her dream business."

Ivy gasps. Then she says, "You're not *giving* it to me."

"What dream business?" Liam asks.

"Jesus Christ, Harrison," I mutter. He, of course, did that on purpose. He wanted to push Ivy into telling Liam about the wedding venue. I love my best friend but he's an idiot sometimes, and he fights dirty. We're going to have to work on that.

"What dream business?" Liam insists.

Ivy turns to him. "I wasn't going to tell you like this. I wanted to show it to you. Tell you all about the ideas I have."

"What. Dream. Business," Liam repeats through gritted teeth.

"I want to open a wedding venue here. Right down on the beach. There's this gorgeous building—"

"That I own and am selling to her for basically nothing," Harrison says.

Ivy rounds on him. "Just shut up, Harrison!" she yells. "You are going to have to learn how to fight *productively* with the four of us because *this* is not going to work!"

Exactly. God, I love her.

Harrison doesn't apologize, but he puts his hands up.

"You're…staying," Liam finally says, his voice rough.

Ivy looks at him again, and she immediately looks like she's going to cry. But she nods. "Yes," she says quietly. "I love it here. And this business idea feels *right*."

"And Ford and Harrison?" Liam asks. "They're part of you staying?"

She nods. "Yes." She steps toward him. "I just don't think there's anything for me in L.A. anymore."

Liam just stands there, looking like she slapped him.

"Ivy," I say quietly.

It takes a second, but she realizes how that sounded. She reaches for Liam. "Liam, I didn't mean…" But she trails off when he pulls away from her.

"Wow, I see what you mean," Harrison says to her. "Now I'm kind of pissed at *you* for hurting him like that. That's not cool."

"Jesus, shut up, Harrison," I mutter.

"I'm just saying that fighting is bonkers with four of us," he says. "I'm annoyed with all of you, but I don't want any of you hurting the others."

Yeah, I get it.

"Fuck, Liam," Harrison says, coming around the counter. "Just quit your job. You don't need it. Stay here with us. We need to be together. I'll give you double your current salary."

And just when I thought Harrison couldn't make it worse. I sigh.

Liam straightens. "For what?" he asks, his voice ominously quiet.

"What do you mean?" Harrison asks.

"What would you give me double my current salary for? What would I do?"

Harrison shrugs. "Nothing. Anything. Whatever you want."

My friend means well. He really does. He loves Liam and wants to make all of his problems go away. That's all this is. But… Harrison's kind of an idiot. An idiot who doesn't have an artistic creative side. An idiot who has never had to worry about money for longer than it takes him to remember where he put his platinum card. An idiot who truly thinks that money can take care of any problem. Because it always has for him.

Until now.

"What I want," Liam says carefully. "Is to be a lead writer on *My Fellow Aliens*!" His voice rises as he continues. "To get the show renewed! To win Best Writer!"

"What? Are you fucking kidding me? I love you!" Harrison shouts back at him. "And you're worried about money and awards? That's more important to you? Seriously?"

Ivy gasps. "Harrison! It's not just money and awards to him. You know him better than that! This is his passion! He's proud of it and *so fucking good* at it. That show is huge, and it's what it is, in large part, because of Liam. They *need* him and he loves it. Just because you don't have any true *passion* for anything, doesn't mean you can demean what Liam does!"

"Whoa," Liam says, frowning at Ivy. "I wouldn't say Harrison doesn't have *any* passion for anything. He loves his family and this town and the people who are important to him so much. He's passionate about them being happy and provided for and supported. That's what he does every single minute of every day. It's why he offered me money."

Ivy stares at Liam. "Are you *defending* him to me while I'm defending you *to him*?"

Liam looks from her to Harrison, then back to her. "Maybe. Yes. I guess. I don't like when you two fight."

This is what the rest of my life looks like, I realize as I watch them argue and change sides and yell at and then protect one another.

These three are going to drive me to an early grave.

I'm here for it all.

I step forward and use my 'dad voice'. I didn't even know I had one of those, but that is definitely what comes out when I say, "Okay, *enough*."

They all turn to look at me with wide eyes.

"Ivy, they're..."

"Always going to be like this," she finishes for me.

I nod.

"I know," she says with a sigh.

"Liam," I say. "You don't have to worry about Ivy and Harrison. Ivy gets him. She's…"

"His goofy soulmate," Liam says, sounding resigned. "I know."

Yeah. She is.

"And Harrison," I say, turning to my friend. "You *know* Liam isn't going back for just a paycheck, so stop being a jackass. And, for the love of God, stop trying to throw money at everything. You don't have to do that."

"That's what I fucking do!" Harrison exclaims. "All I have to offer any of you is money!"

"That's not true!" Ivy protests.

"Come on, Harrison," Liam says at the same time.

"Fine, orgasms and money," Harrison says. "But I have *so much money* and nothing to do with it. I *want* to throw money at the things they need. I want to make your lives easier. I want to have more time with you. I want to feel like I'm *helping you*. Like I did by giving Ivy the building for her new business. Like I did when I bought her house."

We all stop and stare at him. Then look at one another. Then back to him.

"Wait, you bought Ivy's house? The one Brad left her?" I ask.

Harrison sighs. "Yes. I bought the house so we could just be done with it. So she didn't have to worry, and we didn't have to fuck around with showings and we could all just relax. And I…" He shoves a hand through his hair and leans back against the counter. "I planned to drag out the closing and everything so that they'd have to stay in town longer."

I start shaking my head. "Harrison, you *have* to understand that you have more to offer than that. We love *you*. Not the stuff you have or can buy us. We don't want to be in a relationship with you because of your money."

"Easy for you to say," he tells me.

"It's easy for *me* to say too," Liam tells him firmly.

"Really? Because you're leaving," Harrison says with a scowl, pushing off the counter. "And Ivy's only in this relationship with me because I was a tag-along with you and Ford. And Ford's stuck with me because our parents are friends."

Ivy gasps. Liam groans. I want to roll my eyes, but don't.

Harrison looks at Liam. "I hope L.A. is everything you want it to be."

Liam shakes his head. "No, you don't."

Harrison nods. "You're right. I hope it sucks." Then he turns and stomps out of the room.

There's a *long* moment of silence. Then Ivy says, "Wow, and I thought reality TV people were dramatic."

"Better get used to that," I say. "Forever is a long time. And even though he's going to grow up a little yet, drama is always going to be a part of Harrison."

She looks a little sad when I look at her. I'm suddenly worried that our forever is actually slipping away.

But that can't be. "Ivy—" I start.

"Liam—" Ivy starts at the same time.

"I have to get to the airport." Liam glances down the hallway where Harrison disappeared. "I think I'm going to have you just send my stuff. There's not much."

Ivy nods.

He steps toward her. She steps toward him. He pulls her into his arms. She lets out a sob that tears at my heart.

He kisses the top of her head, then meets my eyes. "Take care of them."

I nod.

Then he lets go of her, turns, and walks out of the kitchen. Without a look back.

I get it. Looking back makes it all hurt even more.

When we hear the front door shut, Ivy turns to me. "What the *hell* just happened?"

"Our guys just tried to break up," I tell her, pulling her close and folding her into a hug.

She clings to me tightly. "Tried to?"

"Yeah. It's not going to stick."

"You promise?"

"Yeah. We'll fix it."

"We have to." She tips her head up to look at me. "I really love you, Ford. I want to be with you. But I think it needs to be the four of us."

"I know. It does."

She sighs with relief.

"So do you want to go to L.A. to talk to Liam and I'll talk to Harrison?" I ask. "Or the other way around? Because honestly? I kind of want to strangle my best friend at the moment."

"Same." She gives a soft laugh. "Want to flip a coin?"

I can't believe it, but I feel myself smile. "Or rock, paper, scissors?"

We start to pull apart, but my phone rings just then.

Then Ivy's starts to ring.

I pull mine from my pocket. She grabs hers from the counter.

We look from our phones to each other.

"It's the FBI," she says.

"Me too."

Well, fuck. Looks like fixing our relationship is going to have to wait.

Thanks a lot, Brad.

CHAPTER 33

Liam

"WHEN SHOULD I plan that dinner party?" Toby asks, flinging his arm around me as we leave the writer's room.

I have a headache. Gwenyth was fucking annoying today. She laughed insanely at every one of Andrew's suggestions and said, "Brilliant!" to him at least four times. She even used a British accent when she's from Reseda.

She's a suck up. A pretty, manipulative, chronic cliche abusing suck up.

Who is just trying to get ahead in the industry, like we all are, and who has no idea that I'm a man on the edge right now. Every fiber of my fucking being feels tense, agitated, and lonely as hell.

Harrison offered to pay me a salary to stay in South Carolina. I know he had good intention, but for fuck's sake, does he even hear himself sometimes? I don't want to give up my career and I don't want to be *paid* to be his boyfriend.

I want to be his boyfriend because I'm in love with him and I want him to understand me. It shocked me he didn't get that.

I'm also a little stunned that Ivy has no immediate plans to return to California.

She said there was nothing for her here and whether she meant it to sound the way it did or not, that shit hurt.

What also hurts is that not one of the three of them has reached out to me since I got on that airplane and came home.

Home.

It doesn't have quite the same feeling now that my three favorite people are on the other side of the country.

Yes, three.

I don't know when or how it happened, but in a mere ten days me, Ivy, Harrison, and Ford became a foursome. A fully functioning, love all around poly unit.

I've always loved Ivy. For a year, I've been fighting the truth that I'm in love with Harrison too.

Then seeing how Ford takes care of Ivy and enjoying his incredibly loyal and deep friendship with Harrison and finding a connection with him myself, well, getting them out of my system was never going to happen.

But here I am and they're…there.

I sigh and rub my temples. "Put a pin in the dinner party," I tell Toby, heading for the front door. I need fresh air and a coffee. "Ivy is still in Honeysuckle Harbor."

"What's Honeysuckle Harbor, a lingerie shop? Sex club? Your girl getting a little sexed up for you? I love a good role play session." Toby drops his arm and adjusts his bow tie.

He's the only one who wears a suit daily. Given our many meetings, brainstorming, and bantering, most of the six writers on the show dress like Ross from Friends. Bulky sweaters, loose pants, and sneakers. Toby always looks like he's a salesman on the floor at Saks.

I'm actually wearing old gray joggers and a Star Wars T-shirt that has seen better days. Which was a poor choice because it just reminds me of Harrison and Ford back in South Carolina.

And Ivy.

God, we left things on a fucking terrible note.

We were all frustrated and not on the same page. At all.

"It's neither. It's a town in South Carolina. It's where Brad bought the house for Ivy."

And Harrison and Ford are from and live.

And now presumably Ivy, since she wants to launch a new business there.

I push the front door open harder than I need to and warm air hits me in the face. At least today is overcast. The gloom suits my mood.

"Why on earth is she still there?" Toby makes a face. "It sounds so *gauche*."

And he sounds like my grandmother, but I don't bother to point that out.

"It's actually a very cool place. The people there aren't fake."

"Hmm." He doesn't sound convinced.

I don't really want to have this conversation. "Are you parked down here?" I ask him as he walks down the sidewalk next to me. I'd really prefer to be alone right now.

"No, I'm going to the coffee shop with you. I heard you tell Andrew that's where you were going and I need a double espresso, pronto."

"I'm actually going straight home," I say, instantly changing my mind. I'm not up for either shallow banter or a work bitch session with Toby. "That's what I meant. I got a new coffee maker from Sur La Table."

"The one that can do lattes and cappuccinos and espressos?" Toby stops walking and gives me a steely glare. "Did you get a raise? I'll kill that bitch Andrew."

"No. I'm just a good…saver."

"Well, you definitely don't spend your paychecks on your clothes. See you tomorrow." He gives me a friendly wave that belies his insult and crosses the street.

"Damn it," I mutter. I really did want that coffee and I don't have a fancy as fuck coffee maker at home. I have a twenty-five dollar one from Target.

I miss the coffee maker at Harrison's. It did a perfect brew. I miss the coffee shop in Honeysuckle Harbor, which did not do a perfect brew, but came with atmosphere galore and the excellent company of Sam, Ed, and Walt.

Checking my phone with one hand, I rub my forehead with the other.

No texts. Nothing.

I've called Ivy twice and I've texted Harrison four—okay, five —times. When neither answered, I resorted to texting Ford and even he hasn't responded to me, which seems out of character.

Did something happen?

Is there a hurricane in South Carolina that I haven't heard about? They get those fuckers all the time. What if they're hunkered down with no power, or worse, Harrison's beach house has been sucked into the ocean?

Or what if they're having a great time without me? Laughing, having sex, falling deeper in love? What if it's all *better* without me?

Maybe it's easier with me gone, which is great for them, a virtual hell for me.

I didn't think this through.

A woman walks past me with her little dog. I'm not sure of the breed but it starts barking riotously at me and trying to nip my ankle. I jump back. "Whoa! Back off, Killer."

The brunette gives me a glare and bends down to scoop her dog up, like I'm going to kick it or something.

"I wasn't—

"Go fuck yourself," she says in a haughty tone, nestling her still barking dog against her yoga crop top. Her yoga mat slides down her shoulder.

"Real Zen," I tell her.

"Prick."

Shaking my head, I walk toward my car, knowing full well it's going to take me thirty minutes to drive the three miles to my apartment. I tried to walk to work a few times to avoid the traffic but then Gwenyth made a comment that I was very sweaty and she couldn't concentrate because of it, so the next day I got back in my car and drove to work. After that, I just kind of forgot walking was an option.

That's what happens when you spend your whole life in the same city.

You kind of forget there are other options.

I stop dead in my tracks.

Fuck this.

Pulling my phone out, I scroll until I find Chess Sam.

He gave me his number before I knew he was Harrison's grandfather. I shoot off a text.

> Hey, is everything okay there? No hurricanes or other disasters?

Sam doesn't text me back until I'm walking into my apartment. He's not as attached to his phone as millennials, as he's told me three times.

> No hurricanes. But the FBI is crawling all over town.

I stop and stare at my phone. I know there was an agent trying to get a hold of Ivy, but I guess I figured once she said she didn't know where Brad is, they'd back off.

They're *in* Honeysuckle Harbor? Crawling all over town? That's not good. That definitely involves Ivy. And probably Ford and Harrison. They're Brad's friends. They were business partners in the restaurant in L.A. when it first opened. What the hell has Brad gotten into?

> The FBI? Because of Brad?

I shove the door open to my apartment and head straight to my bedroom to pack an overnight bag.

Yes, sir. They were at his parents, then Ivy's house, now Harrison's. Took all the kids' phones, fyi, in case you've been trying to get a hold of them. Heavy-handed bullshit. Got some lawyers working on it.

Yeah. I need to get back there. I don't care what we said or didn't say in Harrison's kitchen. This is big. They need me. Or, I need to be there, at least. I type quickly.

I'm booking a flight now.

Nah, don't worry about it. Everything is under control here.

What is with these laid-back millionaires? God. I don't care if it's under control or not. Obviously, there's not much I can really *do*, but…I have to go back to South Carolina.

I need to be with the people I love.

CHAPTER 34

Ivy

IT WOULD REALLY SUCK to go through this alone.

That thought keeps going through my head on repeat.

I give a shudder because even being casually interviewed by FBI agents, knowing I had done nothing wrong, it was still a little unnerving.

But I had Harrison and Ford standing by my side through this whole debacle, and I'm so grateful for that. They've been reassuring me, talking to a lawyer, and holding me at night.

On top of the way Liam left, I need their arms around me even more.

As we sit in Raw, the interviews done, and the searches concluded, I feel better that none of Brad's mess is going to land on me, but I'm agitated that I don't have my phone. They confiscated it to do further electronic analysis to make sure I wasn't aware of Brad's illegal activities.

Because of that, I don't even know if Liam made it back to L.A. or if he's trying to reach out to me or Harrison or not.

I'm sure he is. Even though we all got frustrated and angry and Liam left Honeysuckle Harbor upset, it wouldn't be like him to not be in touch.

Without my phone, though, I have no idea.

It's making me incredibly anxious.

Harrison asked his father to text Liam for us to let him know what was going on, and yet we haven't heard anything, so all we can assume is that he's still upset with us.

"You need to eat something," Ford urges me, as I sit at the bar with his father on one side of me and Harrison's father on the other.

"Listen to my son," Ford's dad, Greg, says. "You look pale."

"I'm not sure I can eat."

"I don't blame you. It's not every day you have the FBI on your ass," Bill comments, gesturing to the two agents who are still in Raw, tucking into a seafood platter while they pour over documents.

Harrison, who is on the other side of the bar, serving himself a snifter of bourbon, eyes his father. "Helpful, Dad, thanks. Why are you here again?"

"We just wanted to make sure you kids are okay and that you're not being bullied without benefit of legal counsel. You've got a lawyer right here, you know." He gestures to Ford's father.

"We are very much aware of that." Harrison sips his bourbon and sets it down. "You know we've run everything past him, and we did reach out to the lawyer we've used for the restaurant since Greg is retired."

Ford rubs my back. "I'm going to go get you some soup. You need to eat."

"Okay, thanks." I muster up a smile for Ford. "I appreciate you taking care of me."

"Always," he says simply, leaning in to give me a kiss.

When he heads into the kitchen, Harrison works a martini shaker. "When I see Brad, I'm going to knock him out cold. This is all bullshit. We haven't been able to order any supplies without our computers and Chef has been scrambling to come up with creative dishes based on what food we have in stock."

"You could have just closed for a few days."

Penelope Fraser, who is in her eighties and eats lunch at the bar every single day, pipes in from her usual stool three down from me. "I'd starve without Raw," she proclaims dramatically. "Thank you for not closing."

Harrison pours her a martini and hands it to her with a flourish. "I'd never let that happen to you, Penelope. Over my cold dead body."

What I think is incredible is that if someone has dined in Raw in the last few days and didn't have cash to pay for their meal, Harrison has just been writing it down in a notebook and telling them, "we'll settle up later."

He's been paying the servers tips out of his own pocket.

When I suggested he might never get some of those tabs settled, he and Ford both laughed.

"People here aren't like that," Ford had assured me. "They'll all pay."

"That's a small town for you," Harrison had shrugged. "No one wants to screw over their neighbors."

It's yet another reason to love living here.

Penelope giggles at Harrison's comment now. "You're a sweetheart, Harrison. You always have been. Come here."

He leans in obediently and she pats his cheek. "Don't let this nonsense get you down. I can tell you're fretting."

"I'm fine," he says in protest. "I can handle the Feds. I'm just worried about Ivy."

And Liam.

That is what really has pinched his mouth and given him shadows under his eyes. He told me and Ford he heartily regrets the way he handled Liam's decision to go back to L.A. Without his phone to reach out, he's been tossing and turning in the middle of the night. He thinks he's hiding it, but we know him.

When I suggested he borrow a phone and call him, he'd said that if Liam wanted to talk to us, he would have responded to his dad.

"Well, this business seems to be wrapping up. They told the boys they would have their phones and Raw's computers back by tonight." Greg lifts an oyster. "Since they didn't find any connection between them and Brad."

"I've never been so grateful to have severed business ties with someone," Harrison says, pouring the remaining liquid from the shaker into another glass. He adds an olive and pushes it in front of me. "Here you go, sweetheart. I'm sure you could use this."

"I do need this." I take a tiny sip, letting the vodka slide down my throat and warm my insides. "And I'm glad Brad and I never shared bank accounts. Though I'd like to think if we had, I would have noticed huge deposits of money and called him out on it. But maybe not."

Because honestly, I'm not sure I would have. Brad always had money, and he did paid appearances and made tons of money from the show and the restaurant. If money had appeared in our personal account, I'm not sure I would have questioned its origin.

"Five million is a bit hard to explain away," Bill says.

Even though that number is mind-boggling to me, I still shrug. "Brad is a good liar."

Hell, he convinced me he loved me.

But the depth of his deception is a little overwhelming. He was using the restaurant for an elaborate money laundering and Ponzi scheme. He was taking investor money and using it for personal expenses, as well as creating fake businesses and invoicing the restaurant for services that were never rendered, like electrical work and a new commercial kitchen installation.

It was bold and reckless and I sat there as the agents explained some of it to me, words like "federal mail fraud" and "racketeering" being thrown around.

"Brad is a crook," Greg says. "I feel terrible for the Richardsons. They invested in him opening that restaurant."

That makes me reach for my martini glass. "Oh, no! Do you know how much?"

"I think about a hundred grand."

I chew my bottom lip as Ford emerges from the kitchen. "I'm going to pay them back then with the money from the house sale.

I can't just keep that money and have them going into retirement out that much cash."

"It's not your responsibility but that is definitely the honorable thing to do, Ivy," Bill says, nodding in approval. "Good for you."

Harrison is frowning.

"What?" I ask him.

"Well…that's kind of like me paying the Richardsons back since I bought your house and I feel guilty I didn't already think of that."

It makes my heart twinge. Harrison is still caught up in thinking all he brings to the table is money. "We've had a lot going on. Obviously. You can't think of everything."

Harrison looks slightly sheepish. "I *should* think of everything."

Everyone eyes him. "Is there something else you want to say?" I coax.

"You're going to make me say it?"

"Yes."

Harrison sighs as Ford emerges from the kitchen and moves in beside Harrison. He puts a bowl of bisque in front of me.

"I should have handled Liam needing to go back to work better. I was an asshole."

It's hard for him to admit that, and I appreciate it. I squeeze his hand.

"It wasn't any of our finest moments," Ford says. "But yes, you were an asshole."

Harrison's nose wrinkles, and he lifts his bourbon to his mouth. "I realize that now. I'm sorry. I really am. I just…"

"Love them," Bill fills in the blanks.

"Yes. I love you, and I love Liam. I want you to stay here."

I pick up my spoon. "We all need to work on our communication. This is new. But we can do this, right?" I ask, earnestly. I need to hear he's committed to making this work.

He nods and puts his hand over mine, massaging my fingers.

"Yes. One hundred percent. I've learned my lesson. I've already lost Liam. I can't lose you too, Ivy."

"Why do you think you've lost Liam?" Bill asks. "Didn't he just go back for his job?"

"I don't know. He went back to California really upset with me."

There is a pit in my stomach. "And me. I shouldn't have said there was nothing in California for me. I hurt him."

"So just talk to him," Bill says, like this is the most obvious thing in the world. "I'm sure y'all can work it out."

"Dad, he never answered you when you texted him that we don't have our phones. I think that's a pretty clear message that he's still not ready to talk."

"That shouldn't stop you," Ford's father says.

I look at Ford. In a way, this is what Ford originally wanted—me with him and not Liam.

Yes, he's been sympathetic to my upset, but maybe he's secretly happy it's working out like this.

But to my delight, he's nodding firmly. "Dad is right. This isn't over until we've all talked through our relationship. Liam belongs with us and we need to try to make this work. For all of us."

My heart squeezes. "Thank you," I tell him. "I love you."

Ford smiles. "I love you too." Then he turns to Bill. "Text him again. Tell him we urgently need to talk to him."

Bill obediently pulls out his phone and his reading glasses. He scrolls through his phone, then frowns. "Oh, shit. Look, I typed up the message but then I forgot to hit send."

"*What?*" Harrison roars, reaching over the bar top and yanking his father's phone out of his hand. "Dad! What the fuck?"

"Sorry, son. Sometimes I forget to do that." Bill makes a face like he forgot to get milk at the store, not that he forgot to tell our boyfriend we desperately miss him and want to talk to him but we've had all our electronics confiscated by the FBI.

"Oh, my god!" Harrison runs his hand through his hair and sets the phone down on the bar. He hits send on the text. "William must think I'm a complete insensitive bastard. Even more than he already did." He turns and puts his palms on the back counter, bending over like he's trying to gather his thoughts.

I'm reaching for the phone to just call Liam when a laugh rings out at the table where the agents are seated. I'm momentarily distracted by the fact that Ford's sister, Frannie, is doing a hair flip as she puts down yet another dessert plate in front of the muscular agent.

"That agent has had at least four desserts," Penelope comments. "What a hungry fella."

"I don't think he loves just the pastries," Bill comments. "He's been eyeing Frannie and vice versa all day."

"What?" Ford exclaims, his eyes widening as he studies the interaction.

"That's consorting with the enemy."

The new voice coming from behind us makes me jump a little. I turn. "Oh good grief, Sam, you scared me."

Harrison's grandfather must be the oldest ninja in existence, because I had no idea he had come into Raw.

"Having the Feds on your ass would make anyone jumpy," he says, sounding almost exactly like his son, Bill. Or maybe Bill sounds like him.

At any rate, it only serves to make Harrison even more agitated. "Why is everyone being so fucking casual?" he demands. "This is a disaster!" Then he turns to Penelope. "Sorry for the language, ma'am."

His apology for using a word he uses two dozen times a day is adorable to me.

"No offense, Harrison. Love brings out strong emotions."

"Love?" Sam asks. "I thought we were talking about Brad Richardson being a crook."

"We were but we're also discussing how these kids need to work out their poly relationship," Greg says. "What with Liam decamping to California and all. They're not going to be happy until they're all together."

Harrison has his father's phone to his ear. "Liam isn't picking up."

My heart sinks. What is going on with Liam?

The pastry loving and flirting-with-Frannie FBI agent has stood up and walks over to us. He sets two phones down on the bar. "Harrison and Ford, your phones have been released."

"Thank God." Harrison grabs his and does facial recognition to unlock it. "I'm calling Liam."

"And my phone?" I ask. I have the definite feeling I'm not getting mine back.

"I'm sorry, miss. Yours has been sent to the field office for further analysis. But you're not under suspicion. We just need to see if there is anything useful to our investigation. And you're sure you don't have any idea where Brad might have gone?"

I shake my head. They've already asked me this ten times. "I honestly have no idea. Brad obviously didn't come here and I have no idea where he might go." My initial thought was Mexico but that's only because it seems the easiest. I have no basis for thinking that, so I've kept that to myself. I don't want another round of probing questions I don't have answers for.

"Thank you all for your help and for lunch." The agent gives us a wave. "We'll be in touch."

"What am I going to do without a phone?" I ask to no one in particular. I feel sick to my stomach about Liam.

"I already ordered a new one," Ford says. "It should be here any minute. I got one hour delivery."

"His phone is going straight to voicemail," Harrison announces.

Sam is fiddling with his own phone. "Oh, that's because he's in the air. He has a layover in Denver."

"What?" I gape at him. "Why is he going to Denver?"

"I talked to him yesterday. Told him what was going on. He tried to get a flight last night but they were all booked. He's on a flight now to Denver, then he has a five-hour layover, then he lands in Charleston at…" Sam peers at his phone. "Nine-oh-seven tonight."

Liam is flying back to Honeysuckle Harbor.

Hope surges through me.

"That's great! Oh my god, I'm so relieved."

"Why didn't you tell me that last night?" Harrison asks his grandfather.

"I didn't want to interfere in your love life."

Harrison snorts. "Ivy, grab your purse."

"What? Why?"

A delivery man walks into the restaurant. "Ivy Scott?"

"That's me." I sign for a package. My new phone.

When I look up to see Ford and Harrison are exchanging a look.

"You in?" Harrison asks him.

Ford nods. "All the way."

"On what?" I can't keep up with what's happening.

"We're flying to Denver," Harrison says, breaking out in a grin. "To get our William. You in?"

"Fuck yes," I exclaim, leaping off of my stool. "Sorry, Penelope."

Penelope looks up from her drained martini. "Hmm?"

The dads and Harrison's grandfather all grin at us. "Go get him!" Bill shouts, giving a fist pump in the air.

"Grandpa, we'll talk about why you didn't tell us sooner a bit later. Right now, we have a plane to get on." Harrison launches himself over the bartop, spinning his legs and dropping to the floor.

"It would have taken an extra two seconds to walk around, son," Bill says.

"That's too much time to wait to see the love of my life," Harrison declares.

Ford nods. "I agree." He follows suit over the bartop. Then he glances at his own ass. "Oh, shit, I ripped my pants."

I laugh in delight and lock arms with two of my three guys. "Let's go get our man."

CHAPTER 35

Liam

"ATTENTION PASSENGERS on flight 362 to Charleston."

I tense. I've already had one gate change and my flight has been delayed by thirty minutes.

I've been deep breathing and telling myself that thirty minutes is no big deal.

I booked this flight last minute so the middle seat in row thirty two wasn't awesome, but it was no big deal either.

Or so I told myself.

The woman in the aisle seat was a very nervous flyer and her leg closest to mine bounced the entire flight while she ate from her family sized bag of Ruffles, rustling the bag loudly, the strong scent of cheddar and sour cream surrounding me for two hours and twenty-five minutes. But I squeezed my eyes shut and told myself it was no big deal.

I packed in such a rush I forgot my noise-canceling headphones, so I got to listen to the two guys behind me rehash their entire business meeting and what an asshole Larry is and how hot his VP, Hayley, is. But it was no big deal. I said it repeatedly. It had to be true.

"Due to some mechanical issues, we are going to need to change planes. This is going to take us a little time. The flight is now scheduled to depart at six forty-two. If you choose to leave the gate area, please…"

I tune out the rest of the announcement.

Because that departure time is three fucking hours from now.

I already had a three-hour layover here. Now it's going to be more than six.

This will put me into Charleston after nine p.m.

My "it's no big deal" mantra is *not* going to work much longer.

I need to be in Honeysuckle Harbor.

Now.

I never should have left South Carolina in the first place.

What the fuck was I thinking? I finally fell in love, times *two*, with two people who also love each other, who want to make a life in an awesome little town that has embraced me, made me feel a part of everything, where I've been surrounded by family I can imagine sharing everything with from daily chess matches to town-wide Christmas extravaganzas.

I want to sit at the bar at Raw and watch Harrison charming every person who steps inside. I want to be there when Ivy opens her wedding venue. I want to find a show that Ford and I can watch together and geek out over. I want to joke around and tease with them all. I want to fight with them all. And defend them all. I want to have the hottest, dirtiest, most fun sex of my life with them all. I want to sleep late and have lazy brunches that get crashed by their parents.

Fuck my job. Fuck the TV show.

I'll…write a novel. A sci-fi novel that will hit all the best-seller charts and make me a seven-figure salary of my own.

Or, fuck it, I'll write a sci-fi novel that only ten people will read, but I'll love it, Ford will love it, and I'll let my hot millionaire boyfriend pay my way through life.

I honestly don't care. As long as I'm with Harrison, Ivy, and Ford.

"Are you okay?"

I open my eyes—I didn't realize I'd squeezed them shut, imagining Honeysuckle Harbor and my life with my three loves—and relax my death grip on the arms of the chair I'm sitting in.

A little boy is staring at me. He's probably about eight. He's holding a cinnamon roll from the shop across from our gate with both hands. He's also wearing a T-shirt with an alien on the front. It's not from my show, but it still feels like a sign. Because the alien has a phone to his head (he doesn't really have ears) and is saying, "No intelligent life detected here."

An alien, on a phone, calling me stupid.

Yep. That's a sign.

"Yeah," I tell him. "Pretty much."

"You look like you have a bad headache," he informs me.

Well, that's insightful. "I do," I admit. "But I'll be okay."

"My dad says airports always give him a fucking headache," the boy tells me.

I lift a brow, but his dad isn't wrong. I'd guess ninety percent of the people inside this building have a headache right now.

"Want my cinnamon roll?" the kid asks.

Kind of. But I can't take his cinnamon roll. "Nah, but thanks."

He shrugs. "K, but they're pretty good."

"Maybe I'll go get one in a bit."

He seems to believe I'm going to make it at that point. "K, bye." He heads toward the row of chairs that look out over the runways, climbing up between a man and a woman.

I sigh, then pull my phone out. I open a text and type, "Hey, just need to let you know, I quit. Sorry. We can talk in a couple of days."

Then I send it to Andrew.

I love my job. I'm proud of my job. I'll never get to do something like that again.

But as soon as I press send, I feel a weight lift.

I'll also never feel the way I do about Ivy and Harrison again, and I'll never find a situation like what I've got waiting for me in Honeysuckle Harbor again.

I can write other things.

My phone dings and I open my messages.
But it's not Andrew. It's Sam.

You still in Denver?

Sam insisted on picking me up from the airport when I sent him my itinerary. I figured someone should know where I was and since Ivy, Harrison, and Ford had lost their phones to the FBI, Sam made the most sense.

Yeah. Fucking mechanical issues. Sorry. I'll text once I'm on board.

Nothing to worry about. It's all going to be fine.

I appreciate that. But I'm not going to totally feel that until I'm back at Harrison's house with my three people around me.

Get one of those cinnamon rolls while you wait. I don't know what they do but airport cinnamon rolls are the best.

I blink at his message. I glance toward the kid by the windows.
Wait, was the *cinnamon roll* the sign and not the alien?
Like a sign that everything is really pretty simple and sweet?
Fuck if I know.
My phone dings again. Oh, good. Maybe Sam can follow up on his words of wisdom.
But it's not Sam. It's Andrew.

WHAT THE FUCK ARE YOU TALKING ABOUT!?

I look over at the cinnamon roll shop. Maybe I should get a cinnamon roll before I reply. Maybe I'm fucking this all up.
Another text comes in.

YOU CAN NOT QUIT. I DO NOT ACCEPT YOUR RESIGNATION!!!!!!!!!

Are you aware your caps lock is on?

I'M FUCKING YELLING AT YOU!

Okay, then.

My phone rings. Now Andrew is calling. I grimace and answer. "Hey. Before you say anything, it's a done deal. I'm half-way back to South Carolina."

There's a pause on his end, then he says, "So what?"

I frown. "So, I need to be in South Carolina, Andrew. My… family is there. That's where I need to be. I'm relocating."

Again he asks, "So what?"

"So I can't keep writing for a show in California!" I snap. I realize I raised my voice when several fellow travelers glance over. I lower my voice. "You know I love the show, and honestly, if you give Marley's character to Gwyneth, I'll hate you forever, but, I can't do it."

"You wrote this entire new storyline from South Carolina, right?" he asks.

"Well…yes."

"So obviously you *can* do it."

"But I can't keep doing it."

"Why not?"

I frown. "What do you mean? I can't be in the writer's room in L.A. if I'm living in South Carolina."

"You can write from South Carolina," Andrew says. "Obviously. You can join video calls. And surely you'd be willing to fly in once or twice a month for a couple of days, right?"

My heart starts hammering. "Well…yes."

"Then I don't see a problem. You've been with the show long enough that you know everyone, you know the show, you know how we work." He sighs. "I'm not saying it's ideal, but it's a hell of a lot better than losing you. We *need* you, Liam. You're way too important to the show to just let you go without at least trying to make it work."

I don't know what to say. I sit, staring at the flat gray carpet in front of me, processing his words.

I'm too important.

They need me.

They don't want to lose me.

Well…fuck. That's amazing.

"Liam? Are you there?"

"Yes," I manage. "Yes, I'm here. I…thanks." I clear my throat. "I appreciate all of that."

"So if you can work remotely, if we fly you in just as needed, you'll stay on?"

"Yes," I tell him. "Of course. I definitely want to try that."

"Thank God." He actually sounds relieved. "Okay. Fuck. I thought I was going to have to tell Chris and Bruce you were out. They would have wanted to kill me."

Chris and Bruce are the executive producers. Chris is also the actor who plays Captain Daniels.

I feel myself smiling. "Thanks, Andrew. I appreciate it."

"I don't know what exactly is going on in South Carolina, but Toby said it has to do with Ivy," Andrew says.

Everyone on the show has met Ivy. She's visited me on set and has been to a couple of parties. They all, of course, loved her.

"It does," I tell him. "We're together. In love. I…plan to marry her." That's the god's honest truth.

"Good for you," Andrew says and I can hear the sincerity in his voice. "That's a pretty damned good reason to uproot your life."

I smile. The thing is, I feel like I'm actually putting roots down.

We disconnect and I stretch to my feet. I think I need a cinnamon roll.

I've just taken my place at the back of a surprisingly long line when I hear, "Liam!"

That sounds like…

I turn and see Ivy running toward me.

I feel like the oxygen just got sucked out of my lungs. What the hell? How is this possible?

She darts around a family with two suitcases, two toddlers, and a stroller—seriously, how do people travel like that?—almost plows over a businessman who is too caught up in talking on his phone to notice her, and then is there, throwing herself into my arms.

"Liam! Oh my god!"

I catch her, squeezing her tightly to my body, but over her shoulder I see Harrison jogging toward us.

My heart does a double-flip.

"What are you doing here?" I ask against her hair, taking a deep breath, inhaling her scent.

I let her go as Harrison joins us. "Jesus, you're fast," he tells Ivy. "You didn't even give me a chance to get my shoes back on after security." Then he meets my gaze. "Hi."

"Hi." I frown. "You went through security? You had to take your shoes off?"

"They make people take their shoes off if they're not pre-screened," he says.

I roll my eyes. "Yes, I'm aware. When has that *ever* happened to you?"

"When I fly into an airport in a private plane, but have to get to my boyfriend who is flying commercial out of an entirely separate terminal, so I have to buy a brand new ticket and don't have time to give them all the pertinent information."

I look from him to Ivy. "You had to buy tickets to get to this gate?"

She nods. "But *he* didn't buy anything. Ford did."

I look past her just as Ford comes jogging up. "Jesus, you two. You couldn't have waited three minutes?"

"It's not our fault you look sketchy and had to be patted down," Harrison says.

I look from him, to Ford, to Ivy. I can't believe they're here.

In *Denver*.

"What…how…what the hell are you doing here?" I ask. "How did you even know where I was?"

"Sam," they all say together.

"We intended to come all the way to L.A.," Ivy adds.

"We would have done it two days ago, but we got a little held up," Ford says.

"The FBI," I say. "I heard."

"I can't believe we missed your calls and texts," Ivy says. "I'm so sorry. We felt awful as soon as you left, but they showed up, literally minutes later."

"Sam filled me in," I tell them.

"But what are *you* doing in Denver?" Harrison asks.

He hasn't said anything about being sorry or missing me. He also hasn't touched me yet. I can see wariness in his eyes. But also hope.

I step in closer to him. "I was on my way back to Honeysuckle Harbor."

"Why?"

"Because that's where I want to be. Where I *need* to be."

"Why?"

"Because that's where the loves of my life are," I say simply. "Because being there with them…with *you*…is more important than anything in L.A."

The wariness is starting to melt away. The hope is blooming in his eyes and there's heat there too. "What about your job? The money? The awards?"

"I quit."

Now he steps closer to me, and there's a little growl in his voice. "For me?"

I nod. "And for Ivy."

He reaches up, cupping the back of my neck. "Fuck, Liam. I love that. But I hate that."

"Well…" I say.

He hesitates.

"They won't let me quit. They're insisting I stay on. Work remotely from South Carolina. I'll have to fly to L.A. periodically for a couple of days at a time. But I'll be living, permanently, in Honeysuckle Harbor."

He draws in a deep breath. "Thank God."

"Yeah?" I ask, no longer fighting my smile.

"Yeah. I want you to be happy," he says, with an intensity I'm not expecting. "I really do. I want it to be with us, but it kills me to think that you might be giving something up."

"If I'm with you all, I have everything I really need. We'll figure the rest out."

He takes another deep breath, then blows it out. "Tell me I get to fly you back and forth. And come with you some of the time. That you're going to take my fucking money and let me take care of you that way." His voice is low. And a little bossy.

I lift an eyebrow. "No."

His eyes narrow.

"The show will be flying me back and forth," I say. "As they should. But, I'll let you pay to keep an apartment there. An even nicer one than what I have now. With a much bigger bed. And a huge shower."

When he growls and pulls me close this time, I let him.

He covers my mouth with his, kissing me deeply, thoroughly, pouring all of his relief and possessiveness and love into it.

As our mouths move together, I reach out and grab our girl, pulling her into our arms. Harrison gathers her close too, and I turn to kiss her as well.

Ivy arches close, kissing me hotly, letting me taste her fully.

When I finally release them both, they're breathing hard, their faces flushed.

Just the way I like them.

"Um, are you still in line?"

I look over Ivy's shoulder at the woman standing behind us. A glance in front shows the line for the cinnamon rolls is gone. We're up.

I grin at her, then down at Ivy, then up at Harrison, then over at Ford, who is watching us with his hands in his pockets, a contented smile on his face.

I nod. "Yeah." I move us to the counter, not letting go of either of them fully.

"What can I get you?" the woman behind the counter asks.

"A cinnamon roll," I say. "The biggest you've got. Lots of icing."

She looks at the four of us. "Just one?"

I nod with a grin. "Yeah. We'll share."

CHAPTER 36

Harrison

I WAKE up the next morning to one of my favorite sounds—Ivy's sex moan.

I smile. I don't know who's causing the sound, but honestly, Ford and Liam are equally good at making her sound like that. Then again, Ivy might be causing that sound by herself. I don't hear a buzzing indicating she's getting any battery-powered help, but the girl has fingers after all.

But I need to be sure she knows that even if I'm asleep, if I'm here I'm very happy to be awakened to help her out. I stretch and roll to my right.

I open my eyes and see that Ivy's on her back, neck arched, gorgeous breasts exposed and a lump moving under the sheet, presumably between her legs. Which means I still don't know who it is.

I'm going to guess Ford. Liam probably got up and went to see Sam. My grandfather, after all, deserves a thank you for making sure we got to Denver to intercept Liam rather than going all the way to L.A. And he was the one who stayed in touch with Liam when the rest of us lost our phones.

"Oh my God," Ivy moans, her hands gripping the sheets.

I lean over and run my stubbled chin up over her shoulder to her neck. "My favorite alarm clock," I murmur in her ear.

Almost as if she's just reacting on instinct, she turns toward me, kissing me. I cup her breast, teasing her nipple, and she quickly pulls back, gasping, and then coming.

Fuck, she's gorgeous. I stroke her cheek, wide awake now, my cock throbbing.

God, I get to do this every morning for the rest of my life.

Ford crawls up her body, emerging from under the sheet with a huge grin. He glances at me. "Morning," he says, his tone smug. Then he seals his mouth over Ivy's, kissing her deeply.

The sheet still covers their lower halves but she obviously wraps her legs around him and a moment later his ass is moving up and down as he fucks her.

And I just lie there.

I don't know that I would have ever imagined this a year ago. Or five years ago.

But this is my dream life. It really is. Three people who love me just as I am and who I want to see every day, take care of, share everything with, who just *fit*. They fit into my life, into my family, into my plans perfectly.

They both quickly orgasm, Ivy clinging to Ford and crying out his name, while he groans her name.

He kisses her again, but then rolls to her side opposite of me and she reaches over, looping her arm around my neck and pulling me in for a long kiss.

"Good morning," she says against my mouth.

My hand is sliding down over her belly and she's shifting closer when we hear, "Hello? Anyone home?"

We all freeze.

"Good morning! Hello!"

Yep, that's Ford's mom's voice.

And I'm sure my mom is...

"You're not all still asleep, are you?" my mother calls up the stairs from the kitchen.

I sigh.

"You've got to be kidding me," Ford mutters.

Ivy giggles. He gives her a fake glare.

"They're just so happy that the two of you are living together now," she whispers.

"Yeah, we might need to reconsider that," Ford says quietly.

Ivy gasps. "No! We all have to live together."

He leans in. "But it means we have moms and dads crashing our morning plans every weekend." He nuzzles her neck. "You won't get all the attention that you need."

"I love your mom and dad," she says, tipping her head so he can get at more of her neck.

"But how are we going to keep you satisfied?" I ask, moving in to nuzzle the other side of her neck and sliding my hand lower.

She gives a little moan. "Well, you have a point."

"Do *not* go up there, Daphne," my father calls.

I pull my hand out from between Ivy's legs. I can't help it. It's an instinct.

"I'm not going *all* the way up," she says. "But they might not be able to hear me."

Ivy covers her mouth with her hand to stifle a laugh.

"Oh, you think that's funny?" I ask her, running my hand over her pussy. "You think it's funny that you're going to have to settle for cinnamon rolls and egg bake instead of another orgasm?"

"We could just leave the food on the counter and come back later," Ford's mom says.

Ivy grins up at me. "I really love cinnamon rolls and egg bake."

Ford growls. "You're going to get spanked for that later," he tells her.

She gives a little wiggle. "Oh, no," she says. "That sounds terrible. Cinnamon rolls, egg bake, time with your lovely parents, and a spanking. Please. No."

I can't hold back my laugh. "I love you, you little brat."

Her giggles are quiet but her smile is so sweet, my heart squeezes. "I love you too, Harrison."

I lean in and kiss her. "I know. Everybody loves me."

But she catches my face between her hands when I try to pull back. She looks me directly in the eyes. "I know they do," she says. "But I *love* love you. And I'm so happy to be spending forever with you."

Jesus. This girl. I relax my expression and let her see my real emotions. All the love and awe and happiness she and Ford and Liam inspire. "Forever isn't long enough."

She smiles a smile that I will never get tired of seeing.

Ford reaches over and squeezes my shoulder. "There you go. That wasn't so hard, was it?"

I shake my head and smile at him, too. "Shut up."

He laughs.

Then we hear, "Yep, give me a second, I'll get them."

Liam's here.

We all look at one another.

Ford looks down at Ivy. "Well, are you going to shower and get all cleaned up, or are you ready to let the parents know how we debauch you every chance we have?"

"I think the parents are very aware of the debauching," Liam says from the doorway.

"Hey," I greet. "You have perfect timing."

"Sam got the text from Bill that breakfast was starting."

"So Sam's here too?" Ivy asks, clearly very amused.

"Walt and Ed too," Liam says.

Ivy sits up, laughing. "I need to shower."

She's naked, crawling across me to get out of bed, and there's no way I can keep from running my hand over her ass.

"They could wait ten minutes," I say, giving her a squeeze.

She keeps going.

"Or twenty," Liam adds, his eyes on her too.

"You all need to go down and entertain our guests," she says, padding across the room toward the bathroom.

Her hips have a little extra sway. She loves our eyes all on her.

"I should shower too though," Ford says, pushing up from the bed.

"You don't get to shower with her if Harrison and I have to go downstairs," Liam protests.

"I got dirty with her before they got here," Ford says, smugly, starting for the bathroom.

"Oh, *I'm* the gentleman who lets her sleep, and this is what I get?" Liam calls after them.

I push up from the bed and cross to where he's standing. I cup the back of his neck, pull him in, and kiss him. "You get this." I kiss him again. "And my dad's cinnamon rolls. They really are amazing."

He hugs me. "We'll make Ford and Ivy do the dishes and we can shower together later."

"Deal."

We make our way downstairs and I pause in the doorway to the kitchen for a moment just absorbing the sight of my family, Ford's family, and my grandfather's best friends welcoming Liam into their midst as if he's been a part of their lives for years instead of just days.

God, I love him so much.

And I almost lost him.

How could I have let him go? How could I have not just said, "Let's go," packed up, and gone to L.A. with him?

I'm relieved the show is going to let him work remotely, but I should have been willing to go wherever he went.

I have to be sure he knows that.

I think I'm going to propose to him.

Maybe not today. But someday soon. It should be me. I'm the one who has a hard time with this commitment thing and I need to prove to him I'm done with that.

Liam is it for me. Him and Ivy and Ford.

This is it. Whatever that means, wherever we need to be for them to be happy.

Because I'll be happy as long as I'm with them.

I join them at the table and somehow participate in the conversation without anyone wondering what's going on with me. Eating three cinnamon rolls helps.

But the second Ivy and Ford step into the room, wet hair, big grins, Ford's hand on her ass, I stand up.

"Um, hey, everyone?"

They are all quiet and turn to face me.

"Are you okay, dear?" my mom asks.

"Yes. I'm great."

"You look flushed. Are you sick?" my dad asks.

"He does look flushed," Greg agrees.

"I'm not sick, I'm fine," I assure them.

"You do look tense, though. What's going on?" my grandfather asks.

"I'm trying to tell you," I tell them.

"Is it the FBI?" Ed asks. "Have they found something?"

"No, it's not the FBI. That's all fine," I say.

"Oh good," my mother says. She looks at Regina. "Can you believe that we had the *FBI* here investigating our kids?"

"Well, they weren't really investigating the kids," Dad says. "They're investigating Brad and just questioned the kids."

"Oh, you know what I mean," Mom says. "It was the *FBI*."

"I just can't believe *Brad* did all of that," Regina says. "We've known him since he was born! All those years. And his poor parents."

"Okay!" I say loudly. "I have something to say and it's *not* about the FBI or Brad! I'm not sick, and I'm not tense!"

I'm a little tense, but…

"Then what's wrong?" Liam asks.

I focus on him. "Nothing. Absolutely nothing is wrong." I drop back into my seat and face him. "In fact, everything is completely *right*. Now. Because you're here. Because of you and Ivy."

I look up and find her. She's watching me. The look on her face is so sweet. And I think she knows exactly what I'm about to say.

I give her a wink. She grins.

"So what do you have to say in front of everyone right at this very moment?" Ford asks.

I look at the guy who's been my best friend all of my life. The one who knows me better than anyone. The one who I can't imagine living without and who I now won't ever have to.

Ford also knows what I'm about to say.

"I need to say that…" I look at Liam. "I'm in love with you. Madly. Completely. I've never felt like this before, and I need you to know that I never want to be without you. No matter what that means or where I need to go or what I need to do to make that happen."

Liam is watching me with surprise. But…pleasure.

"Will you marry me, Liam?"

I hear Ivy's little, happy squeak and I see her and Ford hug.

My mom gasps.

My dad slides an arm around her and pulls her into a hug.

My grandfather grins, nodding.

Regina has her hand over her mouth, and Greg is grinning widely.

Then I concentrate on Liam.

He slowly smiles. "Wow."

"Just wow? How about a yes? Or even a fuck yes?" I ask.

"Oh, fuck yes," he says with a nod.

My heart flips over. I lean in. Then I pause, "What was the wow for?"

"You just really took charge there," he says.

I narrow my eyes and lean closer. "Yeah, I did. And I did a hell of a job, didn't I?"

He leans closer too. "Yeah, you did."

I start to kiss him, but he puts a hand on the back of my head, threads his fingers into my hair, and tugs gently. "But let's not make that a regular thing, okay?" he mutters against my mouth.

I laugh lightly. "Okay."

And I'm suddenly happy that our family crashed our brunch plans.

This time.

But as Liam puts his mouth against my ear and says, "I love you so fucking much and I can't wait to get my *fiancé* upstairs," I realize that we're going to need to establish some rules with our family.

Or change the locks.

Or both.

Epilogue

NINE MONTHS LATER

Ford

I **STARE** at my phone in disbelief as a typing bubble pops up in response to my text and then disappears.

I text again, using caps to get my point across.

> **WHERE ARE YOU?**

> I'm not coming.

"You have got to be fucking kidding me," I say to no one in particular and to the universe.

This has to be a joke.

Brad cannot possibly be standing up a second bride a mere nine months after running out on Ivy.

They say prison can change a man, but apparently not in Brad's case.

After taking a plea deal, Brad spent a mere five months in Club Fed, playing checkers with men convicted of white-collar crimes and becoming best friends with an aging mobster. He also fell in love with a woman who randomly wrote to him and they are supposed to be getting married. Today. In Ivy's new wedding venue.

I would hate to see Brad's blushing bride, Lucy, stood up the way Ivy was, and I would really, really hate to see The Ivy Wedding Event Center's debut wedding end in disaster.

> SHUT THE FUCK UP AND GET HERE NOW. I DON'T CARE IF YOU DIVORCE HER NEXT WEEK, GET TO THIS FUCKING WEDDING.

That should get my point across.

I'm in the hallway outside of the groomsmen lounge. Ivy has designed it with a speakeasy vibe, dark and moody, with a leather chesterfield sofa and hunter green walls. Harrison is in there with Brad's fiancée's brother, dressed and ready to wait on the beach for the bride to enter.

Except we have no groom.

Harrison and I weren't even sure we wanted to stand up for Brad after everything he's done in the last year, but in the end he explained to Ivy and to us that he ditched Ivy to save her from the blowback his illegal activities might create. He had gotten in over his head financially, made some really stupid and poor choices, thinking he could pay the money back, then realized his time was up. He deeded the house to Ivy as an apology for not telling her he was stealing money hand over fist.

I can't say I've totally forgiven him, but we've been friends since we were five and Ivy reminded us that if Brad hadn't bailed, our road trip would have never happened and we wouldn't be the happiest—okay only—foursome in Honeysuckle Harbor.

If Ivy can forgive, so can I.

But now I need to go find Ivy, who is dashing around the venue sorting out final details and making sure everything is perfect. Liam is with her, holding anything she needs held, moving furniture as needed, and making sure she has water and caffeine.

Taking a deep breath, I open up the door to the groomsmen room and tell Harrison, "Hey, I need you out here."

We're a team. The four of us. We do everything together.

We're all financially and emotionally invested in making all of our dreams come true. From Harrison's expanding property portfolio, to my desire to expand Raw's product line, to Liam working on a science fiction novel while still writing for his show back in L.A.

And Ivy's event center.

She's poured her heart and soul into this space.

We'll be damned if Brad fucks that up.

"So Brad just texted me that he's not coming," I say to Harrison in a low voice, gesturing for him to follow me.

Harrison's jaw drops. "Get the fuck out of here. I will rip that son of a bitch apart!"

I believe him. He looks ready to throw hands and easily win. "Does Ivy know?"

"We need to go tell her. Together."

He gives a short nod, taking a deep breath and running his fingers through his hair. He visibly restrains himself, because he knows that Ivy doesn't need his anger right now. She needs our support and cool heads to prevail.

Since the four of us have been together, we've learned how to be there for each other with whatever each of us needs at that moment. It's honestly been a fucking beautiful experience to blend my life with that of three other people.

We can get through anything together.

Even Brad 2.0.

But when Harrison and I turn the corner to the main dining space, with floor to ceiling windows, Brad is standing there grinning, arms out.

"Hey! Looking good, boys!"

My stomach drops and I feel instant relief, followed immediately by the urge to punch Brad. "What the fuck was that?" I demand.

He pulls me into a hug. "Just messing with you. God, your face. That was gold, bro."

"Don't bro me," I snap. "You're a dick."

He hugs Harrison and laughs. "Lighten up. I'm the one who's been in the big house. What are you stressing about?"

Harrison shakes his head. "Does Lucy know what a fucking idiot you are?"

"One hundred percent." Brad adjusts his tie. "That's the beauty of meeting a woman when you're at your worst. If she loves you then, she'll love you through anything."

Fair point.

"Jesus," I grumble. "Okay, are you ready? For real?"

"Yep. Let's do this. Where's Ivy? I want to thank her."

"I'm right here."

My heart always skips a beat whenever Ivy walks into the room.

It always stuns me a little how damn lucky I am to have her love me. She gives us a smile as she comes into the room, in a beautiful pale pink dress that shows off her legs. Her hair is pulled back in a sleek ponytail and she has on minimal jewelry. Just the engagement ring that Harrison, Liam, and I designed for her.

I get to marry this woman and spend the rest of my life with her.

"You look beautiful," I tell her, brushing a kiss across her cheek.

"Why thank you. You both are very handsome." She adjusts my tie and leans around me to give Harrison a kiss.

"I could eat you alive," he tells her.

Ivy laughs.

Liam appears in the doorway and says, "It's time to head down to the beach. The very windy and sandy beach."

That makes me grin.

You can take the grump out of L.A....

"It's April, William," Harrison says, going over and kissing him. "It's windy."

"That's my point." But Liam returns his smile. "You look good, Harrison."

"I know."

I roll my eyes and clap Brad on the back.

A minute later, we're lined up next to the arch that has been erected by the water, a few dozen guests rubbing their arms against the chill as they sit in white wooden chairs.

To my shock and surprise, Brad actually tears up when Lucy appears on her father's arm, and strolls across the sand toward him, smiling broadly.

My first instinct was to wonder what kind of a woman marries a man three days out of prison, but then I realized it's not anyone's place to judge who someone chooses to love.

Look at us.

It might not be for everyone, but it works for us. So fucking well.

I steal a peek at Ivy, who has taken a seat in the front row to oversee the ceremony. Liam sits next to her, entwining his fingers with hers.

I give her a wink and she gives me that beautiful smile I get to see every day until I die.

Then I look at Brad.

Thank God this guy is an idiot.

If he hadn't left Ivy at the altar, I wouldn't get to stand by her next year and promise to love her for the rest of my life with Harrison and Liam.

I grin as Brad says, "I do" to Lucy.

Yeah…thanks a lot, Brad.

Thanks for reading **Three Grumpy Groomsmen**! For a free bonus scene with Ivy and her guys go to: https://subscribepage.io/threegrumpygroomsmenbonus

Keep an eye out for the next sexy Emma Foxx why choose rom com, *Three Dirty Dads*, coming soon!

Find Emma on Social

Emma Foxx is the super fun and sexy pen name for two long-time, bestselling romance authors who decided why have just one hero when you can have three at the same time? (they're not sure what took them so long to figure this out)! Emma writes contemporary romances that will make you laugh (yes, maybe out loud in public) and want more…books (sure, that's what we mean ). Find Emma on Instagram, TikTok, and Goodreads.

Also by Emma Foxx

Read more Emma Foxx for more _steamy, fun why-choose rom coms! No cheating, a guaranteed HEA, and the guys are all about her._

Puck One Night Stands

Four Pucking Christmases

Seriously Pucked

Permanently Pucked

Icing It

Some Like It Hot

Light My Fire

Spicy Short Reads